FOUR STORIES

D1111347

Alan Bennett has been one of our leading dramatists since the success of *Beyond the Fringe* in the 1960s. His television series *Talking Heads* has become a modern-day classic, as have many of his works for the stage, including *Forty Years On*, *The Lady in the Van*, *A Question of Attribution*, *The Madness of George III* (together with the Oscar-nominated screenplay *The Madness of King George*) and an adaptation of Kenneth Grahame's *The Wind in the Willows*. His most recent play, *The History Boys*, won six Tonys, the Evening Standard and Critics' Circle award for Best Play, the Laurence Olivier Award for Best New Play and the South Bank Award.

FOUR STORIES

BY

ALAN BENNETT

PROFILE BOOKS

First published in Great Britain in 2006 by
PROFILE BOOKS LTD
3A Exmouth House
Pine Street
London EC1R 0JH
www.profilebooks.com

in association with

LONDON REVIEW OF BOOKS
28 Little Russell Street, London WC1A 2HN
www.lrb.co.uk

THE LAYING ON OF HANDS
First published in 2001 in the London Review of Books
First published in book form in 2001 by Profile Books Ltd

THE CLOTHES THEY STOOD UP IN
First published in 1996 in the London Review of Books
First published in book form in 1998 by Profile Books Ltd

FATHER! FATHER! BURNING BRIGHT
First published in 2000 in the London Review of Books
First published in book form in 2000 by Profile Books Ltd

THE LADY IN THE VAN
First published in 1989 in the London Review of Books
First published in book form in 1999 by Profile Books Ltd

The Lady in the Van is also included in Alan Bennett's collection of prose,
Writing Home, published by Faber & Faber Ltd

1 3 5 7 9 8 6 4 2

Typeset in Quadraat

Printed and bound in Great Britain by Bookmarque Ltd, Croydon, Surrey

ISBN-10: 1 86197 891 7
ISBN-13: 978 1 86197 891 6

CONTENTS

THE LAYING ON OF HANDS

SEATED OBSCURELY towards the back of the church and on a side aisle, Treacher was conscious nevertheless of being much looked at. Tall, thin and with a disagreeable expression, were this a film written forty years ago he would have been played by the actor Raymond Huntley who, not unvinegary in life, in art made a speciality of ill-tempered businessmen and officious civil servants. Treacher was neither but he, too, was nothing to look at. Yet several times he caught women (and it was women particularly) bending forward in their seats to get a better view of him across the aisle; a murmured remark passed between a couple in front, the woman then turning round, ostensibly to take in the architecture but actually to look at him, whereas others in the congregation dispensed with such polite circumspection and just stared.

Unwelcome enough in any circumstances, this scrutiny was not at all what Treacher had had in mind when he had come into the church fully half an hour before the service was due to start, a precaution against having his hand shaken at the door by the vicar. Such redundant clerical conviviality was always distasteful to Treacher but on this occasion he had a particular reason for avoiding it. Luckily the vicar was not to be seen but, early as he was, Treacher had still had to run the gauntlet of a woman in the porch, a reporter presumably, who was making a record of those attending the memorial service. She held out her book for him to sign.

'Name and organisation?'

But Treacher had pushed past as if she were a lowlier form of autograph hunter. 'Not important,' he said, though whether he meant he was not important or that it was not important his name be recorded was not plain.

'I'll put you under "and many other friends",' she had called after him, though in fact he had never met the deceased and did not even know his name.

Somewhere out of the way was what he wanted, where he could see and not be seen and well back on the side aisle he thought he had found it, instead of which the fuller the church became the more he seemed the focus of attention. It was very vexing.

In fact no one was looking at Treacher at all, except when they pretended to look at him in order also to take in someone sitting in the row behind. A worldlier man than Treacher, if worldliness consists in watching television, would have known why. Seated behind him was a thick-set shaven-headed young man in dark glasses, black suit and black T-shirt who, minus the shades and occasionally (and far too rarely, some viewers felt) minus the T-shirt, appeared nightly on the nation's screens in a television soap. The previous week he had stunned his audience when, with no excuse whatsoever, he had raped his mother, and though it later transpired she had been begging for it for some time and was actually no relation at all, nevertheless some vestiges of the nation's fascinated revulsion still clung to him. In life, though, as he was at pains to point out to any chat-show host who would listen, he was a pussy-cat and indeed, within minutes of the maternal rape, he could be found on another channel picking out the three items of antique furniture he would invest in were his budget limited to £500.

None of this Treacher knew, only becoming aware of the young man when an usher spotted him and insisted on shepherding the modest hunk to a more prominent seat off the centre aisle next to a chef who, though famously disgruntled in the workplace, now smilingly shifts along to accommodate the big-thighed newcomer. After his departure Treacher was relieved, though not unpuzzled, to find himself invisible once more and so able to look unobserved at the incoming congregation.

There was quite a throng, with people still crowding through the door and a small queue now stretching over the worn and greasy gravestones that paved this London churchyard. The flanks of the queue were harried by autograph hunters and the occasional photographer, outlying celebrities meekly signing as they shuffled on towards the door. One or two did refuse, on the justifiable grounds that this wasn't a first night (and more of a closing than an opening), but the autograph hunters were impatient of such scruples, considering themselves wilfully thwarted. 'Choosy cow,' one muttered as he turned away from some glacial TV newsreader, brightening only when he spotted an ageing disc jockey he had thought long since dead.

The huddled column pressed on up the steps.

As memorial services go these days it had been billed as 'a celebration', the marrying of the valedictory with the festive convenient on several grounds. For a start it made grief less obligatory, which was useful as the person to be celebrated had been dead some time and tears would have been something of an acting job. To call it a celebration also allowed the congregation to dress up not down, so that though the millinery might be more muted, one could have been forgiven, thought Treacher, for thinking this was a wedding not a wake.

Clive Dunlop, the dead man, was quite young – thirty-four according to the dates given on the front of the Order of Service, though there were some in the congregation who had thought him even younger. Still, it was a shocking age to die, there was no disagreement about that and what little conviviality there might have been was muffled accordingly.

Knowing the deceased, many of those filing into the church in surprisingly large numbers also knew each other, though in the circumstances prevailing at funerals and memorial services this is not always easy to tell as recognition tends to be kept to a minimum – the eye downcast, the smile on hold, any display of pleasure at the encounter or even shared grief postponed until the business of the service is done – however sad the professionally buoyant clergyman will generally assure the congregation that that business is not going to be.

True, there were a number of extravagant one-word embraces, 'Bless!' for instance, and even 'Why?', a despairing invocation that seemed more appropriate for the actual interment which (though nobody seemed quite to know where) appeared to have taken place some six months previously. Extravagant expressions of sorrow seemed out of place here, if only because a memorial service, as the clergyman will generally insist, is a positive occasion, the negative side of the business (though they seldom come out baldly with this) over and done with at the disposal of the body. Because, however upbeat a priest manages to be (and indeed his creed requires him to be), it's hard not to feel that cheerful though the memorial service can be, the actual interment does tend to be a bit of a downer.

Still, discreet funerals and extravagant memorial services are not unusual these days, the finality of death mitigated by staggering it over two stages. 'Of course there'll be a memorial service,' people say, excusing their non-attendance at the emotionally more demanding (and socially less enjoyable) obsequies. And it is generally the case nowadays that anybody who is anybody is accorded a memorial service – and sometimes an anybody who isn't.

Hard to say what Clive was, for instance, though taking note of the numerous celebrities who were still filing in, 'well-connected' would undoubtedly describe him.

Dubbing such a service a celebration was, thought Treacher, a mistake as it could be thought to license a degree of whoopee. The proceedings seemed to include a saxophone solo, which was ominous, and Treacher's misgivings were confirmed when a young man sat down heavily in the pew in front, laid his Order of Service on the ledge then put his cigarettes and lighter beside it.

She was in the next pew, but spotting the cigarettes the spirits of a recently ennobled novelist rose. 'You can smoke,' she whispered.

Her companion shook her head. 'I don't think so.'

'I see no signs saying not. Is that one?'

Fumbling for her spectacles she peered at a plaque affixed to a pillar.

'I think,' said her friend, 'that's one of the Stations of the Cross.'

'Really? Well I'm sure I saw an ashtray as I was coming in.'

'That was holy water.'

In the light of these accessories, more often to be met with in Roman Catholic establishments, it was hardly surprising if some of the congregation were in doubt as to the church's denomination, which was actually Anglican, though a bit on the high side.

'I can smell incense,' said a feared TV interviewer to his actress friend. 'Are we in a Catholic church?'

She had once stabbed a priest to death in a film involving John Mills so knew about churches. 'Yes,' she said firmly.

At which point a plumpish man in a cassock crossed the chancel in order to collect a book from a pew, bowing to the altar en route.

'See that,' said the interviewer. 'The bowing? That's part of the drill. Though it looks a bit pick'n'mix to me. Mind you, that's the trend these days. Ecumenicalism. I talked to the Pope about it once. Sweet man.'

'I missed the funeral,' whispered one woman to her vaguely known neighbour. 'I didn't even know it had happened.'

'Same with me,' the neighbour whispered back. 'I think it was private. What did he die of?'

The sight of a prominent actor in the Royal Shakespeare Company gliding humbly to an empty place in the front row curtailed further discussion, though it was the prototype of several similar conversations going on in various parts of the church. Other people were trying to recall why it was they had failed to attend a funeral which ought to have been high on their lists. Was it in the provinces they wondered, which would account for it, or one of the obscurer parts of South London ... Sydenham, say, or Catford, venues that would be a real test of anybody's friendship?

It had actually been in Peru, a fact known to very few people in the congregation though in the subdued hum of conversation that preceded the start of the service this news and the unease it generated began to spread. Perhaps out of tact the question, 'What did he die of?' was not much asked and when it was sometimes prompted a quizzical look suggesting it was a question best left unput; that, or a sad smile implying Clive had succumbed not to any particular ailment but to the general tragedy that is life itself.

Spoken or unspoken, the uncertain circumstances of the death, its remote location and the shocking prematureness of it contributed to an atmosphere of gloom and, indeed, apprehension in the church. There was conversation but it was desultory and subdued; many people's thoughts seemed to be on themselves. Few of them attended a place of worship with any regularity, their only contact with churches occasions like this, which, as was ruefully remarked in several places in the congregation, 'seemed to be happening all too often these days'.

To Treacher, glancing at the details on the front of the Order of Service it was all fairly plain. He was a single man who had died young. Thirty-four. These days there was not much mystery about that.

'He told me thirty, the scamp,' said one of the many smart women who was craning round to see who was still coming in. 'But then he would.'

'I thought he was younger,' said someone else. 'But he looked after himself.'

'Not well enough,' said her husband, whose wife's grief had surprised him. 'I never understood where the money came from.'

Anyone looking at the congregation and its celebrity assortment could be forgiven for thinking that Clive had been a social creature. This wasn't altogether true and this numinous gathering studded with household names was less a manifestation of his friendships than an advertisement for his discretion.

It was true that many of those present knew each other and virtually all of them knew Clive. But that the others knew Clive not all of them knew and only woke up to the fact when they had settled in their seats and started looking round. So while most memorial services take place in an atmosphere of suppressed recognition and reunion to this one was added an element of surprise, many of those present having come along on the assumption they would be among a select few.

Finding this was far from the case the surprise was not untinged with irritation. Or as a go-for-the-throat Australian wordsmith put it to her companion, 'Why, the two-faced pisshole.'

Diffidence was much to the fore. A leading international architect, one of whose airports had recently sprung a leak, came down the centre aisle, waiting at the end of a pew until someone made room, his self-effacing behaviour and downcast eyes proclaiming him a person of some consequence humbled by the circumstances in which he currently found himself and which might have been allegorically represented on a ceiling, say (although not one of his), as Fame deferring to Mortality. 'Do not recognise me,' his look said. 'I am here only to grieve.'

Actually, compared with the soap-stars he hardly counted as famous at all. The world of celebrity in England, at any rate, is small. Whereas fame in America vaults over the barriers of class and profession, lawyers rubbing shoulders with musicians, politicians and stars of stage and screen, in England, television apart, celebrity comes in compartments, *Who's Who* not always the best guide to who's who. Thus here Fame did not always recognise Reputation or Beauty Merit.

A high official in the Treasury, for instance, had got himself seated next to a woman who kept consulting her powder compact, her renown as bubbling game-show host as wasted on him as his skill in succinct summation was lost on her. Worlds collided but with no impact at all, so while what few lawyers there were knew the politicians and some of the civil servants none of them knew the genial wag who pounced on reluctant volunteers and teased out their less than shamefaced confessions on late-night TV. The small-screen gardeners knew the big-screen heart-throbs but none of them recognised 'someone high up in the Bank of England' ('and I don't mean the window-cleaner,' whispered a man who did).

Much noticed, though, was a pop singer who had been known to wear a frock but was today dressed in a suit of stunning sobriety, relieved only by a diamond clasp that had once belonged to Catherine the Great and which was accompanied by an obligatory security guard insisted on by the insurance company. This bovine young man lounged in the pew picking his fingers, happy already to have pinpointed Suspect No. 1, the Waynflete Professor of Moral Philosophy in the University of Oxford who, timid though he was, clearly had villain written all over him.

In front of the Professor was a member of the Government,

who was startled to find himself opposite his Permanent Secretary, seated on the other side of the aisle.

'I didn't know you knew Dunlop,' the minister said the next day as they plodded through some meeting on carbon monoxide emissions.

'Oh, I knew him from way back,' said the civil servant airily.

'Me too,' said the minister. 'Way back.'

Actually the minister had only met Clive quite recently, just after he became a minister in fact, but this 'way back' in which both of them took refuge was a time so remote and unspecific that anything that might have happened then was implicitly excused by their youth and the temper of the times. 'I knew him in the Sixties' would have been the same, except that Clive was too young for that.

'At some point,' murmured the minister, 'I want you to take me on one side and explain to me the difference between carbon monoxide and carbon dioxide. Fairly star-studded, wasn't it?'

It was, indeed, a remarkable assembly with philanthropy, scholarship and genuine distinction represented alongside much that was tawdry and merely fashionable, so that with only a little licence this stellar, but tarnished throng might, for all its shortcomings, be taken as a version of England.

And 'a very English occasion' was how it was described by the reporter in the *Telegraph* the next day. Not that she was in a position to know as she hadn't bothered to stay for the service. Currently taking down the names of the last few stragglers she compiled her list, procured a programme of the proceedings, then went off to the Design Museum to lunch with a colleague.

'After all,' she said over oeufs en gelée, 'they're all the same these occasions. Like sad cocktail parties without the drinks.'

This one as it turned out wasn't, so she got the sack. But it was a nice lunch.

Also thinking how English these occasions tended to be was the young priest in charge, Father Geoffrey Jolliffe. Father Jolliffe was Anglican but with Romish inclinations that were not so much doctrinal as ceremonial and certainly sartorial. Amiable, gregarious and plump, he looked well in the cloak he generally went about in, a priest with a bit of a swish to him. His first curacy had been in a slum parish where, as he put it, 'They like a bit of that,' and since he did too, his ministry got off to a good start and that he chose to call the Eucharist 'Mass' and himself 'Father' troubled no one. His present parish, St Andrew Upchance on the borders of Shoreditch and the City, was also poor, but he had done a good deal to 'turn it round', an achievement that had not gone unnoticed in the diocese, where he was spoken of as a coming man.

There were, it is true, some of his fellow clergy who found him altogether too much, but as he said himself, 'There's not enough of "too much" these days,' and since he was a lively preacher and old-fashioned when it came to the prayer book, a large and loyal congregation seemed to bear this out.

Used at his normal services to women predominating, to-day Father Jolliffe was not altogether surprised to find so many men turning up. Some of them had been close to Clive, obviously, but that apart, in his experience men needed less cajoling to attend funerals and memorial services than they did normal church (or even the theatre, say) and since men seldom do what they don't want, it had made him wonder why. He decided that where the dead were involved there was always an element of condescension: the deceased had been put in his or her place, namely the grave, and however lavish the tributes with which this was accompanied there was no altering the fact that the situation of the living was altogether superior and to men, in particular, that seemed to appeal.

USUALLY CHEERFUL AND EXPANSIVE, today Father Jolliffe was preoccupied. He had known Clive himself, which accounted for his church being the somewhat out of the way venue for the memorial service. His death had come as an unpleasant surprise, as, like so many in the congregation, he had not known Clive was even ill. It was sad, too, of course, 'a shared sadness' as he planned to say, but for him, as for others in the congregation, it was somewhat worrying also (though he had no plans to say that).

Still, if he was anxious he did not intend to let it affect his performance. 'And,' as he had recently insisted to a Diocesan Selection Board, 'a service is a performance. Devout, sincere and given wholeheartedly for God, but a performance nevertheless.'

The Board, on the whole, had been impressed.

By coincidence the subject of memorial services had come up at the Board when Father Jolliffe, suppressing a fastidious shudder, had heard himself describe such occasions as 'a challenge'. Urged to expand he had shared his vision of the church packed with unaccustomed worshippers come together, as they thought, simply to commemorate a loved one but also (though they might not know it) hungering for that hope and reassurance which it was the clergy's job to satisfy. This, too, had gone down well with the Board though most them, Father Jolliffe included, knew it was tosh.

The truth was memorial services were a bugger. For all its shortcomings in the way of numbers a regular congregation was in church because it wanted to be or at least felt it ought to be. It's true that looking down from the pulpit on his flock Sunday by Sunday Father Jolliffe sometimes felt that God was not much more than a pastime; that these were churchgoers as some people were pigeon-fanciers or collectors of stamps, gentle, mildly eccentric and hanging onto the end of something. Still, on a scale ranging from fervent piety to mere respectability, these regular worshippers were at least like-minded: they had come together to worship God and even with their varying degrees of certainty that there was a God to worship the awkward question of belief seldom arose.

With a memorial service, and a smart one at that, God was an embarrassment and Father Jolliffe was reminded of this when he had his first sight of the congregation. He had left his service book in his stall and nipping across to get it before putting on his robes he was taken aback at the packed and murmuring pews. Few of those attending, he suspected, had on taking their seats bowed their heads in prayer or knew that

that was (once anyway) the form. Few would know the hymns, and still fewer the prayers. Yet he was shortly going to have to stand up and ask them to collaborate in the fiction that they all believed in God (or something anyway) and even that there was an after-life. So what he had said to the Board had been right. It was a challenge, the challenge being that most of them would think this an insult to their intelligence.

How Father Jolliffe was going to cope with this dilemma was interesting Treacher. Indeed it was partly what had brought him to St Andrew's on this particular morning. There were various ways round it, the best of which, in Treacher's view, was not to get round it at all; ignore it in fact, a priest retaining more respect if he led the congregation in prayer with neither explanation nor apology, the assumption being that they were all believers and if not, since they were in the house of God, it behoved them to pretend to be so. Taking the uncompromising line, though, meant that it was hard then for the clergyman to get on those friendly, informal terms with the congregation that such an occasion seemed to require. Treacher did not see this as a drawback. A priest himself, although in mufti, getting on friendly terms with the congregation had never been high on his list.

Father Jolliffe would not have agreed. 'Whatever else it is,' he had told the Board, 'a congregation is first and foremost an audience. And I am the stand-up. I must win them over.' It was another bold-seeming sentiment that had hit the spot, occasioning some laughter, it's true, but also much sage nodding, though not, Father Jolliffe had noticed, from Canon Treacher, who was an archdeacon and not enthusiastic about congregations in the first place. Treacher (and his fiercely sharpened pencil) was the only one of the Board who had made him nervous (the Bishop was a sweetie), so it was a blessing that on this particular morning, thanks to Canon Treacher's precautions, the priest remained unaware of his presence.

The worst tack a priest could adopt at a service such as this, and a trap Treacher was pretty confident Father Jolliffe was going to fall into, was to acknowledge at the start that the congregation (or 'friends' as Treacher had even heard them called) might not subscribe to the beliefs implicit in the hymns and prayers but that they should on no account feel badly about this but instead substitute appropriate sentiments of their own. ('I believe this stuff but you don't have to.') Since in Treacher's experience there would be few in the church with appropriate sentiments still less beliefs to hand, this meant that if the congregation thought of anything at all during the prayers (which he doubted) it was just to try and summon up a picture of the departed sufficient to squeeze out the occasional tear.

Treacher, it has to be said, had some reason for his pessimism. Casting an eye over the Order of Service Treacher noted that in addition to a saxophone solo a fashionable baritone from Covent Garden was down to sing 'Some Enchanted Evening'. With such delights in prospect Father Treacher feared that liturgical rigour would not be high on the list.

What approach he was going to take to the service ('what angle the priest should come at it') Father Jolliffe had not yet decided, though since he was even now being robed in the vestry it might be thought there was not much time. But he had never been methodical, his sermon often no more than a few headings or injunctions to himself on the back of the parish notes: though on this occasion he had not even bothered with that, preferring, as he would have said, to 'wing it'. This was less slipshod than it sounded, as he genuinely believed that in this 'winging' there was an element of the divine. He had never thought it out but felt that the wings were God-sent, an angel's possibly, or another version of 'Thy wings' under the shadow of which he bade the faithful hide Sunday by Sunday.

He slipped out of the vestry and made his way round the outside of the church to join the choir now assembled at the West door. When he had been appointed vicar at St Andrew's processions generally began obscurely at the vestry winding their awkward way round past the pulpit and up the chancel steps. Father Jolliffe felt that this was untheatrical and missing a trick so one of his first innovations was to make the entrance of the choir and clergy bolder and more dramatic, routeing the procession down the centre of the church.

The procession should have been headed and the choir preceded by a crucifer bearing the processional cross (another innovation), but since this was a weekday Leo, the crucifer, had not been able to get time off work. A beefy young man, Leo was a bus driver and Father Jolliffe had always taken quiet pride in that fact and would occasionally cite him at diocesan conferences as a modern update of the calling of the disciples

('Matthew may have been a tax-collector. What's so special about that? Our crucifer happens to be a bus driver'). Though Leo would have much preferred marching down the centre aisle to where he currently was, stuck behind the wheel of a No. 74 inching up Putney High Street, since privatisation religious obligation was no longer accepted as a reason for absence. 'Or believe me, my son,' said the supervisor, 'come Ramadan and our Sikh and Hindu brethren who compose a substantial proportion of the workforce would be up at the mosque when we need them down at the depot. I'm not without religious feeling myself and my sister-in-law was nearly a nun but sorry, no can do.'

Still, what the procession lacked in splendour at the front it made up in dignity at the back, as in addition to Father Jolliffe also attending the service were several other clergymen, one of them indeed a suffragan bishop. None of them was personally known to Father Jolliffe or seemingly to each other, but all were presumably known to Clive. Though got up in all their gear they were not attending in any official capacity (and in the *Telegraph* report of the occasion they would be described as 'robed and in the sanctuary'), but they definitely brought a kick to the rear of the column which was now assembled and waiting to begin its journey towards the chancel.

The organist was meanwhile playing an arrangement of Samuel Barber's 'Adagio for Strings' which many in the congregation were enjoying, having been made familiar with the tune from its frequent airings on Classic FM. Seeing no conclusion in the offing Father Jolliffe pressed a button behind a pillar to alert the organist that they were ready to begin. The Barber now came to a sharp and unceremonious close but since random terminations were not unusual on Classic FM, nobody noticed.

Now from somewhere at the back of the church Father Jolliffe's voice rang out, 'Would you stand' and the church shuffled to its feet. 'We shall sing the first hymn on your Order of Service, "Love Divine All Loves Excelling".'

Once upon a time it would have been enough to announce the hymn and the congregation would have known to stand. Hymns you stand, prayers you kneel. Nowadays it was prayers you sit, hymns you wait and see what other people are going to do. 'Love,' Father Jolliffe reproached himself. 'We must love one another.'

Now the clergy began to follow the choir down the aisle, Father Jolliffe bringing up the rear, singing the hymn without consulting the words, long since off the book and thus free while singing heartily to cast professionally loving glances to right and left, on his pink and generous face an expression of settled benevolence.

He had still not decided how to pitch his opening remarks, trusting even now that something would occur, in some ways the closest he got to faith in God this trust that when it came to the point words would be put into his mouth. As he passed through the worshippers raggedly singing the hymn, Father Jolliffe thought they looked less like a congregation than an audience, smart, worldly and doubtless expecting him to keep God very much on the back burner.

He resented this a little, because, though he was a sophisticated priest and too self-forgiving, his faith was real enough,
though so supple and riddled with irony that God was no
more exempt from censure than the Archbishop of
Canterbury (whom he privately referred to as Old Potato-
Face). Still, he resented having to tailor his beliefs to his
audience and not for the first time wished he was an out and
out Catholic where this problem wouldn't arise. One of the
many grumbles Father Jolliffe had about the English Re-
formation was that it was then that feeling had got into the
service, so you couldn't get away with just saying the words
but had to mean them at the same time.

These thoughts had taken him and the procession to the
chancel, where the choir filed into their pews and the spare
clergy disposed themselves around, while still leaving the
hymn with a couple of verses to run. This gave Father Jolliffe a
chance to think about what he ought to say about Clive and
what he ought not to say.

CLIVE HAD BEEN A MASSEUR; there was no secret about
that. It was something he was very good at and his skill
transcended mere physical manipulation. Many of his clients
attested to a feeling of warmth that seemed to flow through
his fingers and for which there was no orthodox physiological
explanation. 'He has healing hands' was one way of putting it
or (this from the more mystically inclined) 'He has the Touch.'

That Clive was black (though palely so) was thought by

some to account for these healing attributes since it meant (despite his having been born and brought up in Bethnal Green) that he was closer to his origins than were his clients and in touch with an ancient wisdom long since lost to them. Never discouraging these mythic speculations Clive himself had no such illusions, though the pouch to which he sometimes stripped to carry out the massage was rudimentary enough to call up all sorts of primitive musings.

The heat that his clients felt, though, was not fanciful and as a boy had embarrassed Clive and made him reluctant to touch or be touched. The realisation that what he had was not a burden but a gift was a turning point and that, with his calorific propensities, it could be marketed was another. And so the laying on of hands became for him a way of life.

This was not, of course, all. Though Clive was scrupulous never to omit the ceremony of massage, for some it was just the preliminary to a more protracted and intimate encounter and one which might, understandably, come a little dearer. Looking over the crowded church, Father Jolliffe wondered who were here just as grateful patients whose burden of pain Clive had smoothed away and who had come along to com-memorate the easing of a different sort of burden, and of the latter how many were as nervous as he was himself about the legacy that the dead man might have left them.

NOW AS THE HYMN ENDED Father Jolliffe said, 'Will you sit', gave them a moment to settle and then launched

into his preamble. And straightaway came out with something
he had no intention of saying.

'On such occasions as these,' he said, 'a priest will often
preface his remarks with an apology, craving the forgiveness
of the congregation since they have had the advantage of
knowing the deceased whereas he didn't. I make no such apology. I knew Clive and like most of you, I imagine, loved him
and valued his friendship – else why are any of us here?'

Treacher, who was not here for that at all, made a neat note
on the back of his Order of Service.

Father Jolliffe was amazed at himself. Few people in the
congregation were aware he knew Clive and for various reasons, one of which was prudence, he hadn't been planning to
say that he did. Now he had blurted it out and must make the
best of it, though this would be hard as there was so much he
could not say.

For the most part Geoffrey (and there are some circumstances in which it's right he is called Geoffrey and not Father
Jolliffe) . . . for the most part Geoffrey was celibate, though he
attached no virtue to this, knowing it was not abstinence so
much as lack of opportunity that kept him generally unconju-
gate; that and a certain timidity where sex was concerned
which made him, despite his (mild) moral disapproval, bestow
on an enterprising promiscuity such as Clive's an almost
heroic status. No matter that boldness came as naturally to
Clive as diffidence did to Geoffrey or that Clive, of course, was
much better looking and unburdened by Geoffrey's thoughts
of God (and not looking a fool); Geoffrey knew that in what

nowadays is called a one-to-one situation he was what he thought of as shy, so that men who weren't shy, such as Clive, seemed to him warriors, their valour, however profligate, more of a virtue than his own timorous drawing back.

Geoffrey had had experience at first hand of how fly Clive could be. En route for lunch together along the Farringdon Road (not a thoroughfare Geoffrey had ever thought of in a carnal context) Clive had intercepted a male glance that Geoffrey had not even noticed and quick as a fish he had darted away leaving Geoffrey to eat alone and return home disconsolate, where Clive duly came by to give an account of his afternoon. True, Clive was not choosy or how else would he have got into bed with Geoffrey himself, episodes so decorous that for Clive they can scarcely have registered as sex at all, though still tactile enough for Geoffrey, on the news of Clive's death, to be filled with unease.

Being of an Anglo-Catholic persuasion Father Jolliffe practised auricular confession, when he would come clean about his predilections, an ordeal that was somewhat diminished by choosing as his confessor a clergyman whom he knew 'had no problem with that' and being of a similar persuasion himself would place it low down in the hierarchy of possible wickedness. With never much to confess on that particular score, now with Clive gone there was going to be even less.

Somebody coughed. The congregation were waiting and though the pause while Father Jolliffe wrestled with what he should and should not say was understood to be one of deep personal remembrance or even a chance to regain control of his feelings, still, there wasn't all day.

Father Jolliffe plunged on and suddenly it all came right. 'We shall be singing some hymns. We shall pray together and there will be readings and some of Clive's favourite music.' Father Jolliffe paused. 'Prayer may seem to some of you an out-moded activity and hymns too, possibly, but that was not what Clive thought. Clive, as I know personally, was always keen to involve himself in the rites and rituals of the church and were he here he would be singing louder and praying harder than anybody.'

Despite the unintentional disclosure of his friendship with Clive, Father Jolliffe was not displeased with how he (or possibly God) had turned it to good account. Using Clive as a way round any misgivings the congregation might have re the religious side of things was a happy thought. It took the curse off the service very nicely and in the shadows behind the pillar Treacher made another note and this time added a tick.

Actually Geoffrey (we are back to Geoffrey again) knew that where Clive's religious inclinations were concerned he was stretching it a bit. Pious he wasn't and his interest in the rites and rituals of the church didn't go much further than the not unfetching young men who were often helping to perform them, Clive reckoning, not always correctly, that what with the ceremony, the incense and the general dressing-up anyone of a religious disposition was, as he put it, 'halfway there already'. He was particularly keen on vestments, though not in any way Father Jolliffe (sorry) could share with the congregation, having once found Clive in the rectory clad only in his underpants trying on cotta and cope.

Father Jolliffe now led the congregation in prayer, asking them to kneel if they so chose or simply bow their heads so that they could together remember Clive. Heads went down, eyes were closed with only the security guard on the qui vive, scowling across the bowed benches where someone, he felt sure, might be only pretending to pray. At one point he even stood up and turned round lest some wrongdoer could be taking advantage of these unstructured devotions in order to creep up and snatch the clasp. Suspicious, as he put it, 'of this whole prayer thing' he slumped back moodily in his seat as Jolliffe launched into the Collect.

The vicar didn't improvise prayers, Treacher was relieved to note, drawing them from the ample stock of the old prayer book, and saying them briskly and formally as Treacher preferred them to be said. There were few things worse, in Treacher's view, than a priest who gave too much weight to the words of prayers, pausing as if to invest them with heartfelt meaning and thereby impressing the congregation (and himself) with his sincerity. Treacher had even heard the Lord's Prayer delivered in this fashion and found it intolerable and even queasy. But Father Jolliffe, perhaps because of his Catholic leanings, was dry and to the point. 'Say the word, say the word only' seemed to be his motto and Treacher added another tick.

So far, Treacher was bound to admit, Jolliffe was not doing too badly. Even the news of the priest's friendship with the dead man had scarcely counted against him, as the Archdeacon had all along assumed Jolliffe to be homosexual, though without seeing this as a cause for censure or even a necessary obstacle to promotion. Untrammelled by wife or family and with a housekeeper to look after the vicarage (when there were vicarages to look after), their energies channelled, the sex under wraps, once upon a time homosexuals had made excellent priests and still could so long as they were sensible. The homosexuals Treacher preferred were dry, acerbic and, of course, unavowed; A.E. Housman the type that he approved of, minus the poetry, of course, and (though this was less important) minus the atheism. Nowadays, though, discretion had been cast aside and it had all gone splashy, priests feeling in conscience bound to make their proclivities plain, with even Jolliffe's declaration of friendship for the dead man a timorous attempt, Treacher felt, to lay his cards on the table. Which was a mistake, Treacher believing that a priest should no more declare a sexual preference than he should a political one. Even so, Treacher reflected, there was this to be said in Jolliffe's favour that, whatever his shortcomings, he was not she. In Treacher's church there was a place for she, running the jumble sale, or doing the altar flowers; a she could even take the plate round or read the lesson. But there was no place for she at the altar or in the pulpit. So, give Jolliffe his due: he was not she.

N OW THE CONGREGATION SAT and the scheduled part of the service began. The programme had been put together by Pam, a cheerful woman Clive had known since childhood and who was now a producer at the BBC, and Derek, his long-time landlord. Eclectic would be the kindest word to describe it. Treacher, who had no reason to be kind, thought it looked a bit of a ragbag.

First up was a well-known actress and star of a current sitcom who ascends the stairs of the lectern where she reads immaculately a piece about death not really being the end but just like popping next door. It was a regular standard at memorial services and seeing it billed in the programme Treacher had sighed. He believed in death and when he said he believed in God, death was to a large extent what he meant. These days people didn't, or tried not to, always feeling death was unfair, so when they saw it coming to them or their loved ones they made a great song and dance about it.

And these days there was always blame; it was 'down to' someone or other – the school, the doctor, the police – and you must fight back, that was today's philosophy; in the midst of life we are in death was nowadays a counsel for wimps. It didn't used to be like this, he thought. Had it come from America, he wondered. Or Liverpool? Was television to blame? Or Mrs Thatcher? These days he seldom felt well himself but he wasn't complaining. Or perhaps (and here he was trying to be charitable) what was really distasteful was death as leveller. These days people were so anxious to lay hold of anything that marked them out from the rest – the death of their children, for instance, their neglect by hospitals, being fumbled when young or tortured by nuns; even the murder of loved ones would do if it served to single them out. Whereas the good thing about death was that it singled everybody out. It was the one unchanging thing. Treacher smiled.

Father Jolliffe's thoughts were different, though just as wayward and far from Clive. The next reader had a ponytail and Geoffrey found himself wondering at what point in bed the hair was unloosed, shaken out, let down. And by whom? He thought of the curtain of hair falling across the pillow, the signal, perhaps (in addition to other signals), that the body was now on offer. So again he remembered Clive.

Next up was a pianist, another personal acquaintance who comes to the piano in mittens which he then takes off before playing some Schubert, the performance of which, judging by his expression, seems to cause him exquisite pain but which turns to dark-faced anger as during the final section a police car drives past with its siren going.

And so it goes on, under Father Jolliffe's benevolent eye, poems, readings, a succession of 'turns' really, one of which, though, Treacher is pleased to note, is from St Paul's First Letter to the Corinthians, the passage about love, with Father Jolliffe opting for the King James version using charity. He took time at the start of the reading to explain to the congregation that charity was love and not anything to do with flag days or people in doorways. Or if it was to do with people in doorways that was only one of its meanings.

Treacher would have scorned such condescension and let

the congregation make of it what they could but he forbore to mark his card on the point. Still, he would have preferred it if the great rolling cadences of the Authorised Version hadn't been followed by a saxophone rendition of the Dusty Springfield standard 'You Don't Have to Say You Love Me', a number (and there was no other word for it) that occasioned a round of applause, from which Treacher unsurprisingly abstained.

During the saxophone solo Geoffrey's worries about Clive recurred. What had he died of? He wished he knew for certain. Or not. Geoffrey had been in bed with Clive seldom and so tamely that only someone as inexperienced as Geoffrey would have thought himself at risk at all. But it did happen, he knew that; he wasn't even sure if there was some risk in kissing (though there hadn't been much of that either).

The truth was it was God that Geoffrey didn't trust. Irony was always the deity's strong point and to afflict a transgressor as timid as Geoffrey with such a disproportionate penalty might appeal to the Almighty's sense of cosmic fun. It was unfair to God, he knew, but he'd always felt the deity had a mean side and on one of his reports at theological college his tutor had written, 'Tends to confuse God with Joan Crawford.'

Treacher looked at his watch. One or two of the participants had preceded their contributions with a few words about Clive – Clive as assiduous and imaginative hospital visitor, Clive as holiday companion, Clive as lover of Schubert and dogs. Still, though these had lengthened the proceedings a little, Treacher was relieved to note that they were now on the last item before the final hymn, a rendering by an ancient musical comedy actress of 'darling Ivor's' immortal 'Fly Home, Little Heart'. 'Fly home, Clive,' she prefaced it, 'our thoughts go with you.'

As her quavering soprano drifted through the church, Treacher began to make plans to slip away as unobtrusively as he had arrived. Slightly to the Archdeacon's regret he had to concede that Father Jolliffe had not done too badly. He had kept the service moving and each contribution brief: he had not sold God short and even allowing for the saxophone solo and the old lady currently in full, if tiny, voice it had never ceased to be a church service. Treacher had come along hoping to find Father Jolliffe a bit of a clown and over-anxious to please. There had been no evidence of that and he deserved credit. Canon Treacher folded his Order of Service and put it in his pocket. He would nip out during the last hymn.

FATHER JOLLIFFE, too, was pleased the service was over in such good time, though he had some regrets. Varied though the contributions had been he didn't feel they had done justice to Clive and his special charm. Nobody had quite captured his character; an opportunity had been missed. Besides, Father Jolliffe (and he can surely be forgiven) was still somewhat star-struck by his glamorous congregation and understandably wanted to hold onto them for just a little longer. They were such a change from his usual attendance who (while just as precious in the sight of God, of course) were duller and less fun.

So when the old lady finished and was greeted with such sympathetic applause she had to be coaxed from the microphone before she got into an encore, Father Jolliffe on a sudden impulse (with which he subsequently thought God had had something to do) didn't sink to his knees for the final prayers but stood up, moved to the centre of the chancel steps and expressed the hope that anyone with cherished memories of Clive which they would like to share should now feel free to do so. Treacher frowned and fished the Order of Service out of his pocket to check that this was a departure from the published proceedings. Finding that it was and the proceedings had indeed been prolonged he put a large question-mark in the margin.

Father Jolliffe stood on the chancel steps and in the expectant silence the ponderous workings of the clock, fixed on the back wall of the tower, now began to click and whirr preparatory to slowly striking twelve. From experience Father Jolliffe knew that these crankings made speech impossible, so hearing those first admonitory clicks he had learned to pause and wait until the ancient mechanism had run its course.

These necessary cessations often had an opportuneness to them, coming at a pause in a prayer, say, or, as today, at a moment of remembrance, just as year by year the coughing and wheezing ushered in the start of the grandest remembrance of all, the Two-Minute Silence. The unorchestrated pauses, though, were generally less weighty than that but were so repeatedly apposite as to have acquired an almost liturgical significance, the whirring of the cogs and the clanking of the wheels serving to charge the moment, as did the ringing of the bell at the elevation of the Host.

In matters of faith Father Jolliffe might be thought a bit of a noodle but however felicitous the pause in question even he didn't quite identify it as the voice of God. Still, if it was not God speaking, sometimes he felt the Almighty was at least clearing his throat, coughing meaningfully as a reminder of his presence. Father Jolliffe could see no harm in the practice of the presence of God being conflated with the sound of the passage of time, though there were also occasions when the clock's timely intervention irritated him, feeling that there was no need sometimes for the deity to draw attention to himself so obviously. It had something of St Peter and the cock crowing thrice about it, not an incident Father Jolliffe was particularly fond of as it showed Jesus up as a bit of an 'I told you so', which on the quiet the priest felt he sometimes was anyway.

Today, though, the intervention of the clock was useful in that it gave the congregation a moment or two to dwell on what they might want to say about Clive and perhaps as a consequence once twelve had struck people were not slow to respond.

A man was straightaway on his feet testifying to Clive's skill and good humour crewing in a transatlantic yacht race and another to his unsuspected abilities as a gourmet cook, testimonials greeted with incredulity in some sections of the congregation ('Clive?') but elsewhere without surprise. A woman said what a good gardener he was and how he had gone on to paint her kitchen, while someone from Woman's Hour described him as 'bright-eyed and bushy-tailed' and evidenced the large congregation as a testimony to Clive's genius for friendship, a genius incidentally that is generally posthumous and, like 'touching life at many points' (which Clive was also said to have done), is only found in obituaries. On the other hand, 'not suffering fools gladly', another staple of the obituary column, was not said, Clive having suffered fools as a matter of course as this was partly what he was paid for.

A Japanese gentleman now stood up and addressed the congregation in Japanese, a series of emphatic and seemingly impassioned declarations of which no one, even those lucky enough to speak Japanese, understood a word, as the acoustics of the church (designed by Inigo Jones) made it sound like overhearing an argument. Still, whether out of admiration for his boldness in speaking at all or to compensate him for being Japanese and therefore unintelligible, the congregation gave him a round of applause.

He bowed to every corner of the church then sat down, by which time there were already two more people on their feet wanting to have a word. Treacher began to think his estimate of Father Jolliffe to have been wrong. There was no firm hand here and as a woman behind him said, 'It's going on a bit,' the Archdeacon made another adverse note.

Happy to see it go on was a publisher, a portly and pretentious figure who had never met Clive but was there escorting one of his authors (as yet unennobled), a woman with several bestsellers under her belt but whose work had recently taken a feminist turn and who he feared might be looking for a publisher to match. Coming along to the service just as a chore he

had been amazed at the level and variety of celebrity represented and, in the way of publishers, began to scent a book. As
more and more of the congregation stood up and the reminiscences about Clive accumulated the publisher grew steadily
more excited, occasionally clutching his companion's arm or,
like Treacher (but not), scribbling notes on the back of his
Order of Service. He saw the book as quick and easy to produce,
a tape-recording job largely, a collage of interviews each no
more than two or three paragraphs long – a book for people
who preferred newspapers and which read like gossip while
masquerading as sociology. 'A portrait of a generation'.

Her affection for Clive notwithstanding the novelist found
it hard to reciprocate the publisher's enthusiasm, her own
work never having generated a comparable degree of fervour.
A woman would understand. As the publisher jotted down the
names of possible writers she determined to take her next
book where it would be better appreciated. She yawned.

Others were yawning too. Now an elderly couple got up and
left, followed a few minutes later by a younger man, tapping
his watch, portraying helplessness and mouthing 'Sorry' to an
unidentified friend in one of the pews behind.

FATHER JOLLIFFE was now wishing he'd never let the congregation off the leash. They were popping up all over the
place, never fewer than two people on their feet waiting their
turn. Some didn't stand but put a hand up, one of the most
persistent a drab youth in an anorak sitting towards the front

on the aisle. How he had come to know Clive Father Jolliffe could not imagine.

As a woman ended some protracted hymn to Clive's 'nurturing touch' Father Jolliffe managed to get in before the next speaker. 'I feel,' he said tentatively, 'that as time's getting on we ought to think about drawing these delightful reminiscences to a close', a warning word that had the opposite effect to that intended as it galvanised all those who had not yet made up their minds to speak now to try and do so. In particular it made the drab youth start waving his hand as if he were still at school and trying to catch the teacher's eye. He looked as if he was at school, too, in jeans and blue anorak, though he had made some effort to dress up for the occasion by putting on a shirt and tie, the shirt rather too big at the collar and the cuffs almost covering his hands. Father Jolliffe wished he would be more forthright and not wait to be called but just stand up and get on with it like other people were doing, currently a philosopher, well-groomed and bronzed from a sabbatical at Berkeley.

'Though we knew his name was Clive,' he was saying, 'we' – his wife sitting beside him smiled – 'we called him Max, a name I came to feel suited him well. It's not entirely a nice name, not plain certainly or wholesome. In fact Max, really, is the name of a charmer, implying a degree of sophistication, a veneer of social accomplishment. It's urban, metropolitan, the name of someone who could take a vacant place at a poker game, say, and raise no eyebrows, which someone called ... oh, Philip, say, couldn't.'

At this a woman in front turned round. 'I called him Philip.' Then turning to her neighbour. 'He said that was what he felt like inside.'

'I called him Bunny,' said a man on the aisle and this was the signal for other names to be tossed around – Toby, Alex and even Denis, all, however unlikely, attested to and personally guaranteed by various members of the congregation – so that still on his feet to bear witness to the unique appropriateness of Max the philosopher begins to feel a bit of a fool and says lamely, 'Well, he was always Max to us but this was obviously a many-sided man ... which is yet another cause for celebration.' And sits down plumply to a reassuring pat from his wife.

One of the names submitted in contention with Max was Betty, the claims for which had been quite belligerently advanced by a smallish young man in a black suit and shaven head who was sitting towards the front with several other young men similarly suited and shorn, one or two of them with sunglasses lodged on top of their hairless heads.

Now, ignoring the woman whose turn it was and the feebly waving youth, the young man, who gave his name as Carl, addressed the congregation. 'Knowing Clive well I think he would be touched if someone' – he meant himself – 'were to say something about him as a lover?'

A couple who had just got up to go straightaway sat down again. There was a hush, then a woman in the front row said: 'Excuse me. Before you do that I think we ought to see if this lady minds.' She indicated her neighbour, a shabby old woman in a battered straw hat, her place also occupied by a couple of greasy shopping bags. 'She might mind. She is Mr Dunlop's aunt.'

Father Jolliffe closed his eyes in despair. It was Miss Wishart and she was not Clive's aunt at all. Well into her eighties and with nothing better to do Miss Wishart came to every funeral or memorial service that took place at the church, which was at least warm and where she could claim to be a distant relative of the deceased, a pretence not hard to maintain as she was genuinely hard of hearing and so could ignore the occasional probing question. Sometimes when she was lucky (and the relatives were stupid) she even got invited back for the funeral tea. All this Father Jolliffe knew and could have said, but it was already too late as Carl was even now sauntering round to the front pew where Miss Wishart was sitting in order to put the question to her directly.

With set face and making no concessions to her age or sensibilities Carl stood over Miss Wishart. 'Do you mind if we talk about your nephew's sex life?' Her neighbour repeated this in Miss Wishart's ear and while she considered the question, which she heard as having to do with his ex-wife, Carl looked up at Father Jolliffe. 'And you don't object, padre?'

It's often hard these days for the clergy not to think of God as a little old-fashioned and Father Jolliffe was no exception. So if he was going to object it wasn't on grounds of taste or decorum but simply in order to cut the service short. But what he really objected to was the condescension of 'padre' (and even its hint of a sneer) so this made him feel he couldn't object on any grounds at all without the young man thinking he was a ninny.

'No, I've no objection,' he said, 'except' – and he looked boldly down at this small-headed creature – 'I think what we're talking about is love. Clive's love life.' Then, thinking that didn't sound right either, 'His life of love.'

That sounded even worse and the young man smirked.

Treacher sighed. Jolliffe had been given an opportunity to put a stop to all this nonsense and he had muffed it. Had he been in charge he would have put the young man in his place, got the congregation on their knees and the service would have been over in five minutes. Now there was no telling what would happen.

As an indication that the proceedings were descending into chaos Treacher noted that one or two men in the congregation now felt relaxed enough to take out mobile phones and carry on hushed conversations, presumably rearranging appointments for which the length of the service was now making them late. The young man in front pocketed his cigarettes and lighter and strolled up the aisle to slip out of the West door where he found that two or three other like-minded smokers had preceded him. They nattered moodily in nicotine's enforced camaraderie before grinding their fags into the gravestones and rejoining the service at the point where the question about her nephew's sex life had at last got through to Miss Wishart and her neighbour was able to announce the verdict to the congregation. 'His aunt doesn't mind.'

There was a smattering of applause to signify approval of such exemplary open-mindedness in one so old, but since the question Miss Wishart thought she'd been asked was not to do with her nephew's sex life but with his next life, her tolerance hadn't really been put to the test.

'I JUST THOUGHT,' said Carl standing on the chancel steps, 'that it would be kind of nice to say what Clive was like in bed?' It was a question but not one that expected an answer. 'I mean, not in detail, obviously, only that he was good? He took his time and without being, you know, mechanical he was really inventive? I want,' he said, 'to take you on a journey? A journey round Clive's body?'

Treacher sank lower in his seat and Geoffrey's smile lost some of its benevolence as Carl did just that, dwelling on each part, genitals for the moment excepted, with the fervour if not quite the language of the metaphysical poets.

Though it was a body Geoffrey was at least acquainted with, Carl's version of it rang no bells and so he was reassured when he saw one or two in the congregation smiling wistfully and shaking their heads as if Carl had missed the point of Clive's body. Still, Geoffrey hoped nobody was going to feel strongly enough about this discrepancy to offer up a rival version as, however fascinating this material was, he felt there was a limit to what the congregation would stand.

'Do we really want to know this?' a senior official in the Foreign Office muttered to his wife (though in truth he knew some of it already and, unbeknownst to him, so did she).

Actually Geoffrey was surprised at Carl's forbearance in omitting the penis, an intimate survey of which he was obviously capable of providing should he so choose. Perhaps, Geoffrey thought, he was saving it up but if so it was to no purpose as it was while Carl was en route from the scrotum to the anus that suddenly it all got too much and a man was bold enough to shout out: 'Shame.'

Carl rounded on him fiercely. 'No, there was no shame. No shame then and no shame now. If you didn't understand that about Clive, you shouldn't be here.'

After which, though there were no more interruptions, the congregation felt slightly bullied and so took on a mildly mutinous air.

A woman sitting near to the front and quite close to Carl said almost conversationally: 'And you made this journey quite often, did you?'

'What journey?'

'Round Clive's body.'

'Sure. Why?'

'It's just that, while I may be making a fool of myself here,' and she looked round for support, 'I didn't know he was ... that way.'

Several women who were within earshot nodded agreement.

'To me he was – ' and she knew she was on dangerous ground, 'to me, he wasn't that way at all.'

Carl frowned. 'Do you mean gay?'

The woman (she was a buyer for Marks and Spencer's) smiled kindly and nodded.

'Well let me tell you,' said Carl, 'he was "that way".'

Though these exchanges are intimate and conversational they filter back through the congregation where they are greeted with varying degrees of astonishment, some of it audible.

'She didn't know?'

'Who's she kidding?'

'Clive,' the woman went on, 'never gave me to suppose that his sexual preferences were other than normal.'

'It is normal,' shouted Carl.

'I apologise. I mean conventional.'

'It's conventional, too.'

'Straight then,' said the buyer with a gesture of defeat. 'Let's say straight.'

'Say what you fucking like,' said Carl, 'only he wasn't. He was gay.'

Smiling and unconvinced she shook her head but said no more.

During this exchange Geoffrey had been thinking about Carl's hair or lack of it, the gleam of his skull through the blond stubble making him look not unlike a piglet. Once upon a time hair as short as this would have been a badge of a malignant disposition, a warning to keep clear, with long hair indicating a corresponding lenity. With its hint of social intransigence it had become a badge of sexual deviance, which it still seemed to be, though nowadays it was also a useful mask for incipient baldness, cutting the hair short a way of pre-empting the process.

'Fucking' had put a stop to these musings though Carl had said it so casually that for all they were in church no one seemed shocked (Treacher fortunately hadn't heard it) and Father Jolliffe decided to let it pass.

In his fencing match with the buyer from M&S Carl had undoubtedly come out on top but it had plainly disconcerted him and though he resumed his journey round Clive's body, when he got to his well-groomed armpits he decided to call it a day. 'When someone dies so young,' he summed up, 'the pity of it and the waste of it touch us all. But when he or she dies of Aids' – someone in the congregation gave a faint cry – 'there should be anger as well as pity, and a resolve to fight this insidious disease and the prejudice it arouses and not to rest until we have a cure.' Carl sat down to be embraced by two of his friends, his stubbly head rubbed by a third.

H EARING AIDS mentioned for the first time and what had hitherto been vague fears and suspicions now given explicit corroboration many in the congregation found it hard to hide their concern, this death which had hitherto been an occasion for sorrow now a cause for alarm.

One woman sobbed openly, comforted by her (slightly pensive) husband.

A man knelt down and prayed, his companion stroking his back gently as he did so.

'I didn't think you needed to die of it any more,' a round the world yachtswoman whispered to her husband. 'I thought there were drugs.'

Others just sat there stunned, their own fate now prefigured, this memorial service a rehearsal for their own.

One of these, of course, was Father Jolliffe who is professional enough, though, to think this sobering down might be given prayerful expression, all this worry and concern channelled into an invocation not only for Clive but for all the victims of this frightful disease and not merely here but in Africa, Asia and America and so on. The landscape of the petition taking shape in his mind he stood up and faced the congregation. 'Shall we pray.'

As he himself knelt he saw the student-type in the anorak, impervious to the atmosphere obviously, still with his hand up and waving it even more vigorously now. But enough had been said and the priest ignored him.

There is a hush, with Treacher relieved that Father Jolliffe has at last got a grip on the service and is now going to bring these unseemly proceedings to a fitting conclusion.

'Vicar.'

It was the young man in the anorak. His voice was very clear in the silence and those of the congregation who had knelt or just put their heads down now raised them to look and Treacher, who had felt this service could hold no more surprises, said 'Oh God' and would have put his head in his hands had it not been there already.

Even the easy-going Father Jolliffe was taken aback at this

unheard-of interruption. 'I was praying,' he said reproachfully.

He thought the young man blushed but he was looking so worked up it was hard to tell. A long-wristed, narrow-faced, straight-shouldered young man now looking sheepish. 'I did have my hand up before,' he said. 'And besides, it's probably relevant to the prayer.'

Had it not come at such an inopportune moment the notion that a prayer needed to be up to the minute and take account of all relevant information would have merited some thought and indeed might have provided a useful subject for 'Faith and Time', the series of discussion groups Father Jolliffe was currently running after Evensong on Sundays; the topicality of intercession in the light of the omniscience of God, for instance, or prayers taking place in time and God not. As it was the priest found himself staring at the young man, all pastoral feeling suspended, and saying rather crossly, 'Well?'

'My name is Hopkins,' said the young man. 'I'm on my year out. I'm going to do geology. I was in South America looking at rocks.'

Some of this he said loudly enough for the congregation to hear, but other less relevant remarks he gave almost as an aside to the nearby pews, so that somebody out of range said: 'What?'

'On his year out, doing geology,' somebody else called back.

'And?' said somebody else under their breath.

'I got sponsorship from Tilcon,' the young man added redundantly.

Somebody sighed heavily and said: 'Do we need to know this?'

'That was why I was in Peru. The rocks are very good there.'

'Can't hear,' said a well-known commentator on the arts. 'I know about Peru and even I can't hear.'

A woman nearby smiled kindly at the boy, and indicated he should speak up.

'The thing is' – and the speaking up made him sound defiant – 'I was staying in the same hotel as Mr Dunlop when he died, and he didn't die of Aids.'

Finding him so unprepossessing and with no air of authority whatever (and, it has to be said, younger than most of their children) the congregation were disinclined to give him much attention. What had seemed just another tedious reminiscence is at first listlessly received and it's only when the glad message 'Not Aids' begins to be passed round and its significance realised that people start to take notice, some at the back even standing up to get a better view of this unlikely herald.

It takes a little time and while there is some shaking of heads at first, soon smiles begin to break out, people perk up and this nondescript young man suddenly finds himself addressing an audience that hangs on his every word. 'I know there is nothing to be ashamed of whatever it was he died of, but with all due respect to the person who spoke, who obviously knew him much better than I did, all the same I was there when he died and I'm sure his aunt, at least, would like to know it was not Aids.'

'HIV-related,' corrected a man with a ponytail.

'Yes, whatever,' says the student.

'It wasn't Aids,' Miss Wishart's helpful neighbour shouts in her ear. 'Not Aids.'

Meeting an uncomprehending smile from the old lady, she thinks to mime the condition by pointing to her bottom and shaking her head, thereby causing much offence to Carl and his glabrous colleagues and bringing Miss Wishart no nearer enlightenment. The only aids she has come across are deaf aids and hers plainly isn't working.

Hopkins, having given his welcome news, offers no evidence to back it up and now seems disposed to sit down again except that Father Jolliffe, who, if he had been an MP and addressing the House of Commons, would at this point have had to preface his question by declaring an interest, leans over the lectern and says, 'And do you mind telling us Mr ...?'

'Hopkins.'

'Mr Hopkins, do you mind telling us how Mr Dunlop did die?'

The young man blew his nose, carefully wiped it, and put away his handkerchief.

'Well, basically he had been on a trip which took him through some rough country where he was like bitten by some insect or other, you know, the name of which I can't remember, only the doctors at the hospital knew it. He got this fever. He was in the room next door to me at the hotel, to begin with anyway. Then they took him in and that was it basically. I was surprised as it's not a tropical place. The climate's not very different from Sheffield. I come from Sheffield,' he added apologetically.

Hopkins remained on his feet looking round at the congregation and smiling helpfully as if to suggest that if there were any more questions he would be happy to try and answer them. He doesn't have long to wait.

'I do not believe this,' Carl mutters as he gets to his feet though it is not to ask a question. He wholly ignores the student and talks to the church. 'I'm sorry? I thought we'd grown up? I thought we'd learned to look this thing in the face? I never thought I'd still be hearing tales of some ailment picked up in the wilds of Tibet. Or a wasting disease caught from the udders of Nepalese yaks. It's not from a bite. It's not from cat hairs. It's not from poppers nor is it a congenital disease of the dick. It's a virus passed via blood and sex and that's how it's caught. Not from some fucking Peruvian caterpillar. Of course it was Aids. Look at his life. How could it be anything else?'

In the silence that followed, many look desperately at the student in the hope he has something more to offer by way of rebuttal. But at nineteen debate is hardly his strong point. He shrugs awkwardly and sits down shaking his head, long wrists dangling between his knees.

Unpleasant and arrogant though Carl had been, and with a manner seemingly designed to put people's backs up, there were many in the congregation who felt that he was right. They longed passionately to believe in this Peruvian caterpillar and its death-dealing bite. South America was a dangerous place, everyone knew that; there were the pampas, gauchos and regular revolutions. The Maya had perished, so why not Clive? But what Carl had said made sense. Of course it was Aids. No one could screw as much as he had done and go unpunished. So the sentence that had been all too briefly remitted was now reimposed and hopes momentarily raised were dashed once more. But to have been given a vision of peace of mind and then to see it snatched away made the burden even harder to bear.

One couple held each other's hands in mute misery. Which had slept with Clive – or both? What did it matter? Never had they been so close.

Still, the couples who had shared Clive's favours were better placed than husbands or wives who had known him singly. 'What does it signify anyway,' said a fierce-eyebrowed judge, to whom Clive was only someone who occasionally unfroze his shoulder. 'He's dead, that's the essence of it.' His wife, who was keeping very quiet, shifted in her seat slightly as she was suffering from thrush, or that was what she hoped.

Symptoms were back generally. A pitiless quiz-show host found herself with a dry mouth. The suffragan bishop knew he had a rash. A stand-up comedian had a cold sore that didn't seem to clear up and which was masked by make-up. Now it had suddenly begun to itch. He had a powder compact but dared not consult it. Those who were famous, though, knew better than to turn a hair. Their anxiety must be kept private and unshown for they were always under scrutiny. They must wait to share their worries discreetly with friends or, if with the general public, at a decent price from the newspapers concerned.

Husbands who thought their wives didn't know put a face on it (though their wives did know very often). Wives who thought their husbands didn't know (which they generally didn't) masked their distraction in a show of concern for others, one, for instance, patting the shoulder of a man in front who, without looking, took the hand and held it to his cheek.

The congregation had been given a glimpse of peace; the itch had gone, the cough had stilled, the linen was unsoiled; the pores had closed, the pus dried up and the stream ran clear and cool. But that was what it had been, a glimpse only. Now there was to be no healing. There was only faith.

How to put this into prayer. Father Jolliffe clasped his hands and tried once more. 'Shall we pray?'

They settled and waited as he sought for the words.

'May I speak?'

Baulked for a second unbelievable time on the brink of intercession, Father Jolliffe nearly said 'No' (which is what the Archdeacon would have said, who has long since written down: 'Hopeless. Lacks grip.' And now inserts 'totally').

Father Jolliffe searches the congregation to see who it is who has spoken and sees, standing at the back, a tall, distinguished-looking man. 'I am a doctor,' he says.

This is unsurprising because it is just what he looks like. He is dry, kindly faced and yet another one who doesn't speak up. 'I am a doctor,' he repeats. 'Mr Dunlop's doctor, in fact. While his medical history must, of course, be confidential' – 'Must

be what?' somebody says. 'Controversial,' says someone else –
'I think I am not breaking any rules when I say that Mr Dunlop
was a most ... ah ... responsible patient and came to me over a
period of years for regular blood tests.'

'Regular blood tests,' goes round the pews.

'These were generally *à propos* HIV, the last one only a week
before his departure for South America. It was negative. What
this fever was that he died of I'm in no position to say, but contrary to the assertions made by the gentleman who spoke earlier' – he meant Carl – 'it seems to me most unlikely, in fact
virtually impossible, that it was HIV-related. Still,' he smiled
sadly, 'the fact remains that Clive is dead and I can only offer
my condolences to his grieving friends and to his aunt.
Whatever it was her nephew died of, her grief must be
unchanged.'

Miss Wishart is nudged by her neighbour and when the doctor is pointed out to her, smiles happily and gives him a little
wave. She seldom got such a good ride as this.

As the doctor sat down there was a ripple of applause and as
the news filtered to the acoustically disadvantaged areas of the
church it grew and grew. People at the front stood up and
began applauding louder and those further back followed suit
until the whole church was on its feet clapping.

'Good old Clive!' someone shouted.

'Trust Clive,' said someone else and there was even some of
that overhead clapping and wild whoops that nowadays
characterises audiences in a TV studio or at a fashionable first
night.

Seldom even at a wedding had the vicar seen so many happy faces, some openly laughing, some weeping even and many of them embracing one another as they were called on to do in the Communion Service, but never with a fervour or a fellow-feeling so unembarrassed as this. It was, thought Father Jolliffe, just as it should be.

Still, it was hard to say what it was they were applauding: Clive for having died of the right thing (or not having died of the wrong one) and for having been so sensible about his blood tests; the young student for having brought home the news; or the urbane-looking doctor for having confirmed it. Father Jolliffe was glad to see that God came in for some of the credit and mindful of the setting one woman sank to her knees in prayer, and both genders got onto their mobiles to relay the news to partners and friends whose concern for themselves (and for Clive, of course) was as keen as those present in the congregation.

Some wept and, seeing the tears, wondering partners took them as tears for Clive. But funeral tears seldom flow for any-one other than the person crying them and so it was here. They cried for Clive, it is true, but they cried for themselves without Clive, particularly now that his clean and uncompli-cated death meant that he had thankfully left them with noth-ing to remember him by.

Amid the general rejoicing even Carl looked a little more cheerful, though it was hard for him to be altogether whole-hearted, the dead man just having been dropped from a club of which Carl was still a life member and from which he stood no chance of exclusion. There were one or two others in the same boat and knew it, but they clapped too, and tried to rejoice.

Though his companion the novelist was gratefully weeping, the publisher's thanksgiving was less wholehearted. Aids never did sales any harm and gave a tragic momentum even to the silliest of lives, whereas it was hard not to think that there was only bathos in a death that resulted from being bitten by a caterpillar. Still, the geology student seemed naive and possibly suggestible, so Clive's death could be made – and moralistically speaking ought to be made – more ambiguous than it really was. Nobody liked someone who had had as much sex as Clive to get off scot free and that included the idle reader. No, there was a book here even so; the absurd death was just a hiccup and, smiling too, the publisher joined in the clapping.

But clapping whom? Father Jolliffe decided it might as well be God and raising his voice above the tumult he said: 'Now (and for the third time of asking), shall we pray?' This even got a laugh and there was a last whoop before the congregation settled down. 'Let us in the silence remember our friend Clive, who is dead but is alive again.'

This, however hallowed, was not just a phrase. Clive's imagined death had been baneful and fraught with far-reaching implications so that, devoid of these, his real (and more salubrious) demise did seem almost a resurrection. And in that cumbrous silence, laden with prayers unmouthed, loosed from anxiety and recrimination many do now try and remember him, some frowning as they pray with eyes closed but seeing him still, some open-eyed but unseeing of the present, lost in recollection. In the nature of things, these memories are often inappropriate. Some think, for instance, of what Clive felt like, smelled like, recalling his tenderness and his tact. There was the diligence of his application and pictured in more than one mind's eye was that stern and labouring face rising and falling in the conscientious performance of his professional duties.

'I sing his body,' prayed Geoffrey to himself. 'I sing his marble back, his heavy legs' – he had been reading Whitman – 'I sing the absence of preliminaries, the curtness of desire. Dead, but not ominously so, now I extol him.'

'I elevate him,' thought a choreographer (for whom he had also made some shelves), 'a son of Job dancing before the Lord.'

'I dine him,' prayed one of the cooks, 'on quails stuffed with pears in a redcurrant coulis.'

'I adorn him,' imagined a fashion designer. 'I send him down the catwalk in chest-revealing tartan tunic and trews and sporting a tam o'shanter.'

'I appropriate him,' planned the publisher, 'a young man eaten alive by celebrity' (the dust-jacket Prometheus on the rock).

None, though, thought of words and how the bedroom had been Clive's education. It was there that he learned that words mattered, once having been in bed with an etymologist whose ejaculation had been indefinitely postponed when Clive (on being asked if he was about to come too) had murmured, 'Hopefully.' In lieu of discharge, the etymologist had poured his frustrated energy into a short lecture on neologisms which Clive had taken so much to heart he had never said 'hopefully' again.

Nothing surprised him, nothing shocked him. He was not – the word nowadays would be judgmental, but Clive knew that there were some who disliked this word, too, and preferred censorious, but he was not judgmental of that either.

Words mattered and so did names. He knew if someone disliked their name and did not want it said, still less called out, during lovemaking. He knew, too, his clients' various names for the private parts and what he or she preferred to call them and what they preferred him to call them (which was not always the same thing). He knew, too, in the heightened atmosphere of the bedroom how swiftly a misappellation in this regard could puncture desire and shrivel its manifestation.

He brought to the bedroom a power of recall and a grasp of detail that would have taken him to the top of any profession he had chosen to enter. A man who could after several months' interval recall which breast his client preferred caressed could have run the National Theatre or reformed the Stock Exchange. He knew what stories to whisper and when not to tell stories at all and knew, too, when the business was over, never to make reference to what had been said.

Put simply this was a man who had learned never to strike a false note. He was a professional.

Aloud Geoffrey said: 'Let us magnify him before the Lord. O all ye works of the Lord, bless ye the Lord: praise him and magnify him for ever.'

Geoffrey rose to his feet. 'And now we end this service of thanksgiving with John Keble's hymn.'

New every morning is the love ...
Our waking and uprising prove
Through sleep and darkness safely brought
Restored to life and power and thought.

How glumly they had come into the church and how happily now, their burden laid down, do they prepare to go forth. So they sing this mild little hymn as the chorus sings their deliverance in *Fidelio*, or the crowd sings at Elland Road. They sing, distasteful though that spectacle often is, as they sing at the Last Night of the Proms. And singing they are full of new resolve.

Since the news of Clive's death a shadow had fallen across sexual intercourse. Coming together had become wary, the whole business perfunctory and self-serving, and even new relationships had been entered on gingerly. As one wife, not in the know, had complained, 'There is no giving any more.' In some bedrooms where intercourse had not been wholly discontinued prophylactics had appeared for the first time, variously explained by a trivial infection or a sudden sensitivity, but in all cases made out to the unknowing partner as just a minor precaution, not the membrane between life and death.

Now that time of sexual austerity was over. This was the liberation, and many of the couples pressing out of the door looked forward to resuming all those sexually sophisticated manoeuvres that Clive's death and its presumed cause had seen discontinued.

Partners not in the know were taken aback by the gusto with which their long-diffident opposites now went to it, and some, to put it plainly, could scarcely wait to get home in order to have a fuck. And indeed some didn't, one couple sneaking round behind the church to the alcove outside the vestry that sheltered the dustbins and doing it there. They happened both to be friends of Clive and so of the same mind, but several husbands, ignorant of their wives' connection with the dead man, were startled to find themselves unexpectedly fingered and fondled (evidence of the strong tide of relief that was sweeping their partners along) and one, made to park on a double yellow line in the Goswell Road, had to spread a copy of the *Financial Times* over his knees while beneath it his wife gave vent to her euphoria.

For some, though, deliverance would be all too brief. A TV designer, a particular friend of Clive and thus feeling himself more enshadowed than most, was so rapturous at the news of Clive's unportentous death that he celebrated by picking up a dubious young man in Covent Garden, spending a delightful evening and an unprotected night, waking the next morning as anxious as he had been before and in much the same boat.

Still, others thought they had learned their lesson and crowding up the aisles they saw the West door open on a churchyard now bathed in sunlight. The bells were ringing out; the vicar was there shaking hands; truly this had been a thanksgiving and an ending and now the portals were flung open on a new life.

'I presume he had us all on his computer somewhere,' someone said.

'Who cares?' said someone else.

Slowly they shuffled towards the light.

IT WAS NOW WELL PAST LUNCHTIME and the Archdeacon had stomach ache. Anxious to get away before the crowd and unobserved by the vicar, who would surely be shaking all those famous hands, Canon Treacher had got up smartly after the blessing only to find his exit from the pew blocked by a woman doing what she (and Canon Treacher) had been brought up to do, namely, on entering or leaving a church to say a private prayer. It was all Treacher could do not to step over her, but instead waited there fuming while she placidly prayed. She took her time with God, and then, her devotions ended, more time assembling her umbrella, gloves and what she called apologetically 'my bits and bobs' and then when she was finally ready, had to turn back to retrieve her Order of Service, which she held up at Canon Treacher with a brave smile as if to signify that this had been a job well done. By which time, of course, the aisle was clogged with people and Treacher found himself carried slowly but inexorably towards the door where, as he had feared, Father Jolliffe was now busy shaking hands.

Even so, the priest was so deep in conversation with a lead-ing chat-show host that Treacher thought he was going to

manage to sidle by unnoticed. Except that then the priest saw
him and the chat-show host, used to calling the shots with
regard to when conversations began and ended, was startled
to find this chat abruptly wound up as Jolliffe hastened across
to shake Treacher's cold, withdrawing hand.

'Archdeacon. What a pleasure to see you. Did you know
Clive?'

'Who? Certainly not. How should I know him?'

'He touched life at many points.'

It was a joke but Treacher did not smile.

'Not at this one.'

'And did you enjoy the service?' Father Jolliffe's plump face
was full of pathetic hope.

Treacher smiled thinly but did not yield. 'It was ... interesting.'

With Father Jolliffe cringing under the archidiaconal disapproval it ought to have been a chilling moment and, by
Treacher at least, savoured and briefly enjoyed, but it was
muffed when the hostess of a rapid response TV cookery
show, whom the vicar did not know, suddenly flung her arms
round his neck saying, 'Oh, pumpkin!'

Firm in the culinary grasp, Father Jolliffe gazed helplessly
as the Archdeacon was borne away on the slow-moving tide
and out into the chattering churchyard where, holy ground
notwithstanding, Treacher noted that many of the congregation were already feverishly lighting up.

When, a few days later, Treacher delivered his report, it was
not favourable, which saddened the Bishop (who had, though

it's of no relevance, been a great hurdler in his day). Rather mischievously he asked Treacher if he had nevertheless managed to enjoy the service.

'I thought it,' said Treacher, 'a useful lesson in the necessity for ritual. Or at any rate, form. Ritual is a road, a path between hedges, a track along which the priest leads his congregation.'

'Yes,' said the Bishop, who had been here before.

'Leave the gate open, nay tell them it's open as this foolish young man did, and straightaway they're through it, trampling everything underfoot.'

'You make the congregation sound like cattle, Arthur.'

'No, not cattle, Bishop. Sheep, a metaphor for which there is some well-known authority in Scripture. It was a scrum. A free-for-all.'

'Yes,' said the Bishop. 'Still,' he smiled wistfully, 'that gardening girl, the footballer who's always so polite – I quite wish I'd been there.'

Treacher, feeling unwell, now passes out of this narrative, though with more sympathy and indeed regret than his acerbities might seem to warrant. Though he had disapproved of the memorial service and its altogether too heartfelt antics he is not entirely to be deplored, standing in this story for dignity, formality and self-restraint.

Less feeling was what Treacher wanted, the services of the church, as he saw it, a refuge from the prevailing sloppiness. As opportunities multiplied for the display of sentiment in public and on television – confessing, grieving and giving way to anger, and always with a ready access to tears – so it seemed to Treacher that there was needed a place for dryness and self-control and this was the church. It was not a popular view and he sometimes felt that he had much in common with a Jesuit priest on the run in Elizabethan England – clandestine, subversive and holding to the old faith, even though the tenets of that faith, discretion, understatement and respect for tradition, might seem more suited to tailoring than they did to religion.

Once out of the churchyard the Archdeacon lit up, his smoking further evidence that there was more to this man than has been told in this tale. There had briefly been a Mrs Treacher, a nice woman but she had died. He would die soon, too, and the Bishop at least would be relieved.

B ACK AT THE CHURCH, Geoffrey was shaking hands to the finish, with last out, as always, Miss Wishart who was still attesting her supposed connection with the deceased. 'Somebody said something about drinks for my nephew. Where would they be? A sherry was what he preferred only I like wine.'

The priest pointed her vaguely in the direction of the churchyard which with people standing about talking and laughing looked like a cocktail party anyway. He had been asked to drinks himself by a florid and effusive character, a publisher apparently, with a stony-faced woman in tow. He had taken both Geoffrey's hands warmly in his, saying he had this brilliant idea for a book and he wanted to run it past him.

This, taken with the upbeat conclusion of the service, ought to have cheered him, but Father Jolliffe found himself despondent. The presence of the Archdeacon could only mean one thing: he had been vetted. For what he wasn't sure, but for promotion certainly. And equally certainly he had failed to impress. For a start he should not have invited the congregation to participate. He knew that from something that had happened at the Board, when in answer to a question about the kiss of peace and the degree of conviviality acceptable at the Eucharist, he had said that the priest was, in a real sense, the master of ceremonies. This had got a laugh from the Board (the Bishop actually guffawing), except that he had noticed that Treacher was smiling in a different way and making one of his spidery notes: he was not impressed then and he had not been impressed now.

Still had he not, as it were, thrown the service open to the floor, the true circumstances of Clive's death would never have emerged, so he could not regret that. What the Lord giveth the Lord also taketh away. He went back into the now empty church to get out of his gear.

'SHOULD I HAVE SPOKEN?' Hopkins was still slumped in his pew. Now he got up clutching his backpack in front of him like a shield. 'I wondered if it was out of turn.'

'Not at all,' said Geoffrey, noticing that the young man had loosened the unaccustomed tie and undone the top button of his shirt, so that he looked younger still and not so old-fashioned. It was difficult to think of him at Clive's death-bed.

'You did the right thing, Mr Hopkins. There were many people' – he didn't say himself – 'who were grateful. It lifted a burden.'

The boy sat down again cradling his backpack. 'The young guy seemed pretty pissed off. The – ' he hesitated, 'the gay one?'

Hopkins had an unconvincing earring that Geoffrey had not spotted, ear and earring now briefly caught in a shaft of light, a faint fuzz on the fresh pink ear.

'People were upset,' Geoffrey said. 'Clive was ... well, Clive.' He smiled, but the young man still looked unhappy.

'I felt a fool.' He sat hugging his backpack then suddenly brightened up. 'That blonde from *EastEnders* was on my row. Clive never told me he knew her.'

Geoffrey thought that there were probably quite a few things Clive had never told him and wondered if anything had happened between them. Probably not, if only because he imagined there was more on offer in South America and the local talent doubtless more exotic.

He was an awkward boy with big hands. He was the kind of youth Modigliani painted and for a moment Geoffrey wondered if he was attractive, but decided he was just young.

'And that cook who slags people off? He was here too.'

'Yes,' said Geoffrey. 'It was a good turn-out.' Then, feeling he ought to be getting on. 'They're all outside.'

The youth did not notice the hint, still less take it. 'You said you knew Clive?'

'Yes,' said Geoffrey, then added, 'but not well.'

'I'd never seen anybody die before. It was depressing?'

Geoffrey smiled sadly and nodded as if this were an aspect of death that had not occurred to him. The youth was a fool.

'Can I show you something?' The student rooted in his pack then put it on the floor so that the priest could sit beside him. 'I had to go through his stuff after he died. There wasn't much. He was travelling light. Only there was this.'

It was a maroon notebook, long, cloth-covered and meant to fit easily into a pocket. Geoffrey thought he remembered it and ran his hand over the smooth, soft cover.

'Is it a diary?' the priest said.

'Not exactly.'

IN THE CHURCHYARD the party was beginning to break up. One group had arranged to lunch at the Garrick and were moving round saying their farewells while someone looked for a cab. Others were going off to investigate a new restaurant that had opened in a converted public lavatory and of which they'd heard good reports, though tempted to join forces with yet another party who were venturing into one of the last genuine cafés patronised by the porters at Smithfield where the tripe was said to be delicious.

Most of the big stars had left pretty promptly, their cars handily waiting nearby to shield them from too much unmediated attention. The pop star's limo dropped him first then called at the bank so that the security guard could redeposit the clasp and then took him on to a laboratory in Hounslow where, as a change from Catherine the Great, he was mounting vigil over some hamsters testing lip-gloss. Meanwhile, the autograph hunters moved among what was left of the congregation, picking up what dregs of celebrity that remained.

'Are you anybody?' a woman said to the partner of a soap-star, 'or are you just with him?'

'He was my nephew,' said Miss Wishart to anyone who would listen.

'Who, dear?' said one of the photographers, which of course Miss Wishart didn't hear, but she looked so forlorn he took her picture anyway, which was fortunate, as he was later able to submit it to the National Portrait Gallery where it duly featured in an exhibition alongside the stage doorman of the Haymarket and the maître d' of the Ivy as one of 'The Faces of London'.

Soon, though, it began to spit with rain and within a few minutes the churchyard was empty and after its brief bout of celebrity, back to looking as dingy and desolate as it generally did.

'NO, IT ISN'T A DIARY,' said Hopkins. 'It's more of an account book.'

It was divided into columns across the page, each column numbered, possibly indicating a week or a month, the broad left-hand column a list of initials, and in the other columns figures, possibly amounts. The figures were closely packed and as neat as the work of a professional accountant.

'Can you make it out?' said the young man, running his finger down the left-hand column. 'These are people, I take it.'

'They might be,' said Geoffrey. 'I don't quite know.' Having just spotted his own initials, Geoffrey knew only too well, though he noted that the spaces opposite his own name were only occasionally filled in. This was because Clive came round quite spasmodically and wasn't often available when Geoffrey called (now, seeing the number of people on his list, he could see why). When he did come round the visit did not always involve sex ('No funny business' is how Clive put it). Geoffrey told himself that this was because he was a clergyman and that he thus enjoyed a relationship with Clive that was pastoral as well as physical. More often than not this meant he found himself making Clive scrambled eggs, while Clive lay on the sofa watching TV in his underpants, which was about as close to domesticity as Geoffrey ever got. Still, Geoffrey had always insisted on paying for this privilege (hence the entries in the notebook), though really in order to give credence to the fiction that sex wasn't what their friendship was about. Though, since he was paying for it, it wasn't about friendship either, but that managed to be overlooked.

'Did you see a lot of each other? In Peru?'

Geoffrey was anxious to turn the page and get away from those incriminating initials.

'Yes. We had meals together quite often. I could never figure out what he was doing there.'

'What did you eat?' said Geoffrey. 'Eggs?'

'Beans, mostly. He said he was travelling round. Seeing the world.'

As casually as he could, Geoffrey turned the page.

'These figures,' said Hopkins, turning it back. 'What do you think they mean?'

'They're on this page, too,' said Geoffrey turning the page again. 'And here,' turning another.

Hopkins blew his nose, wiped it carefully and put the handkerchief away. 'Is it sex, do you think?'

'Sex?' said Geoffrey with apparent surprise. 'Why should it be sex?' He looked at Hopkins as if the insinuation were his and almost felt sorry for him when the young geologist blushed.

'Clive was a masseur. They may be payments on account – if they're payments at all. I think when he was hard up at one period he used to provide home help, carpentry and so on. It could be that.'

'Yes? You say he was a masseur. He told me he was a writer.'

Geoffrey smiled and shook his head.

'My guess is that it's a sort of diary and I don't feel,' Geoffrey said pompously, 'that one ought to read other people's diaries, do you?'

Hopkins shrank still further and Geoffrey hated himself. He went on leafing through. Against some of the names were small hieroglyphics that seemed to denote a sexual preference or practice, an indication of a client's predilections possibly, of which one or two were obvious. Lips with a line through, for instance, must mean the person with the initials didn't like being kissed; lips with a tick the reverse. But what did a drawing of a foot indicate? Or an ear? Or (in one case) two ears?

None of the drawings was in any sense obscene and were so small and symbolic as to be uninteresting in themselves, but what they stood for – with sometimes a line-up of three or four symbols in a row – was both puzzling and intriguing.

It was a shock, therefore, for Geoffrey to turn the page and come across a note *en clair* that was both direct and naive:

Palaces I have done it in:
Westminster
Lambeth
Blenheim
Buckingham (2)
Windsor

Except Windsor was crossed out with a note, 'Not a palace' and an arrow led from Westminster to a bubble saying 'Lost count'. Written down baldly like this it seemed so childish and unsophisticated as not to be like Clive at all, though as notes for a book, Geoffrey could see it made some sort of sense.

'It's rather sad, really,' Geoffrey went on, still in his pompous mode. 'Why bother to write it down? Who'd be interested?'

'Oh, I keep notes myself,' said Hopkins. Then, as the priest looked up, startled, 'Oh, not about that. Just on rocks and stuff. He told me he was writing a book, but people do say that, don't they? Particularly in South America.'

It's true Clive had spoken of writing a book, or at least of being able to write a book, 'I could write a book,' often how he ended an account of some outrageous escapade. Geoffrey may even have said, 'Why don't you?' though without ever dreaming he would.

Like many who hankered after art, though, Clive was saving it up, if not quite for a rainy day at least until the right opportunity presented itself – prison perhaps, a long illness or a spell in the back of beyond. Which, of course, Peru was and which was why, Geoffrey presumed, he had taken along the book.

Still, he wasn't sure. Clive was always so discreet and even when telling some sexual tale he seldom mentioned names and certainly not the kind of names represented at the memorial service. This iron discretion was, Clive knew, one of his selling points and part of his credit, so not an asset he was likely to squander. Or not yet anyway.

Hopkins seemed to be taking less interest in the diary and when Geoffrey closed the book and put it on the pew between them the young man did not pick it up but just sat staring into space.

Then: 'Of course, if it is sex and those are initials and you could identify them it would be dynamite.'

'Well, a mild sort of dynamite,' said Geoffrey, 'and only if a person,' Geoffrey smiled at the young man, 'only if a person was planning to reveal information ...' He left the sentence unfinished. 'And that would, of course, be ...' and he left this sentence unfinished too, except at that moment a police car blared past outside. Geoffrey sighed. God could be so unsubtle sometimes. 'Besides,' he went on, 'if this is entirely about sex, and I'm not sure it is, it's not against the law, is it?' He wondered how long he could get away with reckoning to be so stupid.

Having found someone, as he thought, more ingenuous than himself the young man was determined to instruct him in the ways of the world. 'No,' he said patiently, 'but it would make a story. Several stories probably. Stories for which newspapers would pay a lot of money.'

'You wouldn't do that, surely?'

'I wouldn't, but someone might.' Hopkins picked up the book. 'I wondered about handing it over to the police.'

'The police?' Geoffrey found himself suddenly angry at the boy's foolishness. 'What for?'

'For safe-keeping?'

'Safe-keeping,' shouted Geoffrey, all pretence of naivety gone. 'Safe-keeping? In which case why bother with the police at all. Just cut out the middleman and give it to the *News of the World*?'

Taken aback by this unexpected outburst Hopkins looked even more unhappy. 'I don't know,' he said, nuzzling his chin on top of his pack. 'I just want to do the right thing.'

The right thing to do was nothing but Geoffrey did not say so. Instead he thought of all the people behind the initials, the troubled novelists, the tearful gardeners and stone-faced soap-stars, Clive's celebrity clientele dragged one by one into the sneering, pitiless light. Something had to be done.

He put his hand on the young man's knee.

He felt Hopkins flinch but kept his hand where he had put it, or not where he had put it, he decided subsequently, but where God had put it. Because tame and timid though such a move might seem (and to someone of Clive's sophistication, for instance, nonchalant and almost instinctive), for Geoffrey it was momentous, fraught with risk and the dread of embarrassment. He had never made such a bold gesture in his life and now he had done it without thinking and almost without feeling.

The young man was unprepossessing and altogether too awkward and angular; in the street he would not have looked at him twice. But there was his hand on the boy's knee. 'What is your name?' he said.

'Greg,' Hopkins said faintly. 'It's Greg.'

Geoffrey had no thought that the presence of his hand on the young man's knee would be the slightest bit welcome nor, judging by the look of panic on his face, was it. Greg was transfixed.

'I am wondering, Greg,' said Geoffrey, 'if we are getting this right. We are talking about what to do with this notebook when strictly speaking, *legally* speaking' – he squeezed the knee slightly – 'it has got nothing to do with us anyway.'

'No?'

'No. The notebook belongs after all to Clive. And now to his estate. And whom does his estate belong to ... or will do eventually?'

Hopkins shook his head.

'His only surviving relative. Miss Wishart!'

The priest loosened his grip on the knee, though lingering there for a moment as if it might be preparatory to travelling further up the young man's leg. This galvanised Hopkins and he got up suddenly. Except that the priest got up too, both crammed together in the close confinement of the pew, the priest seemingly unperturbed and never leaving his face his kind, professional, priestly smile.

Hopkins was now unwise enough to put his hand on the edge of the pew. Geoffrey promptly put his hand on top of it.

'No, no,' said Hopkins.

'No what?' said Geoffrey kindly.

'No, she should keep the book.' Hopkins pulled his hand away in order to retrieve the book still lying on the seat. 'Where can I find her?'

'She comes to church. I can give it to her.' Geoffrey reached for the book and fearful that he was reaching for him too, Hopkins relinquished it without a struggle.

'I can give it to her as a relic of her nephew. The only relic really.' He stroked the book fondly and in that instant Hopkins was out of the pew and on his way to the door. But not quickly enough to avoid the priest's kindly hand pressing into the small of his back and carrying with it the awful possibility that it might move lower down.

'Yes,' Hopkins said, 'give it to her. She's the person.' And stopping suddenly in order to put on his backpack he got rid of the hand, but then found it resting even more horribly on his midriff, so that he gave a hoarse involuntary cry before the priest lifted his hand with a bland smile, converting the gesture almost into a benediction.

'Won't she be shocked?' Hopkins said as he settled the pack on his back. 'She's an old lady.'

'No,' said Geoffrey firmly. 'And I say this, Greg, as her parish priest. It's true she's an old person but I have found the old are quite hard to shock. It's the young one has to be careful with. They are the prudes nowadays.'

Hopkins nodded. Irony and geology obviously did not mix.

'I wondered if you wanted a cup of tea?' Geoffrey stroked the side of his backpack.

'No,' he said hurriedly. 'No, I've got to be somewhere.'

Still widely smiling Geoffrey put out his hand.

They shook hands and the young man dashed out of the door and quickly across the wet gravestones, Geoffrey noting as he did so that he had that over-long and slightly bouncy stride he had always associated with flute-players, train-spotters and other such unworldly and unattractive creatures.

Something strange, though, now happened that Geoffrey would later come to see as prophetic. Or at least ominous. The boy had pulled out a knitted cap and as he stopped to put it on he saw the priest still standing there. Suddenly and unexpectedly the boy smiled and raised his hand. 'I'm sorry,' he called out, and then about to go, he stopped again. 'But thank you all the same.'

Geoffrey sat down in the nearest pew. He was trembling. After a bit he got up and went into the vestry where he opened the safe in which was kept the parish plate, the chalice

(Schofield of London, 1782) and the two patens (Forbes of Bristol, 1718), each in its velvet-lined case. On the shelf below them Geoffrey put Clive's book.

O VER THE FOLLOWING WEEKS Geoffrey would often open up the safe and take a peek at the book, trying to decipher Clive's cryptography and gauge the extent and nature of his activities. None of it shocked him: indeed he found the exercise vaguely exciting and as near to pornography as he allowed himself to come.

Whether it was thanks to the book or to that almost involuntary pass that had allowed him to retain it, Geoffrey found his life changing. Disappointed of immediate promotion he was now more ... well, relaxed and though 'Relax!' is hardly at the core of the Christian message he did feel himself better for it.

So it might be because he was easier with himself or that his unique pass at the geology student had broken his duck and given him more nerve but one way and another he found himself having the occasional fling, in particular with the bus-driving crucifer, who, married though he was, didn't see that as a problem. Nor did Geoffrey's confessor who, while absolving him of what sin there was, urged him to see this and any similar experiences less as deviations from the straight and narrow and more as part of a learning curve. In fairness, this wasn't an expression Geoffrey much cared for, though he didn't demur. He preferred to think of it, if only to himself, as grace.

He still kept the book in the safe, though, as it represented a valorous life he would have liked to lead and still found exciting. It happened that he had been to confession the day before and just as a diabetic whose blood tests have been encouraging sneaks a forbidden pastry so he felt he deserved a treat and went along to the church meaning to take out Clive's book. It was partly to revisit his memory but also because even though he now knew its mysterious notations by heart they still gave him a faint erotic thrill. He knew that this was pathetic and could have told it to no one, except perhaps Clive, and it was one of the ways he missed him.

Pushing open the door of the church he saw someone sitting towards the front and on the side. It was the geology student, slumped in the same pew he had sat in at the memorial service.

'Hail,' said the young man. 'We meet again.' Geoffrey shook hands.

'I meant to come before now,' he said, 'only my car's not been well.'

Geoffrey managed a smile. Seeing him again, Geoffrey thought how fortunate it was that his advance had been rejected. God had been kind. It would never have done.

Hopkins made room for Geoffrey to sit down, just as he had on the first occasion they had talked.

'I came back,' he said, as if it were only that morning he had fled the church. 'I thought about it and I thought, why not?' And now he turned towards Geoffrey and looking him sternly in the eye put his hand on the vicar's knee. 'All right?'

Geoffrey did not speak.

There was a click, then another and the turning of a wheel and faintly, as if from a great way off, Geoffrey heard the cogs begin to grind as the clock gathered itself up and struck the hour.

THE CLOTHES THEY STOOD UP IN

THE RANSOMES HAD BEEN BURGLED. 'Robbed,' Mrs
Ransome said. 'Burgled,' Mr Ransome corrected.
Premises were burgled; persons were robbed. Mr Ransome
was a solicitor by profession and thought words mattered.
Though 'burgled' was the wrong word too. Burglars select;
they pick; they remove one item and ignore others. There is a
limit to what burglars can take: they seldom take easy chairs,
for example, and even more seldom settees. These burglars
did. They took everything.

The Ransomes had been to the opera, to *Così fan tutte* (or *Così*
as Mrs Ransome had learned to call it). Mozart played an
important part in their marriage. They had no children and
but for Mozart would probably have split up years ago. Mr

Ransome always took a bath when he came home from work and then he had his supper. After supper he took another bath, this time in Mozart. He wallowed in Mozart; he luxuriated in him; he let the little Viennese soak away all the dirt and disgustingness he had had to sit through in his office all day. On this particular evening he had been to the public baths, Covent Garden, where their seats were immediately behind the Home Secretary. He, too, was taking a bath and washing away the cares of his day, cares, if only in the form of a statistic, that were about to include the Ransomes.

On a normal evening, though, Mr Ransome shared his bath with no one, Mozart coming personalised via his headphones and a stack of complex and finely-balanced stereo equipment Mrs Ransome was never allowed to touch. She blamed the stereo for the burglary as that was what the robbers were probably after in the first place. The theft of stereos is common; the theft of fitted carpets is not.

'Perhaps they wrapped the stereo in the carpet,' said Mrs Ransome.

Mr Ransome shuddered and said her fur coat was more likely, whereupon Mrs Ransome started crying again.

It had not been much of a *Così*. Mrs Ransome could not follow the plot and Mr Ransome, who never tried, found the performance did not compare with the four recordings he possessed of the work. The acting he invariably found distracting. 'None of them knows what to do with their arms,' he said to his wife in the interval. Mrs Ransome thought it probably went further than their arms but did not say so. She was wondering if the casserole she had left in the oven would get too dry at Gas Mark 4. Perhaps 3 would have been better. Dry it may well have been but there was no need to have worried. The thieves took the oven and the casserole with it.

The Ransomes lived in an Edwardian block of flats the colour of ox-blood not far from Regent's Park. It was handy for the City, though Mrs Ransome would have preferred something further out, seeing herself with a trug in a garden, vaguely. But she was not gifted in that direction. An African violet which her cleaning lady had given her at Christmas had finally given up the ghost that very morning and she had been forced to hide it in the wardrobe out of Mrs Clegg's way. More wasted effort. The wardrobe had gone too.

They had no neighbours to speak of, or seldom to. Occasionally they would run into people in the lift and both parties smiled cautiously. Once they had asked some newcomers on their floor round to sherry, but he had turned out to be what he called 'a big band freak' and she had been a dental receptionist with a timeshare in Portugal, so one way and another it had been an awkward evening and they had never repeated the experience. These days the turnover of tenants seemed increasingly rapid and the lift more and more wayward. People were always moving in and out again, some of them Arabs.

'I mean,' said Mrs Ransome, 'it's getting like a hotel.'

'I wish you wouldn't keep saying "I mean",' said Mr Ransome. 'It adds nothing to the sense.'

He got enough of what he called 'this sloppy way of talking' at work; the least he could ask for at home, he felt, was correct English. So Mrs Ransome, who normally had very little to say, now tended to say even less.

When the Ransomes moved into Naseby Mansions the flats had boasted a commissionaire in a plum-coloured uniform that matched the colour of the building. He had died one afternoon in 1982 as he was hailing a taxi for Mrs Brabourne on the second floor, who had foregone it in order to let it take him to hospital. None of his successors had shown the same zeal in office or pride in their uniform and eventually the function of commissionaire had merged with that of caretaker, who was never to be found on the door and seldom to be found anywhere, his lair a hot scullery behind the boiler room where he slept much of the day in an armchair that had been thrown out by one of the tenants.

On the night in question the caretaker was asleep, though unusually for him not in the armchair but at the theatre. On the look-out for a classier type of girl he had decided to attend an adult education course where he had opted to study English; given the opportunity, he had told the lecturer, he would like to become a voracious reader. The lecturer had some exciting, though not very well-formulated ideas about art and the workplace, and learning he was a caretaker had got him tickets for the play of the same name, thinking the resultant insights would be a stimulant to group interaction. It was an evening the caretaker found no more satisfying than the Ransomes did *Così* and the insights he gleaned limited: 'So far as your actual caretaking was concerned,' he reported to the class, 'it was bollocks.' The lecturer consoled himself with the hope that, unknown to the caretaker, the evening might have opened doors. In this he was right: the doors in question belonged to the Ransomes' flat.

The police came round eventually, though there was more to it than picking up the phone. The thieves had done that anyway, all three phones in fact, neatly snipping off the wire flush with the skirting-board so that, with no answer from the flat opposite ('Sharing time in Portugal, probably,' Mr Ransome said, 'or at a big band concert'), he was forced to sally forth in search of a phone box. 'No joke,' as he said to Mrs Ransome, now that phone boxes doubled as public conveniences. The first two Mr Ransome tried didn't even do that, urinals solely, the phone long since ripped out. A mobile would have been the answer, of course, but Mr Ransome had resisted this innovation ('Betrays a lack of organisation'), as he resisted most innovations except those in the sphere of stereophonic reproduction.

He wandered on through deserted streets, wondering how people managed. The pubs had closed, the only place open a launderette with, in the window, a pay phone. This struck Mr Ransome as a stroke of luck; never having had cause to use such an establishment he had not realised that washing clothes ran to such a facility; but being new to launderettes meant also that he was not certain if someone who was not actually washing clothes was permitted to take advantage of it. However, the phone was currently being used by the sole occupant of the place, an old lady in two overcoats who had plainly not laundered her clothes in some time, so Mr Ransome took courage.

She was standing with the phone pressed to her dirty ear, not talking, but not really listening either.

'Could you hurry, please,' Mr Ransome said, 'this is an emergency.'

'So is this, dear,' said the woman, 'I'm calling Padstow, only they're not answering.'

'I want to call the police,' said Mr Ransome.

'Been attacked, have you?' said the woman. 'I was attacked last week. It's par for the course these days. He was only a toddler. It's ringing but there's a long corridor. They tend to have a hot drink about this time. They're nuns,' she said explanatorily.

'Nuns?' said Mr Ransome. 'Are you sure they won't have gone to bed?'

'No. They're up and down all night having the services. There's always somebody about.'

She went on listening to the phone ringing in Cornwall.

'Can't it wait?' asked Mr Ransome, seeing his effects halfway up the M1. 'Speed is of the essence.'

'I know,' said the old lady, 'whereas nuns have got all the time in the world. That's the beauty of it except when it comes to answering the phone. I aim to go on retreat there in May.'

'But it's only February,' Mr Ransome said. 'I ...'

'They get booked up,' explained the old lady. 'There's no talking and three meals a day so do you wonder? They use it as a holiday home for religious of both sexes. You wouldn't think nuns needed holidays. Prayer doesn't take it out of you. Not like bus conducting. Still ringing. They've maybe finished their hot drink and adjourned to the chapel. I suppose I could ring later, only ...' She looked at the coins waiting in Mr Ransome's hand. 'I've put my money in now.'

Mr Ransome gave her a pound and she took the other 50p besides, saying: 'You don't need money for 999.'

She put the receiver down and her money came back of its own accord, but Mr Ransome was so anxious to get on with his call he scarcely noticed. It was only later, sitting on the floor of what had been their bedroom that he said out loud: 'Do you remember Button A and Button B? They've gone, you know. I never noticed.'

'Everything's gone,' said Mrs Ransome, not catching his drift, 'the air freshener, the soap dish. They can't be human; I mean they've even taken the lavatory brush.'

'Fire, police or ambulance?' said a woman's voice.

'Police,' said Mr Ransome. There was a pause.

'I feel better for that banana,' said a man's voice. 'Yes? Police.' Mr Ransome began to explain but the man cut him short. 'Anyone in danger?' He was chewing.

'No,' said Mr Ransome, 'but ...'

'Any threat to the person?'

'No,' said Mr Ransome, 'only ... '

'Slight bottleneck at the moment, chief,' said the voice. 'Bear with me while I put you on hold.'

Mr Ransome found himself listening to a Strauss waltz.

'They're probably having a hot drink,' said the old lady, who he could smell was still at his elbow.

'Sorry about that,' the voice said five minutes later. 'We're on manual at the moment. The computer's got hiccups. How may I help you?'

Mr Ransome explained there had been a burglary and gave the address.

'Are you on the phone?'

'Of course,' said Mr Ransome, 'only ...'

'And the number is?'

'They've taken the phone,' said Mr Ransome.

'Nothing new there,' said the voice. 'Cordless job?'

'No' said Mr Ransome. 'One was in the sitting-room, one was by the bed ...'

'We don't want to get bogged down in detail,' said the voice. 'Besides, the theft of a phone isn't the end of the world. What was the number again?'

It was after one o'clock when Mr Ransome got back and Mrs Ransome, already beginning to pick up the threads, was in what had been their bedroom, sitting with her back to the wall in the place where she would have been in bed had there been a bed to be in. She had done a lot of crying while Mr Ransome was out but had now wiped her eyes, having decided she was going to make the best of things.

'I thought you might be dead,' she said.

'Why dead?'

'Well, it never rains but it pours.'

'I was in one of these launderettes if you want to know.

It was terrible. What are you eating?'

'A cough sweet. I found it in my bag.' This was one of the sweets Mr Ransome insisted she take with her whenever they went to the opera ever since she had had a snuffle all the way through *Fidelio*.

'Is there another?'

'No,' said Mrs Ransome, sucking. 'This is the last.'

Mr Ransome went to the lavatory, only realising when it was too late that the burglary had been so comprehensive as to have taken in both the toilet roll and its holder.

'There's no paper,' called Mrs Ransome.

The only paper in the flat was the programme from *Così* and passing it round the door Mrs Ransome saw, not without satisfaction, that Mr Ransome was going to have to wipe his bottom on a picture of Mozart.

Both unwieldy and unyielding the glossy brochure (sponsored by Barclays Bank plc) was uncomfortable to use and unsinkable afterwards, and three flushes notwithstanding, the fierce eye of Sir George Solti still came squinting resentfully round the bend of the pan.

'Better?' said Mrs Ransome.

'No,' said her husband and settled down beside her against the wall. However, finding the skirting-board dug into her back Mrs Ransome changed her position to lie at right angles to her husband so that her head now rested on his thigh, a situation it had not been in for many a long year. While telling himself this was an emergency it was a conjunction Mr Ransome found both uncomfortable and embarrassing, but which seemed to suit his wife as she straightaway went off to sleep, leaving Mr Ransome staring glumly at the wall opposite and its now uncurtained window, from which, he noted wonderingly, the burglars had even stolen the curtain rings.

It was four o'clock before the police arrived, a big middle-aged man in a raincoat, who said he was a detective sergeant, and a sensitive-looking young constable in uniform, who didn't say anything at all.

'You've taken your time,' said Mr Ransome.

'Yes,' said the sergeant. 'We would have been earlier but there was a slight ... ah, glitch as they say. Rang the wrong doorbell. The fault of mi-laddo here. Saw the name Hanson and ...'

'No,' said Mr Ransome. 'Ransome.'

'Yes. We established that ... eventually. Just moved in, have you?' said the sergeant, surveying the bare boards.

'No,' said Mr Ransome. 'We've been here for thirty years.'

'Fully furnished, was it?'

'Of course,' said Mr Ransome. 'It was a normal home.'

'A settee, easy chairs, a clock,' said Mrs Ransome. 'We had everything.'

'Television?' said the constable, timidly.

'Yes,' said Mrs Ransome.

'Only we didn't watch it much,' said Mr Ransome.

'Video recorder?'

'No,' said Mr Ransome. 'Life's complicated enough.'

'CD player?'

'Yes,' said Mrs Ransome and Mr Ransome together.

'And my wife had a fur coat,' said Mr Ransome. 'My insurance have a list of the valuables.'

'In that case,' said the sergeant, 'you are laughing. I'll just have a little wander round if you don't mind, while Constable Partridge takes down the details. People opposite see the intruder?'

'Away in Portugal,' said Mr Ransome.

'Caretaker?'

'Probably in Portugal too,' said Mr Ransome, 'for all we see of him.'

'Is it Ransom as in king's?' said the constable. 'Or Ransome as in Arthur?'

'Partridge is one of our graduate entrants,' said the sergeant, examining the front door.

'Lock not forced, I see. He's just climbing the ladder. There wouldn't be such a thing as a cup of tea, would there?'

'No,' said Mr Ransome shortly, 'because there wouldn't be such a thing as a teapot. Not to mention a teabag to put in it.'

'I take it you'll want counselling,' said the constable.

'What?'

'Someone comes along and holds your hand,' said the sergeant, looking at the window. 'Partridge thinks it's important.'

'We're all human,' said the constable.

'I'm a solicitor,' said Mr Ransome.

'Well,' said the sergeant, 'perhaps your missus could give it a try. We like to keep Partridge happy.'

Mrs Ransome smiled helpfully.

'I'll put yes,' said the constable.

'They didn't leave anything behind, did they?' asked the sergeant, sniffing and reaching up to run his hand along the picture-rail.

'No,' said Mr Ransome testily. 'Not a thing. As you can see.'

'I didn't mean something of yours,' said the sergeant, 'I meant something of theirs.' He sniffed again, inquiringly. 'A calling card.'

'A calling card?' said Mrs Ransome.

'Excrement,' said the sergeant. 'Burglary is a nervous business. They often feel the need to open their bowels when doing a job.'

'Which is another way of saying it, sergeant,' said the constable.

'Another way of saying what, Partridge?'

'Doing a job is another way of saying opening the bowels. In France,' said the constable, 'it's known as posting a sentry.'

'Oh, teach you that at Leatherhead, did they?' said the sergeant. 'Partridge is a graduate of the police college.'

'It's like a university,' explained the constable, 'only they don't have scarves.'

'Anyway,' said the sergeant, 'have a scout round. For the excrement, I mean. They can be very creative about it. Burglary in Pangbourne I attended once where they done it halfway up the wall in an eighteenth-century light fitting. Any other sphere and they'd have got the Duke of Edinburgh's Award.'

'You've perhaps not noticed,' Mr Ransome said grimly, 'but we don't have any light fittings.'

'Another one in Guildford did it in a bowl of this pot-pourri.'

'That would be irony,' said the constable.

'Oh would it?' said the sergeant. 'And there was me thinking it was just some foul-arsed, light-fingered little smack-head afflicted with incontinence. Still, while we're talking about bodily functions, before we take our leave I'll just pay a visit myself.'

Too late Mr Ransome realised he should have warned him and took refuge in the kitchen.

The sergeant came out shaking his head.

'Well at least our friends had the decency to use the toilet but they've left it in a disgusting state. I never thought I'd have to do a Jimmy Riddle over Dame Kiri Te Kanawa. Her recording of *West Side Story* is one of the gems of my record collection.'

'To be fair,' said Mrs Ransome, 'that was my husband.'

'Dear me,' said the sergeant.

'What was?' said Mr Ransome, coming back into the room.

'Nothing,' said his wife.

'Do you think you'll catch them?' said Mr Ransome as he stood at the door with the two policemen.

The sergeant laughed.

'Well, miracles do happen, even in the world of law enforcement. Nobody got a grudge against you, have they?'

'I'm a solicitor,' said Mr Ransome. 'It's possible.'

'And it's not somebody's idea of a joke?'

'A *joke*?' said Mr Ransome.

'Just a thought,' said the sergeant. 'But if it's your genuine burglar, I'll say this: he always comes back.'

The constable nodded in sage confirmation; even Leatherhead was agreed on this. 'Come back?' said Mr Ransome bitterly, looking at the empty flat.

'*Come back?* What the fuck for?'

Mr Ransome seldom swore and Mrs Ransome, who had stayed in the other room, pretended she hadn't heard. The door closed.

'Useless,' said Mr Ransome, coming back. 'Utterly useless. It makes you want to swear.'

'Well,' said Mrs Ransome a few hours later, 'we shall just have to camp out. After all,' she said not unhappily, 'it could be fun.'

'Fun?' said Mr Ransome. '*Fun?*'

He was unshaven, unwashed, his bottom was sore and his breakfast had been a drink of water from the tap. Still, no amount of pleading on Mrs Ransome's part could stop him going heroically off to work, with his wife instinctively knowing even in these unprecedented circumstances that her role was to make much of his selfless dedication.

Even so, when he'd gone and with the flat so empty, Mrs Ransome missed him a little, wandering from room to echoing room not sure where she should start. Deciding to make a list she forgot for the moment she had nothing to make a list with and nothing to make a list on. This meant a visit to the newsagents for pad and pencil where, though she'd never noticed it before, she found there was a café next door. It seemed to be doing hot breakfasts, and, though in her opera clothes she felt a bit out of place among the taxi-drivers and bicycle couriers who comprised most of the clientele, nobody took much notice of her, the waitress even calling her 'duck' and offering her a copy of the Mirror to read while she waited for her bacon, egg, baked beans and fried bread. It wasn't a paper she would normally read, but bacon, egg, baked beans and fried bread wasn't a breakfast she would normally eat either, and she got so interested in the paper's tales of royalty and its misdemeanours that she propped it up against the sauce bottle so that she could read and eat, completely forgetting that one of the reasons she had come into the café was to make herself a list.

Wanting a list, her shopping was pretty haphazard. She went off to Boots first and bought some toilet rolls and some paper plates and cups, but she forgot soap. And when she remembered soap and went back for it, she forgot teabags, and when she remembered teabags, she forgot paper towels, until what with trailing halfway to the flats then having to go back again, she began to feel worn out.

It was on the third of these increasingly flustered trips (now having forgotten plastic cutlery) that Mrs Ransome ventured into Mr Anwar's. She passed the shop many times as it was midway between the flats and St John's Wood High Street; indeed she remembered it opening and the little draper's and babies' knitwear shop which it had replaced and where she had been a loyal customer. That had been kept by a Miss Dorsey, from whom over the years she had bought the occasional tray cloth or hank of Sylko but, on a much more regular basis, plain brown paper packets of what in those days were called 'towels'. The closing-down of the shop in the late Sixties had left Mrs Ransome anxious and unprotected and it came as a genuine surprise on venturing into Timothy White's to find that technology in this intimate department had lately made great strides which were unreflected in Miss Dorsey's ancient stock, of which Mrs Ransome, as the last of a dwindling clientele, had been almost the sole consumer. She was old-fashioned, she knew that, but snobbery had come into it too, Mrs Ransome feeling it vaguely classier to have her requirements passed wordlessly across the counter with Miss Dorsey's patient, suffering smile ('Our cross,' it said) rather than taken from some promiscuous shelf in Timothy White's. Though it was not long before Timothy White's went the same way as Miss Dorsey, swallowed whole by Boots. Though Boots too, she felt, was a cut above the nearest chemist, Superdrug, which didn't look classy at all.

The closing-down of Miss Dorsey's (she was found laid across the counter one afternoon having had a stroke) left the premises briefly empty until, passing one morning on the way to the High Street, Mrs Ransome saw that the shop had been taken over by an Asian grocer and that the pavement in front of the window where nothing had previously stood except the occasional customer's pram was now occupied by boxes of unfamiliar vegetables ... yams, pawpaws, mangoes and the like, together with many sacks, sacks, Mrs Ransome felt, that dogs could all too easily cock their leg against.

So it was partly out of loyalty to Mrs Dorsey and partly because it wasn't really her kind of thing that Mrs Ransome had not ventured into the shop until this morning when, to save her trailing back for the umpteenth time to the High Street, she thought she might go in and ask if they had such a thing as boot polish (there were more pressing requirements, as she would have been the first to admit, only Mr Ransome was very particular about his shoes). Though over twenty years had passed, the shop was still recognisably what it had been in Miss Dorsey's day because, other than having introduced a freezer and cold cupboards, Mr Anwar had simply adapted the existing fixtures to his changed requirements. Drawers that had previously been devoted to the genteel accoutrements of a leisured life – knitting patterns, crochet hooks, rufflette – now housed nans and pitta bread; spices replaced bonnets and bootees and the shelves and deep drawers that once were home to hosiery and foundation garments were now filled with rice and chickpeas.

Mrs Ransome thought it unlikely they had polish in stock (did they wear normal shoes?), but she was weary enough to give it a try though, since ox-blood was what she wanted (or Mr Ransome required), she thought vaguely it might be a shade to which they had religious objections. But plump and cheerful Mr Anwar brought out several tins for her kind consideration and while she was paying she spotted a nail-brush they would be needing; then the tomatoes looked nice and there was a lemon, and while she was at it the shop seemed to sell hardware so she invested in a colander. As she wandered round the shop the normally tongue-tied Mrs Ransome found herself explaining to this plump and amiable grocer the circumstances which had led her to the purchase of such an odd assortment of things. And he smiled and shook his head in sympathy while at the same time suggesting other items she would doubtless be needing to replace and which he would happily supply. 'They cleaned you out of house and home, the scallywags. You will not know whether you are coming or going. You will need washing-up liquid and one of these blocks to make the toilet a more savoury place.'

So she ended up buying a dozen or so items, too many for her to carry, but this didn't matter either as Mr Anwar fetched his little boy from the flat upstairs ('I hope I'm not dragging him away from the Koran,' she thought) and he followed Mrs Ransome home in his little white cap, carrying her shopping in a cardboard box.

'Seconds probably,' said Mr Ransome later. 'That's how they make a profit.'

Mrs Ransome didn't quite see how there could be seconds in shoe polish but didn't say so.

'Hopefully,' she said 'they'll deliver.'

'You mean,' said Mr Ransome (and it was old ground), 'you hope they'll deliver. "Hopefully they'll deliver" means that deliveries are touch and go' (though that was probably true too).

'Anyway,' said Mrs Ransome defiantly, 'he stays open till ten at night.'

'He can afford to,' said Mr Ransome. 'He probably pays no wages. I'd stick to Marks and Spencer.'

Which she did, generally speaking. Though once she popped in and bought a mango for her lunch and another time a pawpaw; small adventures, it's true, but departures nevertheless, timorous voyages of discovery which she knew her husband well enough to keep to herself.

The Ransomes had few friends; they seldom entertained, Mr Ransome saying that he saw quite enough of people at work. On the rare occasions when Mrs Ransome ran into someone she knew and ventured to recount their dreadful experience she was surprised to find that everyone, it seemed, had their own burglar story. None, she felt, were so stark or so shocking as to measure up to theirs, which ought in fairness to have trumped outright these other less flamboyant breakins, but comparison scarcely seemed to enter into it: the friends only endured her story as an unavoidable prelude to telling her their own. She asked Mr Ransome if he had noticed this.

'Yes,' he said shortly. 'Anybody would think it happened every day.'

Which, of course, it did but not, he was certain, as definitively, as out and outedly, as altogether epically as this.

'Everything,' Mr Ransome told Gail, his long-time secretary, 'every single thing.'

Gail was a tall, doleful-looking woman, which normally suited Mr Ransome very well as he could not abide much of what he called 'silliness' – i.e. femininity. Had Gail been a bit sillier, though, she might have been more sympathetic, but like everyone else she weighed in with a burglar story of her own, saying she was surprised it hadn't happened before as most people she knew had been burgled at least once and her brother-in-law, who was a chiropodist in Ilford, twice, one of which had been a ram-raid while they were watching television.

'What you have to watch out for is the trauma; it takes people in different ways. Hair loss is often a consequence of burglary apparently and my sister came out in terrible eczema. Mind you,' Gail went on, 'it's always men.'

'Always men what?' said Mr Ransome.

'Who burgle.'

'Well, women shoplift,' said Mr Ransome defensively.

'Not to that extent,' said Gail. 'They don't clean out the store.'

Not sure how he had ended up on the wrong side of the argument, Mr Ransome felt both irritated and dissatisfied, so he tried Mr Pardoe from the firm next door but with no more success. 'Cleaned you out completely? Well, be grateful you weren't in. My dentist and his wife were tied up for seven hours and counted themselves lucky not to be raped. Balaclavas, walkie-talkies. It's an industry nowadays. I'd castrate them.'

That night Mr Ransome took out a dictionary from his briefcase, both dictionary and briefcase newly acquired. The dictionary was Mr Ransome's favourite book.

'What are you doing?' asked Mrs Ransome.

'Looking up "lock, stock and barrel". I suppose it means the same as "the whole shoot".'

Over the next week or so Mrs Ransome assembled the rudiments – two camp beds plus bedding and towels, a card table and two folding chairs. She bought a couple of what she called bean-bags, though the shop called them something else; they were quite popular apparently, even among people who had not been burgled who used them to sit on the floor by choice. There was even (this was Mr Ransome's contribution) a portable CD player and a recording of *The Magic Flute*.

Mrs Ransome had always enjoyed shopping so this obligatory re-equipment with the essentials of life was not without its pleasures, though the need was so pressing that choice scarcely entered into it. Hitherto anything electrical had always to be purchased by, or under the supervision of, Mr Ransome, a sanction that applied even with an appliance like the vacuum cleaner, which he never wielded, or the dishwasher, which he seldom stacked. However, in the special circumstances obtaining after the burglary, Mrs Ransome found herself licensed to buy whatever was deemed necessary, electrical or otherwise; not only did she get an electric kettle, she also went in for a microwave oven, an innovation Mr Ransome had long resisted and did not see the point of.

That many of these items (the bean-bags, for instance) were likely to be discarded once the insurance paid out and they acquired something more permanent, did not diminish Mrs Ransome's quiet zest in shopping for them. Besides, the second stage was likely to be somewhat delayed as the insurance policy had been stolen too, together with all their other documents, so compensation, while not in doubt, might be slow in coming. In the meantime they lived a stripped-down sort of life which seemed to Mrs Ransome, at least, not unpleasant.

'Hand to mouth,' said Mr Ransome.

'Living out of a suitcase,' said Croucher, his insurance broker.

'No,' said Mr Ransome. 'We don't have a suitcase.'

'You don't think,' asked Croucher, 'it might be some sort of joke?'

'People keep saying that,' said Mr Ransome.

'Jokes must have changed since my day. I thought they were meant to be funny.'

'What sort of CD equipment was it?' said Croucher.

'Oh, state of the art,' said Mr Ransome. 'The latest and the best. I've got the receipts somewhere ... oh no, of course. I was forgetting.'

Though this was a genuine slip it was perhaps fortunate that the receipts had been stolen along with the equipment which they were for, because Mr Ransome was telling a little lie. His sound equipment was not quite state of the art, as what equipment is? Sound reproduction is not static; perfection is on-going and scarcely a week passes without some technical advance. As an avid reader of hi-fi magazines, Mr Ransome often saw advertised refinements he would dearly have liked to make part of his listening experience. The burglary, devastating though it had been, was his opportunity. So it was at the moment when he woke up to the potential advantages of his loss that this most unresilient of men began, if grudgingly, to bounce back.

Mrs Ransome, too, could see the cheerful side of things, but then she always did. When they had got married they had kitted themselves out with all the necessities of a well-run household; they had a dinner service, a tea service plus table linen to match; they had dessert dishes and trifle glasses and cakestands galore. There were mats for the dressing-table, coasters for the coffee table, runners for the dining table; guest towels with matching flannels for the basin, lavatory mats with matching ones for the bath. They had cake slices and fish slices and other slices besides, delicate trowels in silver and bone the precise function of which Mrs Ransome had never been able to fathom. Above all there was a massive many-tiered canteen of cutlery, stocked with sufficient knives, forks and spoons for a dinner party for twelve. Mr and Mrs Ransome did not have dinner parties for twelve. They did not have dinner parties. They seldom used the guest towels because they never had guests. They had transported this paraphernalia with them across thirty-two years of marriage to no purpose at all that Mrs Ransome could see, and now at a stroke they were rid of the lot. Without quite knowing why, and while she was washing up their two cups in the sink, Mrs Ransome suddenly burst out singing.

'It's probably best,' said Croucher, 'to proceed on the assumption that it's gone and isn't going to come back. Maybe someone fancied a well-appointed middle-class home and just took a short cut.'

He stood at the door.

'I'll get a cheque to you as soon as I can. Then you can start rebuilding your lives. Your good lady seems to be taking it well.'

'Yes,' said Mr Ransome, 'only she keeps it under.'

'No outstanding jewellery or anything of that sort?'

'No. She's never really gone in for that sort of thing,' said Mr Ransome. 'Luckily she was wearing her pearls to the opera.'

'She had a necklace on tonight,' said Croucher. 'Rather striking, I thought.'

'Did she?' Mr Ransome hadn't noticed.

When they were at the card table having their supper Mr Ransome said: 'Have I seen that necklace before?'

'No. Do you like it? I bought it at the grocer's.'

'The *grocer's*?'

'The Indian shop. It was only 75p. I can't wear my pearls all the time.'

'It looks as if it came out of a cracker.'

'I think it suits me. I bought two. The other one's green.'

'What am I eating?' said Mr Ransome. 'Swede?'

'A sweet potato. Do you like it?'

'Where did you get it?'

'Marks and Spencer.'

'It's very nice.'

A couple of weeks after the burglary (everything now dated from that) Mrs Ransome was sitting on her bean-bag in front of the electric fire, her legs stuck out in front of her, contemplating her now rather scuffed court shoes, and wondering what she ought to do next. It was the same with a death, she thought:

so much to do to begin with, then afterwards nothing.

Nevertheless (and further to her thoughts at the sink) Mrs Ransome had begun to see that to be so abruptly parted from all her worldly goods might bring with it benefits she would have hesitated to call spiritual but which might, more briskly, be put under the heading of 'improving the character'. To have the carpet almost literally pulled from under her should, she felt, induce salutary thoughts about the way she had lived her life. War would once have rescued her, of course, some turn of events that gave her no choice, and while what had happened was not a catastrophe on that scale she knew it was up to her to make of it what she could. She would go to museums, she thought, art galleries, learn about the history of London; there were classes in all sorts nowadays – classes which she could perfectly well have attended before they were deprived of everything they had in the world, except that it was everything they had in the world, she felt, that had been holding her back. Now she could start. So, plumped down on the bean-bag on the bare boards of her sometime lounge, Mrs Ransome found that she was not unhappy, telling herself that this was more real and that (though one needed to be comfortable) an uncushioned life was the way they ought to live.

It was at this point the doorbell rang.

'My name is Briscoe,' the voice said over the intercom. 'Your counsellor?'

'We're Conservatives,' said Mrs Ransome.

'No,' said the voice. 'The police? Your trauma? The burglary?'

Knowing the counsellor had come via the police Mrs Ransome had expected someone a bit, well, crisper. There was nothing crisp about Ms Briscoe, except possibly her name and she got rid of that on the doorstep.

'No, no. Call me Dusty. Everybody does.'

'Were you christened Dusty?' asked Mrs Ransome, bringing her in. 'Or is that just what you're called?'

'Oh no. My proper name is Brenda but I don't want to put people off.'

Mrs Ransome wasn't quite sure how, though it was true she didn't look like a Brenda: whether she looked like a Dusty she wasn't sure as she'd never met one before.

She was a biggish girl who, perhaps wisely, had opted for a smock rather than a frock and with it a cardigan so long and ample it was almost a dress in itself, one pocket stuffed with her diary and notebook, the other sagging under the weight of a mobile phone. Considering she worked for the authorities Mrs Ransome thought Dusty looked pretty slapdash.

'Now you are Mrs Ransome? Rosemary Ransome?'

'Yes.'

'And that's what people call you, is it? Rosemary?'

'Well, yes' (insofar as they call me anything, thought Mrs Ransome).

'Just wondered if it was Rose or Rosie?'

'Oh no.'

'Hubby calls you Rosemary, does he?'

'Well, yes,' said Mrs Ransome, 'I suppose he does,' and

went to put the kettle on, thus enabling Dusty to make her first note: 'Query: Is burglary the real problem here?'

When Dusty had started out counselling, victims were referred to as 'cases'. That had long since gone; they were now clients or even customers, terms Dusty to begin with found unsympathetic and had resisted. Nowadays she never gave either designation a second thought – what her clients were called seemed as immaterial as the disasters that befell them. Victims singled themselves out; be it burglary, mugging or road accidents, these mishaps were simply the means by which inadequate people came to her notice. And everybody given the chance had the potential to be inadequate. Experience, she felt, had turned her into a professional.

They took their tea into the sitting-room and each sank onto a bean-bag, a manoeuvre Mrs Ransome was now quite good at, though with Dusty it was more like a tumble. 'Are these new?' said Dusty, wiping some tea from her smock. 'I was with another client yesterday, the sister of someone who's in a coma, and she had something similar. Now Rosemary, I want us to try and talk this through together.'

Mrs Ransome wasn't sure whether this was the same as 'talking it over'. One seemed a more rigorous, less meander-ing version of the other, the difference in their choice of prepositions not boding well for fruitful discourse. 'More structured,' Dusty would have said, had Mrs Ransome ven-tured to raise the point, but she didn't.

Mrs Ransome now described the circumstances of the bur-glary and the extent of their loss, though this made less of an

impression on Dusty than it might have done as the diminished state in which the Ransomes were now living – the bean-
bags, the card table, etc. – seemed not so much a deprivation
to Dusty as it did a style.

Though this was more tidy it was the minimalist look she
had opted for in her own flat.

'How near is this to what it was before?' said Dusty.

'Oh we had a lot more than this,' said Mrs Ransome. 'We
had everything. It was a normal home.'

'I know you must be hurting,' said Dusty.

'Hurting what?' asked Mrs Ransome.

'You. You are hurting.'

Mrs Ransome considered this, her stoicism simply a question of grammar, 'Oh. You mean I'm hurt? Well, yes and no.
I'm getting used to it, I suppose.'

'Don't get used to it too soon,' said Dusty. 'Give yourself
time to grieve. You did weep at the time, I hope?'

'To begin with,' said Mrs Ransome. 'But I soon got over it.'

'Did Maurice?'

'Maurice?'

'Mr Ransome.'

'Oh ... no. No. I don't think he did. Well,' and it was as if
she were sharing a secret, 'he's a man, you see.'

'No, Rosemary. He's a person. It's a pity that he didn't let
himself go at the time. The experts are all more or less agreed
that if you don't grieve, keep it all bottled up, you're quite
likely at some time in the future to go down with cancer.'

'Oh dear,' said Mrs Ransome.

'Of course,' said Dusty. 'Men do find grieving harder than women. Would it help if I had a word?'

'With Mr Ransome? No, no,' said Mrs Ransome hastily. 'I don't think so. He's very ... shy.'

'Still,' said Dusty, 'I think I can help you ... or we can help each other.' She leaned over to take Mrs Ransome's hand but found she couldn't reach it so stroked the bean-bag instead.

'They say you feel violated,' said Mrs Ransome.

'Yes. Let it come, Rosemary. Let it come.'

'Only I don't particularly. Just mystified.'

'Client in denial,' Dusty wrote as Mrs Ransome took away the teacups. Then she added a question-mark.

As she was going Dusty suggested that Mrs Ransome might try to see the whole experience as a learning curve and that one way the curve might go (it could go several ways apparently) was to view the loss of their possessions as a kind of liberation – 'the lilies of the field syndrome', as Dusty called it. 'Lay not up for yourself treasures on earth-type-thing.' This notion having already occurred to Mrs Ransome she nevertheless didn't immediately take the point because Dusty referred to their belongings as 'their gear', a word which, if it meant any-thing to Mrs Ransome, denoted the contents of her handbag, lipstick, compact etc., none of which she had in fact lost. Though thinking about it afterwards she acknowledged that to lump everything, carpets, curtains, furniture and fittings all under the term 'gear' did make it easier to handle. Still it wasn't a word she contemplated risking on her husband.

Truth to tell (and though she didn't say so to Mrs Ransome)

it was advice Dusty only proffered half-heartedly anyway. The more she saw of the lilies of the field syndrome the less faith she had in it. She'd had one or two clients who'd told her that a hurtful burglary had given them a clue how to live, that from now on they would set less store by material possessions, travel light etc. Six months later she'd gone back on a follow-up visit to find them more encumbered than ever. Lots of people could give up things, Dusty had decided; what they couldn't do without was shopping for them.

When Mrs Ransome said to Dusty that she didn't particularly miss her belongings she had been telling the truth. What she did miss – and this was harder to put into words – was not so much the things themselves as her particular paths through them. There was the green bobble hat she had had, for instance, which she never actually wore but would always put on the hall table to remind her that she had switched the immersion heater on in the bathroom. She didn't have the bobble hat now and she didn't have the table to put it on (and that she still had the immersion heater must be regarded as a providence). But with no bobble hat she'd twice left the immersion on all night and once Mr Ransome had scalded his hand.

He too had had rituals to forego. He had lost the little curved scissors, for instance, with which he used to cut the hair in his ears – and that was only the beginning of it. While not especially vain he had a little moustache which, if left to itself, had a distasteful tendency to go ginger, a tinge which Mr Ransome kept in check with the occasional touch of hair dye.

This came out of an ancient bottle Mrs Ransome had tried on her roots years ago and then instantly discarded, but which was still kept at the back of the bathroom cupboard. Locking the bathroom door before applying it to the affected part, Mr Ransome had never admitted to what he was doing, with Mrs Ransome in her turn never admitting that she knew about it anyway. Only now the bathroom cupboard was gone and the bottle with it, so in due course Mr Ransome's moustache began to take on the tell-tale orange tinge he found so detestable. Asking her to buy another bottle was one answer but this would be to come clean on the years of clandestine cosmetics. Buying a bottle himself was another. But where? His barber was Polish and his English just about ran to short back and sides. An understanding chemist perhaps, but all the chemists of Mr Ransome's acquaintance were anything but understanding, staffed usually by bored little sluts of eighteen unlikely to sympathise with a middle-aged solicitor and his creeping ginger.

Unhappily tracing its progress in Mrs Ransome's powder compact, kept in the bathroom now as the only mirror in the flat, Mr Ransome cursed the burglars who had brought such humiliation upon him and lying on her camp bed Mrs Ransome reflected that not the least of what they had lost in the burglary were their little marital deceptions.

Mr Ransome had been told that while the insurance company would not pay for the temporary rental of a CD player (not regarded as an essential) it would sanction the hire of a TV. So one morning Mrs Ransome went out and chose the

most discreet model she could find and it was delivered and
fitted that same afternoon. She had never watched daytime
television before, feeling she ought to have better things to
do. However, when he had gone she found the engineer had
left the set switched to some sort of chat show in which an
overweight American couple were being questioned by a black
lady in a trouser suit about how, as the black lady put it,
'they related to one another sexually'.

The man, slumped in his seat with his legs wide apart, was
describing in as much detail as the woman in the trouser suit
would allow what he, as he put it, 'asked of his marriage',
while the woman, arms folded, knees together but too plump
to be prim, was explaining how 'without being judgmental, he
had never taken the deodorant on board'.

'Get a load of that body language,' said the lady in the
trouser suit, and the audience, mystifyingly to Mrs Ransome
who did not know what body language was, erupted in jeers
and laughter.

'The things people do for money,' thought Mrs Ransome,
and switched it off.

The next afternoon, waking from a doze on her bean-bag,
she switched on again and found herself watching a similar
programme with another equally shameless couple and the
same hooting, jeering audience, roaming among them with a
microphone a different hostess, white this time but as imper-
turbable as the first and just as oblivious of everybody's bad
manners, even, it seemed to Mrs Ransome, egging them on.

These hostesses (for Mrs Ransome now began to watch

regularly) were all much of a muchness, big, bold and, Mrs Ransome thought, with far too much self-confidence (she thought this was what they meant by 'feisty' and would have looked it up in Mr Ransome's dictionary but wasn't sure how it was spelled). They had names that defied gender: Robin, Bobby, Troy and some, like Tiffany, Page and Kirby, that in Mrs Ransome's book weren't names at all.

The presenters and their audience spoke in a language which Mrs Ransome, to begin with anyway, found hard to understand, talking of 'parenting' and 'personal interaction', of 'fine-tuning their sex-lives' and 'taking it up the butt'. It was a language of avowal and exuberant fellowship. 'I hear what you're saying,' they said, smacking each other's hands. 'I know where you're coming from.'

There was Felicia, who wanted long and loving sexual inter-action and Dwight, her husband, who just had hungry hands and no marital skills. They both, it was generally agreed, needed to talk, and here in front of this jeering throng, hungry for sensation, was the place they had chosen to do it, finally, as the credits rolled, falling hungrily upon one another, mouth glued to mouth while the audience roared its approval and the presenter looked on with a sadder and wiser smile. 'Thank you people,' she said, and the couple kissed on.

What Mrs Ransome could never get used to was how unabashed the participants were, how unsheepish and how none of these people was ever plain shy. Even when there was a programme about shyness no one who took part was shy in any sense that Mrs Ransome understood it; there was no hanging back and no shortage of unblushing participants willing to stand up and boast of their crippling self-consciousness and the absurdities to which overwhelming diffidence and self-effacingness had brought them. No matter how private or intimate the topic under discussion, none of these eager vociferous people had any shame. On the contrary, they seemed to vie with one another in coming up with confessions of behaviour that grew ever more ingeniously gross and indelicate; one outrageous admission trumped another, the audience greeting each new revelation with wild whoops and yells, hurling advice at the participants and urging them on to retail new depravities.

There were, it's true, rare occasions when some of the audience gave vent not to glee but to outrage, even seeming for a moment, presented with some particularly egregious confession, to be genuinely shocked; but it was only because the presenter, glancing covertly at the audience behind the speaker's back, had pulled a wry face and so cued their affront. The presenter was an accomplice, Mrs Ransome thought, and no better than anyone else, even going out of her way to remind participants of yet more inventive and indelicate acts that they had earlier confided to her in the presumed privacy of the dressing-room. When she jogged their memories they went through an elaborate pantomime of shame (hiding their heads, covering face with hands, shaking with seemingly helpless laughter), all this to indicate that they had never expected such secrets to be made public, let alone retailed to the camera.

Still, Mrs Ransome felt, they were all better than she was. For what none of these whooping, giggling (and often quite obese) creatures seemed in no doubt about was that at the basic level at which these programmes were pitched people were all the same. There was no shame and no reserve and to pretend otherwise was to be stuck up and a hypocrite. Mrs Ransome felt that she was certainly the first and that her husband was probably the second.

The contents of the flat were insured for £50,000. It had originally been much less, but being a solicitor and a careful man besides, Mr Ransome had seen to it that the premium had kept pace with the cost of living. Accordingly, this modest agglomeration of household goods, furniture, fixtures and fittings had gone on over the years gently increasing in value; the stereo and the Magimix, the canteen of cutlery, the EPNS salad servers, the tray cloths and tablemats and all the apparatus of that life which the Ransomes had the complete equipment for but had never managed to lead, all this had marched comfortably in step with the index. Durable, sober, unshowy stuff, bought with an eye to use not ornament, hardly diminished by breakage or loss, dutifully dusted and polished over the years so that it was scarcely even abraded by wear or tear – all this had gone uneventfully forward until that terrible night when the column had been ambushed and this ordinary, unpretentious little fraternity was seemingly wiped out and what Mrs Ransome modestly called 'our things' had vanished for ever.

So at any rate the insurance company concluded and in due course a cheque arrived for the full value plus an unforeseen increment payable in the absence of any previous claims and which served to cover disruption and compensate for distress.

'The extra is for our trauma,' said Mrs Ransome, looking at the cheque.

'I prefer to call it inconvenience,' Mr Ransome said. 'We've been burgled, not knocked down by a bus. Still, the extra will come in handy.'

He was already working out a scheme for an improved stereo system plus an update on his CD player combined with high definition digital sound and ultra-refinement of tone, all to be fed through a pair of majestic new speakers in hand-crafted mahogany. It would be Mozart as he had never heard him before.

Mrs Ransome was sitting contentedly in a cheap cane rocking-chair she had found a few weeks earlier in a furniture store up the Edgware Road. It was an establishment which, before the burglary, she would never have dreamed of going into, with garish suites, paintings of clowns and, flanking the door, two lifesize pottery leopards. A common shop she would have thought it once, as a bit of her still did, but Mr Anwar had recommended it and sure enough the rocking-chair she'd bought there was wonderfully comfortable and, unlike the easy chair in which she used to sit before the burglary, good for her back. Now that the insurance cheque had come through she planned on getting a matching chair for Mr Ransome, but in the meantime she had bought a rug to put the chair on, and, sewn with a design of an elephant, it glowed under the light from a brass table lamp bought at the same shop. Sitting with what Mr Anwar had told her was an Afghan prayer rug round her shoulders she felt in the middle of the bare sitting-room floor that she was on a cosy and slightly exotic little island.

For the moment Mr Ransome's island was not so cosy, just a chair at the card table on which Mrs Ransome had put the one letter that constituted the day's post. Mr Ransome picked up the envelope. Smelling curry, he said: 'What's for supper?'

'Curry.'

Mr Ransome turned the letter over. It looked like a bill. 'What sort of curry?'

'Lamb,' said Mrs Ransome. 'With apricots. I've been wondering,' she said. 'Would white be too bold?'

'White what?' said Mr Ransome, holding the letter up to the light.

'Well,' she said hesitantly. 'White everything really.'

Mr Ransome did not reply. He was reading the letter.

'You mustn't get too excited,' Mr Ransome said as they were driving towards Aylesbury. 'It could be somebody's sense of humour. Another joke.'

Actually their mood was quite flat and the countryside was flat too; they had scarcely spoken since they had set off, the letter with Mr Ransome's pencilled directions lying on Mrs Ransome's lap.

'Left at the roundabout,' thought Mr Ransome.

'It's left at the roundabout,' Mrs Ransome said.

He had telephoned the storage firm that morning to have a

girl answer. It was called Rapid'n'Reliant Removals'n'Storage, those 'n's, Mr Ransome thought, a foretaste of trouble; nor was he disappointed.

'Hello. Rapid'n'Reliant Removals'n'Storage. Christine Thoseby speaking. How may I help you?'

Mr Ransome asked for Mr Ralston, who had signed the letter.

'At the present time of speaking Mr Ralston is in Cardiff. How may I help you?'

'When will he be back?'

'Not until next week. He's on a tour of our repositories. How may I help you?'

Her repeated promises of help notwithstanding, Christine had the practised lack of interest of someone perpetually painting her nails and when Mr Ransome explained that the previous day he had received a mysterious invoice for £344.36 re the storage of certain household effects, the property of Mr and Mrs Ransome, all Christine said was: 'And?' He began to explain the circumstances but at the suggestion that the effects in question might be stolen property Christine came to life.

'May I interject? I think that's very unlikely, quite frankly, I mean, Rapid'n'Reliant were established in 1977.'

Mr Ransome tried a different tack. 'You wouldn't happen to know whether any of these household effects you're holding includes some old stereo equipment?'

'Can't help you there, I'm afraid. But if you have any items in storage with Rapid'n'Reliant they'll show up on the C47, of which you should have a copy. It's a yellow flimsy.'

Mr Ransome started to explain why he didn't have a flimsy but Christine cut him short.

'I wouldn't know that, would I, because I'm in Newport Pagnell? This is the office. The storage depot is in Aylesbury. You can be anywhere nowadays. It's computers. Actually the person who could help you at Aylesbury is Martin but I happen to know he's out on a job most of today.'

'I wonder whether I ought to go down to Aylesbury,' Mr Ransome said, 'just to see if there's anything there.'

Christine was unenthusiastic. 'I can't actually stop you,' she said, 'only they don't have any facilities for visitors. It's not like a kennels,' she added inexplicably.

Mr Ransome having told her the storage firm was in a business park, Mrs Ransome, who was not familiar with the genre, imagined it situated in a setting agreeably pastoral, a park that was indeed a park and attached to some more or less stately home, now sensitively adapted to modern requirements; the estate dotted with workshops possibly; offices nestling discreetly in trees. At the hub of this centre of enterprise she pictured a country house where tall women with folders strode along terraces, typists busied themselves in gilded saloons beneath painted ceilings, a vision which, had she thought to trace it back, she would have found to have derived from those war films where French châteaux taken over by the German High Command bustle with new life on the eve of D-Day.

It was as well she didn't share these romantic expectations with Mr Ransome who, the secretary of several companies and so acquainted with the reality, would have given them short shrift.

It was only when she found herself being driven round a bleak treeless ring-road lined with small factories and surrounded by concrete and rough grass that Mrs Ransome began to revise her expectations.

'It doesn't look very countrified,' Mrs Ransome said.

'Why should it?' said Mr Ransome, about to turn in at some un-Palladian metal gates.

'This is it,' said Mrs Ransome, looking at the letter.

The gates were set in a seven-foot high fence topped with an oblique pelmet of barbed wire so that the place looked less like a park than a prison. Fixed to an empty pillbox was a metal diagram, painted in yellow and blue, showing the whereabouts of the various firms on the estate. Mr Ransome got out to look for Unit 14.

'You are here,' said an arrow, only someone had inserted at the tip of the arrow a pair of crudely drawn buttocks.

Unit 14 appeared to be a few hundred yards inside the perimeter, just about where, had the buttocks been drawn to scale, the navel might have been. Mr Ransome got back in the car and drove slowly on in the gathering dusk until he came to a broad low hangar-like building with double sliding doors, painted red and bare of all identification except for a warning that guard dogs patrolled. There were no other cars and no sign of anybody about.

Mr Ransome pulled at the sliding door, not expecting to find it open. Nor was it.

'It's locked,' said Mrs Ransome.

'You don't say,' Mr Ransome muttered under his breath,

and struck out round the side of the building, followed more slowly by Mrs Ransome, picking her way uncertainly over the rubble and clinkers and patches of scrubby grass. Mr Ransome felt his shoe skid on something.

'Mind the dog dirt,' said Mrs Ransome. 'It's all over this grass.' Steps led down to a basement door. Mr Ransome tried this too. It was also locked, a boiler room possibly.

'That looks like a boiler room,' said Mrs Ransome.

He scraped his shoe on the step.

'You'd think they'd make them set an example,' Mrs Ransome said.

'Who?' said Mr Ransome, slurring his polluted shoe over some thin grass.

'The guard dogs.'

They had almost completed a circuit of the hangar when they came on a small frosted window where there was a dim light. It was open an inch or two at the top and was obviously a lavatory, and faintly through the glass Mrs Ransome could see standing on the window-ledge the blurred shape of a toilet roll. It was doubtless a coincidence that it was blue, and forget-me-not blue at that, a shade Mrs Ransome always favoured in her own toilet rolls and which was not always easy to find. She pressed her face to the glass in order to see it more clearly and then saw something else.

'Look, dear,' Mrs Ransome said. But Mr Ransome wasn't looking. He was listening.

'Shut up,' he said. He could hear Mozart.

And floating through the crack of the lavatory window

came the full, dark, sumptuous and utterly unmistakable tones of Dame Kiri Te Kanawa.

'Per pietà, ben mio,' she was singing, 'perdona all 'error d'un alma amante.'

And out it drifted into the damp dusk, rising over Rapid'n'Reliant at Unit 14 and Croda Adhesives at Unit 16 and Lansyl Selant Applicators plc at Unit 20 (Units 17–19 currently under offer).

'O Dio,' sang Dame Kiri. 'O Dio.'

And the perimeter road heard it and the sheathed and stunted saplings planted there and the dirty dribble of a stream that straggled through a concrete culvert to the lumpy field beyond, where a shabby horse contemplated two barrels and a pole.

Galvanised by the sound of the Antipodean songstress Mr Ransome clambered up the fall pipe and knelt painfully on the window-sill. Clinging to the pipe with one hand he prised open the window an inch or two further and forced his head in as far as it would go, almost slipping off the sill in the process.

'Careful,' said Mrs Ransome.

Mr Ransome began to shout. 'Hello. Hello?'

Mozart stopped and somewhere a bus went by.

In the silence Mr Ransome shouted again, this time almost joyfully. 'Hello!'

Instantly there was bedlam. Dogs burst out barking, a siren went off and Mr and Mrs Ransome were trapped and dazzled by half a dozen security lights focused tightly on their shrinking forms. Petrified, Mr Ransome clung desperately to the lavatory window while Mrs Ransome plastered herself as closely as she could against the wall, one hand creeping (she hoped unobtrusively) up the window-sill to seek the comfort of Mr Ransome's knee.

Then, as suddenly as it had begun, the commotion stopped; the lights went out, the siren trailed off and the barking of the dogs modulated to an occasional growl. Trembling on the sill Mr Ransome heard a door pushed back and unhurried steps walking across the forecourt.

'Sorry about that, people,' said a male voice. 'Burglars, I'm afraid, measures for the detection and discouragement of.'

Mrs Ransome peered into the darkness but still half-blinded by the lights could see nothing. Mr Ransome slithered down the fall pipe to stand beside her and she took his hand.

'This way chaps and chapesses. Over here.'

Mr and Mrs Ransome stumbled across the last of the grass onto the concrete where silhouetted against the open door stood a young man.

Dazed, they followed him into the hangar and in the light they made a sorry-looking pair. Mrs Ransome was limping because one of her heels had broken and she had laddered both her stockings. Mr Ransome had torn the knee of his trousers; there was shit on his shoes and across his forehead where he had pressed his face into the window was a long black smudge.

The young man smiled and put out his hand. 'Maurice. Rosemary. Hi! I'm Martin.'

It was a pleasant open face and though he did have one of

those little beards Mrs Ransome thought made them all look like poisoners, for a warehouseman one way and another he looked quite classy. True he was wearing the kind of cap which had once been the distinctive head-gear of American golfers but now seemed of general application, and a little squirt of hair with a rubber band round it coming out of the back, and, again like them all nowadays, his shirt tail was out; still, what gave him a certain air in Mrs Ransome's eyes was his smart maroon cardigan. It was not unlike one she had picked out for Mr Ransome at a Simpson's sale the year before. Loosely knotted around his neck was a yellow silk scarf with horses' heads on it. Mrs Ransome had bought Mr Ransome one of those too, though he had worn it only once as he decided it made him look like a cad. This boy didn't look like a cad; he looked dashing and she thought that if they ever got their belongings back she'd root the scarf out from the wardrobe and make her husband give it another try.

'Follow moi,' said the young man and led them down a cold uncarpeted corridor.

'It's so nice to meet you at long last,' he said over his shoulder, 'though in the circumstances I feel I know you already.'

'What circumstances?' said Mr Ransome.

'Bear with me one moment,' said Martin.

Mr and Mrs Ransome were left in the dark while the young man fiddled with a lock.

'I'll just illuminate matters a fraction,' he said and a light came on in the room beyond.

'Come in,' said Martin and he laughed.

Tired and dirty and blinking in the light, Mr and Mrs Ransome stumbled through the door and into their own flat.

It was just as they had left it in the evening they had gone to the opera. Here was their carpet, their sofa, their high-backed chairs, the reproduction walnut-veneered coffee table with the scalloped edges and cabriole legs and on it the latest number of the *Gramophone*. Here was Mrs Ransome's embroidery, lying on the end of the sofa where she had put it down before going to change at a quarter to six on that never-to-be-forgotten evening. There on the nest of tables was the glass from which Mr Ransome had had a little drop of something to see him through the first act of *Così*, still (Mrs Ransome touched the rim of the glass with her finger) slightly sticky.

On the mantelpiece the carriage clock, presented to Mr Ransome to mark his twenty-five years with the firm of Selvey, Ransome, Steele and Co., struck six, though Mrs Ransome was not sure if it was six then or six now. The lights were on, just as they had left them.

'A waste of electricity, I know,' Mr Ransome was wont to say, 'but at least it deters the casual thief,' and on the hall table the evening paper left there by Mr Ransome for Mrs Ransome, who generally read it with her morning coffee the following day.

Other than a cardboard plate with some cold half-eaten curry which Martin neatly heeled under the sofa, mouthing 'Sorry', everything, every little thing was exactly as it should be; they might have been at home in their flat in Naseby

Mansions, St John's Wood and not in a hangar on an industrial estate on the outskirts of nowhere.

Gone was the feeling of foreboding with which Mrs Ransome had set out that afternoon; now there was only joy as she wandered round the room, occasionally picking up some cherished object with a smile and an 'Oh!' of reacquaintance, sometimes holding it up for her husband to see. For his part Mr Ransome was almost moved, particularly when he spotted his old CD player, his trusty old CD player as he was inclined to think of it now, not quite up to the mark, it's true, the venerable old thing, but still honest and old-fashioned; yes, it was good to see it again and he gave Mrs Ransome a brief blast of *Così*.

Watching this reunion with a smile almost of pride, Martin said: 'Everything in order? I tried to keep it all just as it was.'

'Oh yes,' said Mrs Ransome, 'it's perfect.'

'Astonishing,' said her husband.

Mrs Ransome remembered something. 'I'd put a casserole in the oven.'

'Yes,' said Martin, 'I enjoyed that.'

'It wasn't dry?' said Mrs Ransome.

'Only a touch,' said Martin, following them into the bedroom. 'It would perhaps have been better at Gas Mark 3.'

Mrs Ransome nodded and noticed on the dressing-table the piece of kitchen paper (she remembered how they had run out of Kleenex) with which she had blotted her lipstick three months before.

'Kitchen,' said Martin as if they might not know the way, though it was exactly where it should have been, and exactly how too, except that the casserole dish, now empty, stood washed and waiting on the draining-board.

'I wasn't sure where that went,' said Martin apologetically.

'That's all right', said Mrs Ransome, 'it lives in here.' She opened the cupboard by the sink and popped the dish away.

'That was my guess,' said Martin, 'though I didn't like to risk it.' He laughed and Mrs Ransome laughed too.

Mr Ransome scowled. The young man was civil enough, if over-familiar, but it all seemed a bit too relaxed. A crime had been committed after all, and not a petty one either; this was stolen property; what was it doing here?

Mr Ransome thought it was time to take charge of the situation.

'Tea?' said Martin.

'No thank you,' said Mr Ransome.

'Yes please,' said his wife.

'Then,' said Martin, 'we need to talk.'

Mrs Ransome had never heard the phrase used in real life as it were and she looked at this young man with new-found recognition: she knew where he was coming from. So did Mr Ransome.

'Yes, indeed,' said Mr Ransome, decisively, sitting down at the kitchen table and meaning to kick off by asking this altogether too pleased with himself young man, what this was all about.

'Perhaps,' said Martin, giving Mrs Ransome her tea, 'perhaps you would like to tell me what this is all about. I mean with all due respect, as they say.'

This was too much for Mr Ransome.

'Perhaps,' he exploded, 'and with all due respect, you'd like to tell me why it is you're wearing my cardigan.'

'You never wore it much,' said Mrs Ransome placidly. 'Lovely tea.'

'That isn't the point, Rosemary.' Mr Ransome seldom used her Christian name except as a form of blunt instrument. 'And that's my silk scarf.'

'You never wore that at all. You said it made you look like a cad.'

'That's why I like it,' said Martin, happily, 'the cad factor. However all good things come to an end, as they say.' And unhurriedly (and quite unrepentantly, thought Mr Ransome) he took off the cardigan, unknotted the scarf and laid them both on the table.

Pruned of these sheltering encumbrances, Martin's T-shirt, the message of which had hitherto only been hinted at, now fearlessly proclaimed itself, 'Got a stiffy? Wear a Jiffy!' and in brackets 'drawing on back'. As Mr Ransome eased forward in his chair in order to shield his wife from the offending illustration, Mrs Ransome slightly eased back.

'Actually,' said Martin, 'we've worn one or two of your things. I started off with your brown overcoat which I just tried on originally as a bit of a joke.'

'A joke?' said Mr Ransome, the humorous qualities of that particular garment never having occurred to him.

'Yes. Only now I've grown quite fond of it. It's great.'

'But it must be too big for you,' said Mrs Ransome.

'I know. That's why it's so great. And you've got tons of scarves. Cleo thinks you've got really good taste.'

'Cleo?' said Mrs Ransome.

'My partner.'

Then, catching sight of Mr Ransome by now pop-eyed with fury, Martin shrugged. 'After all, it was you who gave us the green light.' He went into the sitting-room and came back with a folder, which he laid on the kitchen table.

'Just tell me,' said Mr Ransome with terrible calmness, 'why it is our things are here.'

So Martin explained. Except it wasn't really an explanation and when he'd finished they weren't much further on.

He had come in to work one morning about three months ago ('February 15,' Mrs Ransome supplied helpfully) and unlocking the doors had found their flat set out just as it had been in Naseby Mansions and just as they saw it now – carpets down, lights on, warm, a smell of cooking from the kitchen.

'I mean,' said Martin happily, 'home.'

'But surely,' Mr Ransome said, 'you must have realised that this was, to say the least, unusual?'

'Very unusual,' said Martin. Normally, he said, home contents were containered, crated and sealed, and the container parked in the back lot until required. 'We store loads of furniture, but I might go for six months and never see an armchair.'

'But why were they all dumped here?' said Mrs Ransome.

'Dumped?' said Martin. 'You call this dumped? It's beautiful, it's a poem.'

'Why?' said Mr Ransome.

'Well, when I came in that morning, there was an envelope on the hall table ...'

'That's where I put the letters normally,' said Mrs Ransome.

'... an envelope,' said Martin, 'containing £3000 in cash to cover storage costs for two months, well clear of our normal charges I can tell you. And,' said Martin, taking a card out of the folder, 'there was this.'

It was a sheet torn from the *Delia Smith Cookery Calendar* with a recipe for the hotpot which Mrs Ransome had made that afternoon and which she had left in the oven. On the back of it was written: 'Leave exactly as it is,' then in brackets, 'but feel free to use.' This was underlined.

'So, where your overcoat was concerned and the scarves etc., I felt,' Martin searched for the right word, 'I felt that that was my *imprimatur*.' (He had been briefly at the University of Warwick.)

'But anybody could have written that,' Mr Ransome said.

'And leave £3000 in cash with it?' said Martin. 'No fear. Only I did check. Newport Pagnell knew nothing about it. Cardiff. Leeds. I had it run through the computer and they drew a complete blank. So I thought: "Well, Martin, the stuff's here. For the time being it's paid for, so why not just make yourself at home?" So I did. I could have done with the choice of CDs being a bit more eclectic, though. My guess is you're a Mozart fan?'

'I still think,' said Mr Ransome testily, 'you might have made more enquiries before making so free with our belongings.'

'It's not usual, I agree,' said Martin, 'only why should I? I'd no reason to ... smell a rat?'

Mr Ransome took in (and was irritated by) these occasional notes of inappropriate interrogation with which Martin (and the young generally) seemed often to end a sentence. He had heard it in the mouth of the office boy without realising it had got as far as Aylesbury ('And where are you going now, Foster?' 'For my lunch?'). It seemed insolent, though it was hard to say why and it invariably put Mr Ransome in a bad temper (which was why Foster did it).

Martin on the other hand seemed unconscious of the irritation he was causing, his serenity so impervious Mr Ransome put it down to drugs. Now he sat happily at the kitchen table and while Mr Ransome fussed round the flat on the look-out for evidence of damage or dilapidation or even undue wear and tear, Martin chatted comfortably to Rosemary, as he called her.

'He just needs to lighten up a bit,' said Martin as Mr Ransome banged about in the cupboards.

Mrs Ransome wasn't sure if lighten up was the same as brighten up but catching his drift smiled and nodded.

'It's been like playing houses,' said Martin. 'Cleo and I live over a dry-cleaners normally.'

Mrs Ransome thought Cleo might be black but she didn't like to ask.

'Actually,' and Martin dropped his voice because Mr Ransome was in the pantry cupboard counting the bottles of wine in the rack, 'actually it's perked things up between us two. Change of scene, you know what they say.'

Mrs Ransome nodded knowledgeably; it was a topic frequently touched on in the afternoon programmes.

'Good bed,' whispered Martin, 'the mattress give you lots of – what's the word? – purchase.' Martin gave a little thrust with his hips. 'Know what I mean, Rosemary?' He winked.

'It's orthopaedic,' Mrs Ransome said hastily. 'Mr Ransome has a bad back.'

'I'd probably have one too if I'd lived here much longer.' Martin patted her hand. 'Only joking.'

'What I don't understand,' said Mr Ransome, coming into the kitchen while Martin still had his hand over his wife's (Mr Ransome didn't understand that either), 'what I don't understand is how whoever it was transported our things here could remember so exactly where everything went.'

'Trouble ye no more,' said Martin and he went out into the hall and brought back a photograph album. It was a present Mr Ransome had bought Mrs Ransome when he was urging her to find a hobby. He had also bought her a camera which she had never managed to fathom so that the camera never got used, nor did the album. Except that now it was full of photographs.

'The polaroid camera,' Martin said, 'the blessings thereof.'

There were a dozen or so photographs for every room in the flat on the night in question; general views of the room, corners of the room, a close-up of the mantelpiece, another of the desk-top, every room and every surface recorded in conscientious detail, much as if, had her flat been the setting for a film, the continuity assistant would have recorded them.

'And our name and address?' Mr Ransome said.

'Simple,' said Martin. 'Open ...'

'Any drawer,' said he and Mrs Ransome together.

'All these photographs,' Mrs Ransome said. 'Whoever they are, they must have no end of money. Don't they make it look nice.'

'It is nice,' said Martin. 'We're going to miss it.'

'It's not only that all our things are in the right place,' Mr Ransome said. 'The rooms are in the right place too.'

'Screens,' said Martin. 'They must have brought screens with them.'

'There's no ceiling,' said Mr Ransome triumphantly. 'They didn't manage that.'

'They managed the chandelier,' said his wife. And so they had, suspending it from a handy beam.

'Well I don't think we need to prolong this stage of the proceedings any longer than we have to,' said Mr Ransome. 'I'll contact my insurance company and tell them our belongings have been found. They will then doubtless contact you over their collection and return. There doesn't seem to be anything missing but at this stage one can't be sure.'

'Oh, there's nothing missing,' said Martin. 'One or two After Eights perhaps, but I can easily replenish those.'

'No, no,' said Mrs Ransome, 'that won't be necessary. They're ...' and she smiled, 'they're on the house.'

Mr Ransome frowned and when Martin went off to find the various pro-formas he whispered to Mrs Ransome that they would have to have everything cleaned.

'I don't like to think what's been going on. There was a bit of kitchen paper on your dressing-table with what was almost certainly blood. And I've a feeling they may have been sleeping in our bed.'

'We'll exchange flimsies,' said Martin. 'One flimsy for you. One flimsy for me. Your effects. Do you say "effects" when a person's still around? Or is it just when they're dead?'

'Dead,' said Mr Ransome authoritatively. 'In this case it's property.'

'Effects,' said Martin. 'Good word.'

Standing on the forecourt as they were going Martin kissed Mrs Ransome on both cheeks. He was about the age their son would have been, Mrs Ransome thought, had they had a son.

'I feel like I'm one of the family,' he said.

'Yes,' thought Mr Ransome; if they'd had a son this is what it would have been like. Irritating, perplexing. Feeling got at. They wouldn't have been able to call their lives their own.

Mr Ransome managed to shake hands.

'All's well that ends well,' said Martin, and patted his shoulder. 'Take care.'

'How do we know he wasn't in on it?' said Mr Ransome in the car.

'He doesn't look the type,' said Mrs Ransome.

'Oh? What type is that? Have you ever come across a case like this before? Have you ever heard of it? What type does it take, that's what I'd like to know?'

'We're going a little fast,' said Mrs Ransome.

'I shall have to inform the police, of course,' Mr Ransome said.

'They weren't interested before so they'll be even less interested now.'

'Who are you?'

'Beg pardon?'

'I'm the solicitor. Who are you? Are you the expert?'

They drove in silence for a while.

'Of course, I shall want some compensation. The distress. The agony of mind. The inconvenience. They're all quantifiable, and must be taken into account in the final settlement.'

He was already writing the letter in his head.

In due course, the contents of the flat came back to Naseby Mansions, a card pinned to one of the crates saying, 'Feel Free to Use. Martin'. And, in brackets, 'Joke'. Mr Ransome insisted that everything must be put back just as it had been before, which might have proved difficult had it not been for the aide-mémoire in the form of Mrs Ransome's photograph album. Even so the gang who returned the furniture were less meticulous than the burglars who had removed it, besides being much slower. Still, the flat having been decorated throughout and the covers washed, hoovered or dry-cleaned, the place gradually came to look much as it had done before and life returned to what Mrs Ransome used to think of as normal but didn't now, quite.

Quite early on in the proceedings, and while Mr Ransome was at the office, Mrs Ransome tried out her cane rocking-chair and rug in the now much less spartan conditions of the lounge, but though the chair was as comfortable as ever the ensemble didn't look right and made her feel she was sitting in a department store. So she relegated the chair to the spare room where from time to time she visited it and sat reviewing her life. But no, it was not the same and eventually she put the chair out for the caretaker who incorporated it into his scheme of things in the room behind the boiler, where he was now trying to discover the books of Jane Austen.

Mr Ransome fared better than his wife, for although he had had to reimburse the insurance company over their original cheque he was able to claim that having already ordered some new speakers (he hadn't) this should be taken into account and allowance made, which it duly was, thus enabling him to invest in some genuinely state of the art equipment.

From time to time over the next few months traces of Martin and Cleo's brief occupation would surface – a contraceptive packet (empty) that had been thrust under the mattress, a handkerchief down the side of the settee and, in one of the mantelpiece ornaments, a lump of hard brown material wrapped in silver paper. Tentatively Mrs Ransome sniffed it, then donned her Marigold gloves and put it down the lavatory, assuming that was where it belonged, though it was only after several goes that it was reluctantly flushed, Mrs Ransome sitting meanwhile on the side of the bath, waiting for the cistern to refill, and wondering how it came to be on the mantelpiece in the first place. A joke possibly, though not one she shared with Mr Ransome.

Strange hairs were another item that put in regular appearances, long fair ones which were obviously Martin's, darker crinklier ones she supposed must be Cleo's. The incidence of these hairs wasn't split evenly between Mr and Mrs Ransome's respective wardrobes; indeed, since Mr Ransome didn't complain about them, she presumed he never found any, as he would certainly have let her know if he had.

She, on the other hand, found them everywhere – among her dresses, her coats, her underwear, his hairs as well as hers, and little ones as well as long ones, so that she was left puzzling over what it was they could have been up to that wasn't constrained by the normal boundaries of gender and propriety. Had Martin worn her knickers on his head, she wondered (in one pair there were three hairs); had the elastic on her brassière always been as loose as it was now (two hairs there, one fair, one dark)?

Still, sitting opposite Mr Ransome in his earphones of an evening, she could contemplate with equanimity, and even a small thrill, that she had shared her underclothes with a third party. Or two third parties possibly. 'You don't mean a third party,' Mr Ransome would have said, but this was another argument for keeping quiet.

There was one reminder of the recent past, though, that they were forced to share, if only by accident. They had had their supper one Saturday evening after which Mr Ransome was planning to record a live broadcast of Il Seraglio on Radio 3. Mrs Ransome, reflecting that there was never anything on TV worth watching on a Saturday night, had settled down to read a novel about some lacklustre infidelities in a Cotswold setting while Mr Ransome prepared to record. He had put in a tape that he thought was blank but checking it on the machine was startled to find that it began with a peal of helpless laughter. Mrs Ransome looked up. Mr Ransome listened long enough to detect that there were two people laughing, a man and a woman and since they showed no sign of stopping was about to switch it off when Mrs Ransome said: 'No, Maurice. Leave it. This might be a clue.'

So they listened in silence as the laughter went on, almost uninterrupted, until after three or four minutes it began to slacken and break up and whoever it was who was still laughing was left panting and breathless, this breathlessness gradually modulating into another sound, the second subject as it were, a groan and then a cry leading to a rhythmic pumping as stern and as purposeful as the other had been silly and light-hearted. At one point the microphone was moved closer to catch a sound that was so moist and wet it hardly seemed human.

'It sounds,' said Mrs Ransome, 'like custard boiling,' though she knew that it wasn't. Making custard must seldom be so effortful as this seemed to be, nor is the custard urged on with affirmative yells, nor do the cooks cry out when, in due course, the custard starts to boil over.

'I don't think we want to listen to this, do we?' Mr Ransome said and switched over to Radio 3, where they came in on the reverent hush that preceded the arrival of Claudio Abbado.

Later when they were in bed Mrs Ransome said: 'I suppose we'd better return that tape?'

'What for?' said Mr Ransome. 'The tape is mine. In any case, we can't. It's wiped. I recorded over it.'

This was a lie. Mr Ransome had wanted to record over it, it's true, but felt that whenever he listened to the music he would remember what lay underneath and this would put paid to any possible sublimity. So he had put the tape in the kitchen bin. Then, thinking about it as Mrs Ransome was in the bathroom brushing her teeth, he went and delved among the potato peelings and old teabags, and, picking off a tomato skin that had stuck to it, he hid the cassette in the bookcase behind a copy of *Salmon on Torts*, a hidey hole where he also kept a cache of photographs of some suburban sexual acts, the legacy of a messy divorce case in Epsom that he had conducted a few years before. The bookcase had, of course, gone to Aylesbury along with everything else but had been returned intact, the hiding place seemingly undetected by Martin.

Actually it had not been undetected at all: the photographs had been what he and Cleo had been laughing about on the tape in the first place.

Not a secret from Martin, nor were the snaps a secret from Mrs Ransome who, idly looking at the bookcase one afternoon and wondering what to cook for supper, had seen the title *Salmon on Torts* and thought it had a vaguely culinary sound to it. She had put the photographs back undisturbed but every few months or so would check to see that they were still there. When they were she felt somehow reassured.

So sometimes now when Mr Ransome sat in his chair with his earphones on listening to *Magic Flute* it was not *Magic Flute* he was listening to at all. Gazing abstractedly at his reading wife his ears were full of Martin and Cleo moaning and crying and taking it out on one another again and again and again. No matter how often he listened to the tape Mr Ransome never ceased to be amazed by it; that two human beings could give themselves up so utterly and unreservedly to one another and to the moment was beyond his comprehension; it seemed to him miraculous.

Listening to the tape so often he became every bit as familiar with it as with something by Mozart. He came to recognise Martin's long intake of breath as marking the end of a mysterious bridging passage (Cleo was actually on hands and knees, Martin behind her) when the languorous andante (little mewings from the girl) accelerated into the percussive allegro assai (hoarse cries from them both) which in its turn gave way to an even more frantic coda, a sudden rallentando ('No, no, not yet,' she was crying, then, 'Yes, yes, yes') followed by panting, sighing, silence and finally sleep. Not an imaginative man, Mr Ransome nevertheless found himself thinking that if one built up a library of such tapes it would be possible to bestow on them the sexual equivalent of Köchel numbers, even trace the development of some sort of style in sexual intercourse, with early, middle and late periods, the whole apparatus of Mozartean musicology adapted to these new and thwacking rhythms.

Such were Mr Ransome's thoughts as he sat across from his wife, who was having another stab at Barbara Pym. She knew he wasn't listening to Mozart though there were few obvious signs and nothing so vulgar as a bulge in his trousers. No, there was just a look of strain on Mr Ransome's face, which was the very opposite of the look he had when he was listening to his favourite composer; an intensity of attention and a sense that, were he to listen hard enough, he might hear something on the tape he had previously missed.

Mrs Ransome would listen to the tape herself from time to time but lacking the convenient camouflage of Mozart she confined her listening experiences to the afternoons. Getting out her folding household steps she would pull down *Salmon on Torts* then reach in behind it for the tape (the photographs seemed as silly and laughable to her as they had to Martin and Cleo). Then, having poured herself a small sherry, she would settle down to listen to them making love, marvelling still after at least a dozen hearings at the length and persistence of the process and its violent and indecorous outcome. Afterwards she would go and lie on the bed, reflecting that this was the same bed on which it had all happened and think again about it happening.

These discreet (and discrete) epiphanies apart, life after they had recovered their possessions went on much the same as it had before they lost them. Sometimes, though, lying there on the bed or waiting to get up in the morning, Mrs Ransome would get depressed, feeling she had missed the bus; though what bus it was or where it was headed she would have found it hard to say. Prior to the visit to Aylesbury and the return of their things, she had, she thought, persuaded herself that the burglary had been an opportunity, with each day bringing its crop of small adventures – a visit from Dusty, a walk down to Mr Anwar's, a trip up the Edgware Road. Now, re-ensconced among her possessions, Mrs Ransome feared that her diversions were at an end; life had returned to normal but it was a normal she no longer relished or was contented with.

The afternoons particularly were dull and full of regret. It's true she continued to watch the television, no longer so surprised at what people got up to as she once had been but even (as with Martin and Cleo) mildly envious. She grew so accustomed to the forms of television discourse that she occasionally let slip a tell-tale phrase herself, remarking once, for instance, that there had been a bit of hassle on the 74 bus.

'Hassle?' said Mr Ransome. 'Where did you pick up that expression?'

'Why?' said Mrs Ransome innocently. 'Isn't it a proper word?'

'Not in my vocabulary.'

It occurred to Mrs Ransome that this was the time for counselling; previously an option it had now become a necessity, so she tried to reach Dusty via her helpline.

'I'm sorry but Ms Briscoe is not available to take your call,' said a recorded voice, which was immediately interrupted by a real presence.

'Hello. Mandy speaking. How may I help you?'

Mrs Ransome explained that she needed to talk to somebody about the sudden return of all the stolen property. 'I have complicated feelings about it,' said Mrs Ransome and tried to explain.

Mandy was doubtful. 'It might come under post-traumatic

stress syndrome,' she said, 'only I wouldn't bank on it. They're clamping down on that now we're coming to the end of this year's financial year, and anyway it's meant for rape and murder and whatnot, whereas we've had people ringing up who've just had a bad time at the dentist's. You don't feel the furniture's dirty, do you?'

'No,' said Mrs Ransome. 'We've had everything cleaned anyway.'

'Well, if you've kept the receipts I could ring Bickerton Road and get them to give you something back.'

'Never mind,' said Mrs Ransome, 'I expect I shall cope.'

'Well, it's what we all have to do in the end, isn't it?' said Mandy.

'What's that?' said Mrs Ransome.

'Cope, dear. After all, that's the name of the game. And the way you've described it,' Mandy said, 'it seems a very *caring* burglary.'

Mandy was right, though it was the caringness that was the problem. Had this been a burglary in the ordinary way it would have been easier to get over. Even the comprehensive removal of everything they had in the world was something Mrs Ransome could have adjusted to; been 'positive' about, even enjoyed. But it was the wholesale disappearance coupled with the meticulous reconstruction and return that rankled. Who would want to rob them to that degree and having robbed them would choose to make such immaculate reparations? It seemed to Mrs Ransome that she had been robbed twice over, by the loss, first, of her possessions, then of the chance to transcend that loss. It was not fair, nor did it make sense; she thought perhaps this was what they meant when they talked about 'losing the plot'.

People seldom wrote to the Ransomes. They had the occasional card from Canada where Mr Ransome had some relatives of his mother who dutifully kept up the connection; Mrs Ransome would write back, her card as flavourless as theirs, the message from Canada little more than 'Hello. We are still here,' and her reply, 'Yes, and so are we.' Generally, though, the post consisted of bills and business communications and picking them up from the box downstairs in the lobby Mrs Ransome scarcely bothered to look them through, putting them unsifted on the hall table where Mr Ransome would deal with them before he had his supper. On this particular morning she'd just completed this ritual when she noticed that the letter on top was from South America, and that it was not addressed to Mr M. Ransome but to a Mr M. Hanson. This had happened once before, Mr Ransome putting the misdirected letter in the caretaker's box with a note asking him or the postman to be more careful in future.

Less tolerant of her husband's fussing than she once had been, Mrs Ransome didn't want this performance again so she put the letter on one side so that after her lunch she could go up to the eighth floor, find Mr Hanson's door and slip it underneath. At least it would be an outing.

It was several years since she had been up to the top of the Mansions. There had been some alterations, she knew, as Mr Ransome had had to write a letter of complaint to the landlords about the noise of the workmen and the dirt in the lift; but, as tenants came and went, someone was always having something done somewhere and Mrs Ransome came to take renovation as a fact of life. Still, venturing out of the lift she was surprised how airy it all was now; it might have been a modern building so light and unshadowed and spacious was the landing. Unlike their dark and battered mahogany, this woodwork had been stripped and bleached and whereas their hallway was covered in stained and pockmarked orange floor covering, this had a thick smoky blue fitted carpet that lapped the walls and muffled every sound. Above was a high octagonal skylight and beneath it an octagonal sofa to match. It looked less like the hallway of a block of mansion flats than a hotel or one of the new hospitals. Nor was it simply the decoration that had changed. Mrs Ransome remembered there being several flats but now there seemed to be only one, no trace of the other doors remaining. She looked for a name on this one door just to be sure but there was no name and no letter-box. She bent down intending to slip the letter from South America underneath but the carpet was so thick that this was difficult and it wouldn't go. Above Mrs Ransome's head and unseen by her, a security camera, which she had taken for a light fitting, moved round like some clumsy reptile in a series of silent jerks until it had her in frame. She was trying to press the pile of the carpet down when there was a faint buzz and the door swung silently open.

'Come in,' said a disembodied voice and holding up the letter as if it were an invitation Mrs Ransome went in.

There was no one in the hall and she waited uncertainly, smiling helpfully in case someone was watching. The hall was identical in shape to theirs but twice the size and done up like the lobby in the same blond wood and faintly stippled walls. They must have knocked through, she thought, taken in the flat next door, taken in all the flats probably, the whole of the top floor one flat.

'I brought a letter,' she said, more loudly than if there had been someone there. 'It came by mistake.'

There was no sound.

'I think it's from South America. Peru. That is if the name's Hanson. Anyway,' she said desperately, 'I'll just put it down then go.'

She was about to put the letter down on a cube of transparent perspex that she took to be a table when she heard behind her an exhausted sigh and turned to find that the door had closed. But as the door behind her closed so, with a mild intake of breath, the door in front of her opened, and through it she saw another doorway, this one with a bar across the top, and suspended from the bar a young man.

He was pulling himself up to the bar seemingly without much effort, and saying his score out loud. He was wearing grey track suit bottoms and earphones and that was all. He had reached eleven. Mrs Ransome waited, still holding up the letter and not quite sure where to look. It was a long time since she had been so close to someone so young and so naked, the trousers slipping down low over his hips so that she could see the thin line of blond hair climbing the flat belly to his navel.

He was tiring now and the last two pull-ups, nineteen and twenty, cost him great effort and after he had almost shouted 'twenty' he stood there panting, one hand still grasping the bar, the earphones low round his neck. There was a faint graze of hair under his arms and some just beginning on his chest and like Martin he had the same squirt of hair at the back though his was longer and twisted into a knot.

Mrs Ransome thought she had never seen anyone so beautiful in all her life.

'I brought a letter,' she began again. 'It came by mistake.'

She held it out to him but he made no move to take it, so she looked round for somewhere to put it down.

There was a long refectory table down the middle of the room and by the wall a sofa that was nearly as long, but these were the only objects in the room that Mrs Ransome would have called proper furniture. There were some brightly coloured plastic cubes scattered about which she supposed might serve as occasional tables, or possibly stools. There was a tall steel pyramid with vents which seemed to be a standard lamp. There was an old-fashioned pram with white-walled tyres and huge curved springs. On one wall was a dray-horse collar and on another a cavalier's hat and next to it a huge blown-up photograph of Lana Turner.

'She was a film star,' the young man said. 'It's an original.'

'Yes, I remember,' Mrs Ransome said.

'Why, did you know her?'

'Oh no,' Mrs Ransome said. 'Anyway, she was American.'

The floor was covered in a thick white carpet which she

imagined would show every mark though there were no marks that she could see. Still, it didn't seem to Mrs Ransome to add up, this room, and with one of the walls glass, giving out on to a terrace, it felt less like a room than an unfinished window display in a department store, a bolt of tweed flung casually across the table what it needed somehow to make sense.

He saw her looking.

'It's been in magazines,' he said. 'Sit down,' and he took the letter from her.

He sat at one end of the sofa and she sat at the other. He put his feet up and if she had put her feet up too there would still have been plenty of room between them. He looked at the letter, turning it over once or twice without opening it.

'It's from Peru,' Mrs Ransome said.

'Yes,' he said, 'thanks,' and tore it in two.

'It might be important,' said Mrs Ransome.

'It's always important,' said the young man, and dropped the pieces on the carpet.

Mrs Ransome looked at his feet. Like every bit of him that she could see they were perfect, the toes not bent up and useless like her own, or Mr Ransome's. These were long, square-cut and even expressive; they looked as if at a pinch they could deputise for the hands and even play a musical instrument.

'I've never seen you in the lift,' she said.

'I have a key. Then it doesn't have to stop at the other floors.' He smiled. 'It's handy.'

'Not for us,' said Mrs Ransome.

'That's true,' and he laughed, unoffended. 'Anyway, I pay extra.'

'I didn't know you could do that,' said Mrs Ransome.

'You can't,' he said.

Mrs Ransome had an idea he was a singer, but felt that if she asked he might cease to treat her as an equal. She also wondered if he was on drugs. Silence certainly didn't seem to bother him and he lay back at his end of the sofa, smiling and completely at ease.

'I should go,' said Mrs Ransome.

'Why?'

He felt in his armpit then waved an arm at the room.

'This is all her.'

'Who?'

He indicated the torn-up letter. 'She did the place up. She's an interior decorator. Or was. She now ranches in Peru.'

'Cattle?' said Mrs Ransome.

'Horses.'

'Oh,' said Mrs Ransome. 'That's nice. There can't be too many people who've done that.'

'Done what?'

'Been an interior decorator then ... then ... looked after horses.'

He considered this. 'No. Though she was like that. You know, sporadic.' He surveyed the room. 'Do you like it?'

'Well,' said Mrs Ransome, 'it's a little strange. But I like the space.'

'Yes, it's a great space. A brilliant space.'

Mrs Ransome hadn't quite meant that but she was not unfamiliar with the concept of space as they talked about space
a lot in the afternoons, how people needed it, how they had to
be given it and how it had not to be trespassed on.

'She did the place up,' he said, 'then of course she moved
in.'

'So you felt,' said Mrs Ransome (and the phrase might have
been her first faltering steps in Urdu, it seemed so strange on
her lips), 'you felt that she had invaded your space.'

He pointed one beautiful foot at her in affirmation.

'She did. She did. I mean take that fucking pram ...'

'I remember those,' said Mrs Ransome.

'Yes, well, sure, only *apparently*,' he said, 'though it wasn't
apparent to me, that is not there as a pram. It is there as an
object. And it had to be just on that fucking spot. And because
I, like, happened to move it, like half an inch, madam went
ballistic. Threatened to take everything away. Leave the place
bare. As if I cared. Anyway, she's history.'

Since she was in Peru Mrs Ransome felt that she was geography too, a bit, but she didn't say so. Instead she nodded
and said: 'Men have different needs.'

'You're right.'

'Are you hurting?' Mrs Ransome said.

'I was hurting,' the young man said, 'only now I'm stepping
back from it. I think you have to.'

Mrs Ransome nodded sagely.

'Was she upset?' she asked, and she longed to take hold of
his foot.

'Listen,' he said, 'this woman was always upset.' He stared out of the window.

'When did she leave you?'

'I don't know. I lose track of time. Three months, four months ago.'

'Like February?' said Mrs Ransome. And it wasn't a question.

'Right.'

'Hanson, Ransome,' she said. 'They're not really alike but I suppose if you're from Peru ...'

He didn't understand, as why should he, so she told him, told him the whole story, beginning with them coming back from the opera, and the police and the trek out to Aylesbury, the whole tale.

When she'd finished, he said: 'Yeah, that sounds like Paloma. It's the kind of thing she would do. She had a funny sense of humour. That's South America for you.'

Mrs Ransome nodded, as if any gaps in this account of events could be put down to the region and the well-known volatility of its inhabitants; the spell of the pampas, the length of the Amazon, llamas, piranha fish – compared with phenomena like these what was a mere burglary in North London? Still, one question nagged.

'Who'd she have got to do it with such care?' Mrs Ransome asked.

'Oh, that's easy. Roadies.'

'Roadies?' said Mrs Ransome. 'Do you mean navvies?'

'A stage crew. Guys who do set-ups. Picked the lock. Took

the photographs. Dismantled your set up, put it up again in Aylesbury. Designer job probably. They're doing it all the time one way or another. No problem, nothing too much trouble ... provided you pay extra.' He winked. 'Anyway,' and he looked round the sparsely-furnished room, 'it wouldn't be such a big job. Is your place like this?'

'Not exactly,' Mrs Ransome said. 'Ours is ... well ... more complicated.'

He shrugged. 'She could pay. She was rich. Anyway,' he said, getting up from the sofa and taking her hand, 'I'm sorry you've been inconvenienced on my account.'

'No,' said Mrs Ransome. 'It was well, you know, kind of weird to begin with but I've tried to be positive about it. And I think I've grown, you know.'

They were standing by the pram.

'We had one of these once,' Mrs Ransome said. 'Briefly.' It was something she had not spoken of for thirty years.

'A baby?'

'He was going to be called Donald,' Mrs Ransome said, 'but he never got that far.'

Unaware that a revelation had been made the young man stroked his nipple reflectively as he walked her out into the hall.

'Thank you for clearing up the mystery,' she said and (the boldest thing she had ever done in her life) touched him lightly on his bare hip. She was prepared for him to flinch but he didn't, nor was there any change in his demeanour, which was still smiling and relaxed. Except that he also must have thought something out of the ordinary was called for because, taking her hand, he raised it to his lips and kissed it.

One afternoon a few weeks later Mrs Ransome was coming into Naseby Mansions with her shopping when she saw a van outside and crossing the downstairs lobby she met a young man with a cavalier's hat on and wearing a horse collar round his neck. He was pushing a pram.

'Is he going?' she asked the young man.

'Yeah.' He leaned on the pram. 'Again.'

'Does he move often?'

'Look, lady. This guy moves house the way other people move their bowels. All this' – and he indicated the pram, the horse collar and the cavalier's hat – 'is getting the elbow. We're going Chinese now, apparently.'

'Let me help you with that,' Mrs Ransome said, taking the pram as he struggled to get it through the door. She wheeled it down the ramp, rocking it slightly as she waited while he disposed the other items inside the van.

'A bit since you pushed one of those,' he said as he took it off her. She perched with her shopping on the wall by the entrance, watching as he packed blankets round the furniture, wondering if he was one of the roadies who had moved them. She had not told Mr Ransome how the burglary had come to pass. It was partly because he would have made a fuss, would have insisted on going up to the top floor to have a word with the young man personally. ('Probably in on it too,' he would have said.) It was a meeting Mrs Ransome had not been able to contemplate without embarrassment. As the van drove off she waved, then went upstairs.

End of story, or so Mrs Ransome thought, except that one Sunday afternoon a couple of months later Mr Ransome suffered a stroke. Mrs Ransome was in the kitchen stacking the dishwasher and hearing a bump went in and found her husband lying on the floor in front of the bookcase, a cassette in one hand, a dirty photograph in the other, and *Salmon on Torts* open on the floor. Mr Ransome was conscious but could neither speak nor move.

Mrs Ransome did all the right things, placing a cushion under his head and a rug over his body before ringing the ambulance. She hoped that even in his stricken state her efficiency and self-possession would impress her prostrate husband, but looking down at him while she was waiting to be connected to the appropriate service, she saw in his eyes no sign of approval or gratitude, just a look of sheer terror.

Powerless to draw his wife's attention to the cassette clutched in his hand, or even to relinquish it, her helpless husband watched as Mrs Ransome briskly collected up the photographs, something at the very back of his mind registering how little interest or surprise was occasioned by this tired old smut. Lastly (the klaxon of the ambulance already audible as it raced by the park) she knelt beside him and prised the cassette free of his waxen fingers before popping it matter of factly into her apron pocket. She held his hand for a second (still bent to the shape of the offending cassette) and thought that perhaps the look in his eyes was now no longer terror but had turned to shame; so she smiled and squeezed his hand, saying, 'It's not important,' at which point the ambulance men rang the bell.

Mr Ransome has not come well out of this narrative; seemingly impervious to events he has, unlike his wife, neither changed nor grown in stature. Owning a dog might have shown him in a better light, but handy though Naseby Mansions was for the park, to be cooped up in a flat is no life for a dog; a hobby would have helped, a hobby other than Mozart, that is, the quest for the perfect performance only serving to emphasise Mr Ransome's punctiliousness and general want of warmth. No, to learn to take things as they come he would have been better employed in the untidier arts, photography, say, or painting watercolours; a family would have been untidy too, and, though it seems it was only Mrs Ransome who felt the loss of baby Donald (and though Mr Ransome would have been no joke as a father), a son might have knocked the corners off him a little and made life messier – tidiness and order now all that mattered to him in middle age. When you come down to it, what he is being condemned for here is not having got out of his shell, and had there been a child there might have been no shell.

Now he lies dumb and unmoving in Intensive Care and 'shell' seems to describe it pretty well. Somewhere he can hear his wife's voice, near but at the same time distant and echoing a little as if his ear was a shell too and he a creature in it. The nurses have told Mrs Ransome that he can certainly hear what she is saying, and thinking that he may not survive not so much the stroke as the shame and humiliation that attended it, Mrs Ransome concentrates on clearing that up first. 'If we can get on a more sensible footing in the sex department,' she thinks, 'we may end up regarding this stroke business as a blessing.'

So, feeling a little foolish that the conversation has of necessity to be wholly one-sided, Mrs Ransome begins to talk to her inert husband, or rather, since there are other patients in the ward, murmur in his ear; from the corner of his left eye Mr Ransome's view of her just the slightly furry powdered slope of her well-meaning cheek.

She tells him how she has known about what she calls 'his silliness' for years and that there is nothing to feel ashamed of, for it's only sex after all. Inside his shell Mr Ransome is trying to think what 'ashamed' is, and even 'feeling' he's no longer quite sure about, let alone 'sex'; words seem to have come unstuck from their meanings. Having been sensible about Mr Ransome's silliness just about brings Mrs Ransome to the end of her emotional vocabulary; never having talked about this kind of thing much leaves her for a moment at a loss for words. Still, Mr Ransome, though numb, is at the same time hurting and they plainly need to talk. So, holding his limp hand lightly in hers, Mrs Ransome begins to whisper to him in that language which she can see now she was meant to acquire for just this sort of eventuality.

'I find it hard to verbalise with you, Maurice,' she begins. 'We've always found it hard to verbalise with each other, you and me, but we are going to learn, I promise.' Pressing her lips up against his unflinching ear she sees in close-up the stiff little grey hairs he regularly crops with the curved scissors during his locked sessions in the bathroom. 'The nurses tell me you will learn to talk again, Maurice, and I will learn along with you, we will learn to talk to one another together.' The words swirl around his ear, draining into it uncomprehended. Mrs Ransome speaks slowly. It is like spooning pap into the mouth of a baby; as one wipes the mouth of the untaken food so Mrs Ransome could almost wipe the ear clean of the curd of the unheeded words.

Still, and she deserves credit for this, she persists.

'I'm not going to be, you know, judgmental, Maurice, because I personally have nothing to be judgmental about.' And she tells him how she too has secretly listened to the cassette.

'But in future, Maurice, I suggest we listen to it together, make it a part of honing up on our marital skills ... because at the end of the day, love, marriage is about choices and to get something out of it you have to put something in.'

Out it tumbles, the once tongue-tied Mrs Ransome now possessed of a whole lexicon of caring and concern which she pours into her husband's ear. She talks about perspectives and sex and how it can go on joyful and unrestrained until the very brink of the grave and she adumbrates a future of which this will be a part and how once he gets back on his feet they will set aside quality time which they will devote to touching one another.

'We have never hugged, Maurice. We must hug one another in the future.'

Festooned as he is with tubes and drains and monitors, hugging Mr Ransome ill is no easier than hugging Mr Ransome well, so Mrs Ransome contents herself with kissing his hand. But having shared with him her vision of the future – tactile, communicative, convivial – she now thinks to top it off with some *Così*. It might just do the trick, she thinks.

So, careful not to dislodge any other of Mr Ransome's many wires, which are not channels of entertainment at all, Mrs Ransome gently positions the earphones on his head. Before slipping the cassette into the player she holds it before his unblinking eyes.

'*Così*,' she articulates. And more loudly: 'Mozart?'

She switches it on, scanning her husband's unchanging face for any sign of response. There is none. She turns the volume up a little, but not loud, mezzo forte, say. Mr Ransome, who has heard the word 'Mozart' without knowing whether it is a person or a thing or even an articulated lorry, now cringes motionless before a barrage of sounds that are to him utterly meaningless and that have no more pattern or sense than the leaves on a tree, only the leaves on the tree seem to be the notes and there is someone in the tree (it is Dame Kiri) shrieking. It is baffling. It is terrible. It is loud.

Perhaps it is this last awful realisation that Mozart does not make sense or it is because Mrs Ransome, finding there is still no response, decides to up the volume yet further, just as a last shot, that the sounds vibrate in Mr Ransome's ears and it is the vibration that does it; but at any rate something happens in his head, and the frail sac into which the blood has leaked now bursts, and Mr Ransome hears, louder and more compelling than any music he has ever heard, a roaring in his ears; there is a sudden brief andante, he coughs quietly and dies.

Mrs Ransome does not immediately notice that the numb hand of her husband is now not even that; and it would be hard to tell from looking at him, or from feeling him even, that anything has happened. The screen has altered but Mrs Ransome does not know about screens. However since Mozart does not seem to be doing the trick she takes the earphones from her husband's head and it's only as she is disentangling the frivolous wires from the more serious ones that she sees something on the screen is indeed different and she calls the nurse.

Marriage to Mrs Ransome had often seemed a kind of parenthesis and it's fitting that what she says to the nurse ('I think he's gone') is here in parenthesis too, and that it is this last little parenthesis that brings the larger parenthesis to a close. The nurse checks the monitor, smiles sadly and puts a caring hand on Mrs Ransome's shoulder, then pulls the curtain round and leaves husband and wife alone together for the last time. And so, the brackets closed that opened thirty-two years before, Mrs Ransome goes home a widow.

Then there is a fitting pause. And television having schooled her in the processes of bereavement and the techniques of grieving, Mrs Ransome observes that pause; she gives herself ample time to mourn and to come to terms with her loss and generally speaking where widowhood is concerned she does not put a foot wrong.

It seems to her as she looks back that the burglary and everything that has happened since has been a kind of apprenticeship. Now, she thinks, I can start.

FATHER! FATHER!
BURNING BRIGHT

Father! Father! Burning Bright was the original title of a BBC television film I wrote in 1982 but which was subsequently entitled *Intensive Care*. The main part, Midgley, had been hard to cast, though when I was writing the script I thought it was a role I might play myself until, that is, I got to the scene where Midgley goes to bed with Valery, the slatternly nurse. That, I thought, effectively ruled me out as I didn't fancy having to take my clothes off under the bored appraisal of an entire film crew.

Not that it would have been the first time. Back in 1966 I was acting in a BBC TV comedy series I had written which included a weekly spot, 'Life and Times in NW1', in one episode of which I was supposedly in bed with a neighbour's wife. The scene was due to be shot in the studio immediately after a tea break, and rather than brave the scrutiny of the TV crew, I thought that during the break I might sneak on to the set and be already in bed when the crew returned. So I tiptoed into the studio in my underpants, failing to notice that a lighting rig had been positioned behind the bedroom door. When I opened it there was an almighty crash, the lights came down and everybody rushed into the studio to find me sprawled in my underpants among the wreckage and subject to a far more searching and hostile scrutiny than would otherwise have been the case. No more bedroom scenes for me, I thought.

However, the role of Midgley proved hard to cast and after a lot of toing and froing, including what was virtually an audition, I found myself playing the part. Like some other leading roles that I have written, it verged on the anonymous, all the fun and jokes put into the mouths of the supporting characters while Midgley, whom the play is supposed to be about, never managed to be much more than morose.

It was in the hope of finding more to the character than this that I decided, before the shooting started, to write the story up in prose. When I'd finished I showed it to the director in the hope that it might help him to appreciate what the screenplay was about. He received it politely enough and in due course gave me it back, I suspect without having read it, directors tending to form their own ideas about a text, one script from the author hard enough to cope with without wanting two.

So I put it away in a drawer in 1982 where it has remained ever since. I've dusted it off and published it now, I suppose, as part of an effort to slim down my *Nachlass* and generally tidy up.

ON THE MANY OCCASIONS Midgley had killed his father, death had always come easily. He died promptly, painlessly and without a struggle. Looking back, Midgley could see that even in these imagined deaths he had failed his father. It was not like him to die like that. Nor did he.

The timing was good, Midgley acknowledged that. Only his father would have managed to stage his farewell in the middle of a 'Meet The Parents' week. It was not a function Midgley enjoyed. Each year he was dismayed how young the parents had grown, the youth of fathers in particular. Most sported at least one tattoo, with ears and noses now routinely studded. Midgley saw where so many of his pupils got it from. One father wore a swastika necklace, of the sort Midgley had wondered if he felt justified in confiscating from a boy. And a mother he had talked to had had green hair. 'Not just green,' muttered Miss Tunstall, 'bright green. And then you wonder the girls get pregnant.'

That was the real point of these get-togethers. The teachers were appalled by the parents but found their shortcomings reassuring. With parents like these, they reasoned, who could blame the schools? The parents, recalling their own teachers as figures of dignity and authority, found the staff sloppy. Awe never entered into it, apparently. 'Too human by half' was their verdict. So both Nature and Nurture came away, if not satisfied, at any rate absolved. 'Do you wonder?' said the teachers, looking at the parents. 'They get it at school,' said the parents.

'Coretta's bin havin' these massive monthlies. Believe me, Mr Midgley, I en never seen menstruatin' like it.' Mrs Azakwale was explaining her daughter's poor showing in Use of English. 'She bin wadin' about in blood to her ankles, Mr Midgley. I en never out of the launderette.' Behind Mrs Azakwale, Mr Horsfall listened openly and with unconcealed scepticism, shaking his head slowly as Midgley caught his eye. Behind Mr Horsfall, Mr Patel beamed with embarrassment as the large black woman said these terrible things so loudly. And beyond Mr Patel, Midgley saw the chairs were empty.

Mrs Azakwale took Coretta's bloodstained track-record over to the queue marked Computer Sciences, leaving Midgley faced with Mr Horsfall and Martin.

Mr Horsfall did not dye his hair nor wear an earring. His

hair was now fashionably short but only because he had never got round to wearing it fashionably long. Nor had his son Martin ever ventured under the drier; his ears, too, were intact. Mr Horsfall was a detective sergeant.

'I teach Martin English, Mr Horsfall,' said Midgley, wishing he had not written 'Hopeless' on Martin's report, a document now gripped by Mr Horsfall in his terrible policeman's hand.

'Martin? Is that what you call him?'

'But that's his name.' Midgley had a moment of wild anxiety that it wasn't, that the father would accuse him of not even knowing the name of his son.

'His name's Horsfall. Martin is what we call him, his mother and me. For your purposes I should have thought his name was Horsfall. Are you married?'

'Yes.'

Horsfall was not impressed. He had spent long vigils in public toilets as a young constable. Many of the patrons had turned out to be married and some of them teachers. Marriage involved no medical examination, no questionnaire to speak of. Marriage for these people was just the bush they hid behind.

'What does my son call you?'

'He calls me Mr Midgley.'

'Doesn't he call you sir?'

'On occasion.'

'Schools ...' Horsfall sniffed.

His son ought to have been small, nervous and bright, Midgley the understanding schoolteacher taking his part

against his big, overbearing parent. He would have put books
into his hands, watched him flower so that in time to come the
boy would look back and think 'Had it not been for him ...' Such
myths sustained Midgley when he woke in the small hours of
the morning and drowsed during the middle period of the afternoon. But they were myths. Martin was large and dull. He was
not unhappy. He would not flower. He was not even embarrassed. He was probably on his father's side, thought Midgley,
as he sat there looking at his large inherited hands, and occasionally picked at one of a scattering of violet-painted warts.

'What worries me,' said Horsfall, 'is that he can scarcely
put two words together.'

This was particularly hurtful to a man who, in his professional capacity, specialised in converting the faltering confessions of semi-illiterates into his plain policeman's prose. He
could do it. At four o'clock in the morning after a day spent
combing copses and dragging ponds, never mind house-to-
house enquiries, he could do it. Why not his son?

'You show me up, Martin, having to come along here. I
don't grudge coming along here. But what I would like to have
come along here as is a proud father. To be told of your
achievements. Be shown your name in gilt letters on the hon-
ours board. Martin Horsfall. But no. What is it? It's
Geography: Poor. History: Poor. English: Hopeless. PE: Only
fair. Why Martin?'

'Why Mr Midgley? And why hopeless? Geography: Poor.
History: Poor. English: Hopeless. Is he hopeless or are you?'

'He doesn't try.'

'Do you challenge him? We challenge him at home. His mother and I challenge him. Does he get challenged at school? I don't see it.' Horsfall looked round but caught the eye of Mr Patel, who was smiling in anticipation of his interview. Mr Patel's son was clever. Blacks, Indians. That was why. Challenge. How could there be any challenge?

'I never had chances like he had. And I dare say you didn't. We never had chances like that, Martin.'

At the 'we' Midgley flinched, suddenly finding himself handcuffed to Horsfall in the same personal pronoun.

'A school like this. Modern buildings. Light. Air. Sporting facilities tip-top. Volleyball. If somebody had come up to me when I was your age and said, "There are facilities for volley-ball," I would have gone down on my knees. What do you say?'

The question Horsfall was asking his son had no obvious answer. Indeed, it was not really a question at all. 'Justify your life'; that was what this dull and dirty youth was being asked to do. Not seeing that justification was necessary, the son was silent and the father waited.

And it was in the middle of this silence that Miss Tunstall came up to say the hospital had telephoned. Except that, sensing this was not simply a silence but an essential part of what was being said, she did not immediately interrupt but made little wavings with her hand behind Mr Horsfall's head, who – a policeman and ever on the watch for mockery – turned round. So it was to him that Miss Tunstall gave the bad news (a man in any case used to transactions with ambulances, hospitals and all the regimes of crisis).

'The hospital's just rung. Mr Midgley's father's been taken ill.' And only then, having delivered her message, did she look at Midgley, who thus heard his father was dying at second-hand and then only as a kind of apology.

'They're ringing the ward,' said Midgley. 'It's a fall, apparently.' One ear was in Miss Tunstall's office, the other fifty miles away in some nowhere behind a switchboard.

'You want to pray it's not his hip,' said Miss Tunstall. 'That's generally the weak spot.' She had a mother of her own. 'The pelvis heals in no time, surprisingly.' She did not sound surprised. Her mother had broken her pelvis and she had thought it was the beginning of the end. 'No. It's when it's the hip it's complicated.'

'Switchboard's on the blink,' said a voice.

'Join the club,' said another. 'I've been on the blink all day.'

'It's the dreaded lurgi,' said the first voice.

'Hello,' said Midgley. But there was silence.

'She took a nasty tumble in Safeway's last week,' went on Miss Tunstall. 'They do when they get older. It's what you must expect.' She expected it all the time. 'Their bones get brittle.'

She cracked her fingers and adjusted the spacing.

'Maintenance,' said a new voice.

'I've been wrongly connected,' said Midgley.

'It's these ancillary workers,' said Miss Tunstall. 'Holding the country to ransom. Other people's suffering is their bread and butter.' She was wanting to get on with a notice about some boys acting the goat in the swimming baths but felt she ought to wait until Midgley had heard one way or the other. Her mother was eighty-two. The last twenty years had not been easy and had she known what was in store she thought now she would probably have stabbed her mother to death the second she turned sixty. These days it would only have meant a suspended sentence or if the worst came to the worst open prison. Miss Tunstall had once been round such an institution with the school and found it not uncongenial. A picnic in fact.

'Records are on the warpath again,' said a voice in Midgley's ear.

'It never rains,' said another.

'Should I be sterilisin' this?' said a black voice.

'Search me, dear,' said an emancipated one.

'Hello,' said Midgley. 'HELLO.'

Softly Miss Tunstall began to type.

Midgley thought of his father lying in bed, dying but not wanting to be any trouble.

'No joy?' said Miss Tunstall, uncertain whether it would be better to underline 'the likelihood of a serious accident'. 'And then they wonder why people are stampeding to BUPA.'

Midgley decided he had been forgotten, then a crisp voice suddenly said, 'Sister Tudor.'

'I'm calling about a patient, a Mr Midgley.'

Noiselessly Miss Tunstall added an exclamation mark to 'This hooliganism must now STOP!' and waited, her hands spread over the keys.

'What is the patient's name?'

'Midgley,' said Midgley. 'He came in this morning.'

'When was he admitted?'

'This morning.'

'Midgley.' There was a pause. 'We have no Midgley. No Midgley has been admitted here. Are you sure you have the right ward?'

'He was admitted this morning. I was told he was seriously ill.'

'Oh yes.' Her tone changed. 'Midgley. What is your name?'

'Midgley.'

'Are you next of kin?'

'My father is dead,' he thought. 'Only the dead have next of kin.'

'I'm his son.'

Miss Tunstall folded her hands in her lap.

'He's not at all well.' The tone was reproachful rather than sympathetic. 'We think he's had a stroke. He's been lying on the floor. He ought to have been in hospital sooner. There's now the question of pneumonia. It's touch and go.'

'It's touch and go,' said Midgley, putting the phone down.

'How old is he?' said Miss Tunstall, noticing she had typed 'tooling' for 'fooling'.

'He's seventy-four.'

Her mother was eighty-two. She ripped out the paper and wound in another sheet. Life was unfair.

The door opened.

'Been on the phone again Midgley?' said the headmaster. 'I'm the one who has to go cap in hand to the Finance Committee.'

'Mr Midgley's father's ill,' said Miss Tunstall, once again the apologetic herald. 'Apparently it's touch and go.'

And she started typing like the wind.

'Of course you can go. Of course you must go. One's father. There can be no question. A filial obligation.' Midgley was in the headmaster's study. 'It's awkward, of course. But then it always is.' It was death. It was a reshuffling of the timetable.

Midgley's thoughts were with his father in Intensive Care.

'Was he getting on in years?'

No effort was being spared to keep him alive and in the present and yet grammatically he kept slipping into the past.

'He's seventy-four.'

'Seventy-four. Once upon a time I thought that was old. You won't be gone long? What, three, four days?' In his mind the headmaster roughed out a timetable whereby Midgley senior could decently die, be buried and Midgley junior be back in harness. Radical surgery on the timetable might still be avoided.

'Let me see. It's English, Integrated Humanities and Creative Arts, nothing else, is there?'

'Environmental Studies.'

The headmaster groaned. 'That's the awkward one. Pilbeam's off on another course. That's the trouble with the environment, it involves going on courses. I'll be glad when the environment is confined to the textbooks.'

'Ah well,' said the headmaster. 'It can't be helped.' He had never understood the fuss people made about their parents. 'Both of mine were despatched years ago. A flying bomb.' He made it sound like a victory for common sense.

'He must have fallen and not been able to get up,' said Midgley. 'He was lying there two days.'

'An all too familiar scenario these days,' said the headmaster. 'Isolated within the community. Alone in the crowd. You must not feel guilty.'

'I generally go over at weekends,' said Midgley.

'It will give Tomlinson an opportunity to do some of his weird and wonderful permutations with the timetable. Though I fear this one will tax even Tomlinson's talents.'

The headmaster opened the door.

'One must hope it is not as grave as it appears. One must hope he turns the corner. Corners seem to have gone out of medicine nowadays. In the old days the sick were always turning them. Illness is now much more of a straight road. Why is that?'

It was not a question he wanted answering.

'Antibiotics?' said Midgley, lingering.

'Sometimes one has the impression modern medicine encourages patients to loiter.' It was Midgley who was taking his time.

'Mistakenly, one feels. God speed.'

Miss Tunstall had finished the notice about acting the goat in the swimming baths and the headmaster now glanced through it, taking out his pen. She made a start on another notice about the bringing of pupils' cars to school, one of the head's 'privilege not a right' notices. Midgley still hesitated.

'I'm not sure if we've couched this in strong enough terms, Daphne.'

'It's as you dictated it.'

'I have no doubt. But I feel more strongly about it now. Nothing else is there, Midgley?'

Midgley shook his head and went out.

'A boy slips. Is pushed and we are talking about concussion. A broken neck. A fatality, Daphne. I intend to nail the culprits. I want them to know they will be crucified.'

'Shall I put that?'

The headmaster looked at her sharply and wondered if Miss Tunstall was through the menopause.

'We must find a paraphrase. But first the problems caused by this business of Midgley *père*. Ask Tomlinson to step over will you, Daphne. Tell him to bring his coloured pencils. And a rubber.'

'TOMATO or my jam?'

'Tomato.'

The hospital was fifty miles away. His wife was making him sandwiches. He sat in his raincoat at the kitchen table, watching her apply a faint smear of Flora to the wholemeal bread.

'I wanted to go over this last weekend,' said Midgley. 'I would have gone over if your Margaret hadn't suddenly descended.'

'You knew they were coming. They'd been coming for weeks. It's one of the few things Mother's got to look forward to.' Mrs Midgley's mother was stood staring out of the window. 'Don't blame our Margaret.'

'I just never expected it,' said Midgley.

If you expected something it didn't happen.

'I expected it,' said his wife, putting on a shiny plastic apron emblazoned with a portrait of Sylvia Plath.

'I expected it. Last time I went over he came to the door to wave me off. He's never done that before. Bless him.' She slipped on a pair of padded Union Jack mittens and sinking to her knees before the oven gave the Shift a trial blast. 'I think people know.'

'He does come to the door,' said Midgley. 'He always comes to the door.' And it was true he did, but only, Midgley felt, to show that the visit had been so short it needed extending. Though once, catching sight of him in the rear-view mirror, waving, Midgley had cried.

'He was trying to tell me something,' said his wife. 'I know a farewell when I see one.' A fine spray misted the oven's pale grey walls. 'Shouldn't you be going?'

'Is it Saturday today?' said her mother.

Ten minutes later Midgley was sitting on the stairs and his wife had started hoovering.

'I'm not going to let him down. I want to be there when he goes,' shouted Midgley.

The vacuum was switched off.

'What?'

'He loved me.'

'I can't think why,' said Midgley's wife. 'It's not as if you take after him,' and she switched on again, 'not one little bit.'

'Joyce,' her mother called, 'when is that chiropodist coming?'

Midgley looked at his watch. It was three o'clock. At ten past Mrs Midgley took to dusting. It was always assumed the housework put her in a bad temper. The truth was if she was in a bad temper she did the housework. So it came to the same thing.

'He had strength,' she said, dusting a group of lemonade bottles of various ages. 'Our Colin is going to be strong. He loved Colin.'

'Does he know?' asked Midgley.

'Yes. Only it hasn't hit him yet.'

Hoarse shouting and a rhythmic drumming on the floor indicated that his son was seeking solace in music.

'When it does hit him,' said his mother, picking at a spot of rust on a recently acquired Oxo tin, 'he is going to be genuinely heartbroken. There's always a gap. It was on *Woman's Hour*. Poor old Frank.'

'I've never understood,' said Midgley, 'why you call him Frank. He's my father.'

She looked at the 1953 Coronation mug, wondering if it was altogether too recent an artefact to have on display.

'He has a name. Frank is his name.'

It was not only the date, the Coronation mug was about the only object in the house Midgley had contributed to the decor, having been issued with it in 1953 when he was at primary school.

'I call him Dad,' said Midgley.

'He's not Dad, is he? Not my dad, I call him Frank because that's the name of a person. To me he is a person. That's why we get on.'

She was about to hide the mug behind a cast-iron money-box in the shape of a grinning black man, then thought better of it. They had too many things. And there would be more coming from his dad. She cheered up slightly.

Her husband kissed her and opened the back door.

'It isn't though,' he said.

'It isn't what?'

'Why you get on. Treating him like a person.'

Seeing her stood there in her silly apron he felt sorry for her, and wished he had kept quiet.

'You get on,' he said (and because he was sorry for her tried to make it sound as if she was justified), 'you get on because you both despise me.'

'Listen.' She brought him away from the door and closed it. Mrs Barnes next door, who had once described their marriage as uninhibited, was putting out a few opportune clothes. 'Your father is seventy-four. He is dying. Considering the time you've been hanging about here he is possibly already dead yet you resent the fact that he and I were friends. I seem to have married someone very low down in the evolutionary chain. You might want one or two tissues.' And she darted at him and thrust them into his pocket.

Midgley opened the door again.

'It's just that when you and he were together I didn't exist.'

'I am married,' she shouted, 'to the cupboard under the sink.' A remark made more mysterious to Mrs Barnes by the sound of a passing ice-cream van playing the opening bars of the 'Blue Danube'.

'He is *dying*, Denis. Will you exist now? Will that satisfy you?' She was crying.

'I'll make it right, Joyce,' said Midgley. 'I'll be there when he goes. I'll hold his hand.'

He held hers, still in their Union Jack mittens. 'If I let him down now he'd stay with me the rest of my life. I did love him, Joyce.'

'I *want* him to stay with you the rest of your life. That's what I want. I think of his kindness. His unselfishness. His unflagging courtesy. The only incredible thing is that someone so truly saintly should have produced such a pill of a son.'

She took off Sylvia Plath and hung her behind the door. She had stopped crying.

'But I suppose that's your mother.'

'Shut up about my mother,' said Midgley.

His mother was a sore point. 'My mother is dead.'

'So is your father by now probably. Go!'

Midgley took her by the shoulders.

'Things will change then, you'll see. I'll change. I'll be a different person. I can ... go. Live! Start!' He kissed her quickly and warmly and ran from the door down the little drive towards the van. His wife rushed to the door to catch him.

'Start?' she shouted. 'Start what? You're thirty-nine.'

'They had another do today,' Mrs Barnes told her husband that evening. 'It doesn't say much for a university education.'

COMING OFF the Leeds and Bradford Ring Road Midgley stopped at a zebra to let an old man cross. The old man held up a warning hand, and slowly moved across, glowering at the car. Midgley revved his engine and the old man stopped, glared and went on with seemingly deliberate slowness. Someone behind hooted. Midgley did not wait for the old man to reach the kerb but drove off with a jerk. Glancing in his mirror Midgley saw the old man slip and nearly fall.

At the hospital the first person he saw was Aunty Kitty, his father's sister. She said nothing, kissing him wordlessly, her eyes closed to indicate her grief lay temporarily beyond speech. The scene played she took his arm (something he disliked) and they followed the signs to Intensive Care.

'I thought you'd have been here a bit since,' said his aunty. 'I've been here since two o'clock. You'll notice a big change.' They were going down a long featureless corridor. 'He's not like my brother. He's not the Frank I knew.' Visitors clustered at the doors of wards, waiting their turn to sit beside the beds of loved ones. Aunty Kitty favoured them with a brave smile. 'I don't dislike this colour scheme,' she said. 'I've always liked oatmeal. His doctor's black.'

Intensive Care had a waiting room to itself, presumably, Midgley thought, for the display of Intensive Grief, and there was a woman crying in the corner. 'Her hubby's on the critical list,' mouthed Aunty Kitty. 'Their eldest girl works for Johnson and Johnson. They'd just got back from Barbados. The nurse is white but she's not above eighteen.' The nurse came in. 'This is my nephew,' said Aunty Kitty.

'Mr Midgley's son. Your father's got a room to himself, love.'

'They all do,' said the nurse, 'at this stage.'

Midgley's father lay propped up against the pillows, staring straight ahead through the window at a blank yellow wall. His arms lay outside the coverlet, palms upward as if accepting his plight and awaiting some sort of deliverance. They had put him into some green hospital pyjamas, with half-length sleeves the functionalism of which seemed too modish to Midgley, who had only ever seen his father in bed in striped pyjamas, or sometimes his shirt. The garment was open and a monitor clung to his chest, and above the bed the television screen blipped steady and regular. Midgley watched it for a moment.

'Dad,' he said to himself.

'Dad. It's me, Denis.'

He put himself between the bed and the window so that if his father could see he would know he was there. He had read that stroke victims were never unconscious, just held incommunicado. 'In the most solitary confinement,' the article had said, the writer himself a doctor and too much taken with metaphor.

'It's all right, Dad.'

He took a chair and sat halfway down the bed, putting his hand over his father's inert palm.

His father looked well in the face, which was ruddy and worn, the skin of his neck giving way sharply to the white of his body. The division between his known head and the unknown body had shocked Midgley when he had first seen it as a child, when his dad took him swimming at the local baths. It was still the same. He had never sat in the sun all his life.

'I'm sorry, Dad,' said Midgley.

'Are you next of kin?' It was another nurse.

'Son.'

'Not too long then.'

'Is the doctor around?'

'Why? What do you want to know? There's nothing wrong, is there? No complaints?'

'I want to know how he is.'

'He's very poorly. You can see.'

She looked down at her left breast and lifted a watch.

'Doctor'll be round in about an hour. He's very busy.'

'I wonder where he is,' said Aunty Kitty.

'She said he was busy.'

They were back in the waiting room.

Aunty Kitty looked at him with what he imagined she imagined was a look of infinite sadness, mingled with pity ('Sorrow and love flow mingling down' came into his mind from the hymn). 'Not the doctor, your dad, love. Behind that stare he's somewhere, wandering. You know,' she said vaguely, 'in his mind. Where is he?'

She patted his hand.

'I don't suppose with having been to university you believe in an after-life. That's always the first casualty.'

For a while she read the small print on her pension book

and Midgley thought about his childhood. Nurses came and went, leading their own lives and a man wiped plastic-covered mattresses in the corridor. Every time a nurse came near he made remarks like 'It's all right for some' or 'No rest for the wicked'. Once the matron glided silently by, majestic and serene on her electric trolley. 'They're a new departure,' said Aunty Kitty. 'I could do with one of those. I'll just pop and have another peep at your dad.'

'What does that look on his face mean?' she said when she came back. Midgley thought it meant he should have gone over to see him last Sunday. It meant that his dad had been right about him all along and now he was dying and whose fault was that? That was what it meant. 'This unit was opened by the Duchess of Kent,' said Aunty Kitty. 'They have a tip-top kidney department.'

The fascinations of medicine and royalty were equal in Aunty Kitty's mind and whenever possible she found a connection between the two. Had she been told she was dying but from the same disease as a member of the Royal Family she would have died happy.

'There's some waiting done in hospitals,' she said presently. 'Ninety per cent of it's waiting. Would you call this room oatmeal or cream?'

A young man came through, crying.

'His wife was in an accident,' Aunty Kitty explained. 'One of those head-on crashes. The car was a write-off. Did you come in your van?'

Midgley nodded.

'You'll be one of these two-car families, then? Would you say she was black?' A Thai nurse looked in briefly and went out again. 'You don't see that many of them. She's happen a refugee.'

Midgley looked at his watch. It was an hour since he had spoken to the nurse. He went in and stood at the desk but there was no one about. He stood at the door of his father's room. He had not moved, his unseeing eyes fixed on a window-cleaner, who with professional discretion carefully avoided their gaze.

'I always thought I'd be the first to go,' said Aunty Kitty, looking at an advertisement in *Country Life*. 'Fancy. Two swimming pools. I could do without two swimming pools. When you get to my age you just want somewhere you can get round nicely with the hoover. They've never got to the bottom of my complaint. They lowered a microscope down my throat but there was nothing. I wouldn't live in Portugal if they paid me. Minstrels' gallery, I shouldn't know what to do with a minstrels' gallery if I had one. Mr Penry-Jones wanted to put me on this machine the Duke of Gloucester inaugurated. This body-scan thing. Only there was such a long waiting-list apparently.'

A nurse came through.

'She's the one I was telling you about. I asked her if your dad was in a coma or just unconscious. She didn't know. They're taking them too young these days.'

'Aunty,' said Midgley.

'It isn't as if she was black. Black you don't expect them to know.'

'What was my dad like?'

Aunty Kitty thought for a moment.

'He never had a wrong word for anybody. He'd do anybody a good turn. Shovel their snow. Fetch their coal in. He was that type. He was a saint. You take after your mother more.'

'I feel I lack his sterling qualities,' said Midgley some time later. 'Grit. Patience. Virtues bred out of adversity.'

'You wouldn't think they'd have curtains in a hospital, would you?' said Aunty Kitty. 'You wouldn't think curtains would be hygienic. I'm not keen on purple anyway.'

'Deprivation for instance,' said Midgley.

'What?'

'I was never deprived. That way he deprived me. Do you understand?'

'I should have gone to secondary school,' she said. 'I left at thirteen, same as your dad.'

'I know I had it easier than he did,' said Midgley. 'But I was grateful. I didn't take it for granted.'

'You used to look bonny in your blazer.'

'It isn't particularly enjoyable, education.' Midgley had his head in his hands. 'I had what he wanted. Why should that be enjoyable?'

'Mark's got his bronze medal,' said Aunty Kitty. 'Did you not ought to be ringing round?'

'About the bronze medal?'

'About your dad.'

'I'll wait till I've seen the doctor.'

It was half-past six.

'They go on about these silicon chips, you'd think they'd get all these complaints licked first, somebody's got their priorities wrong. Then he's always been a right keen smoker has Frank. Now he's paying the price.'

Midgley fell asleep.

'Robert Donat had bronchitis,' said Aunty Kitty.

'MR MIDGLEY.' The doctor shook his shoulder. 'Denis,' said Aunty Kitty, 'it's doctor.'

He was a pale young Pakistani, and for a moment Midgley thought he had fallen asleep in class and was being woken by a pupil.

'Mr Midgley?' He was grave and precise, twenty-six at the most.

'Your father has had a stroke.' He looked at his clipboard. 'How severe it is hard to tell. When he was brought in he was suffering from hypothermia.'

Aunty Kitty gave a faint cry. It was a scourge that had been much in the news.

'He must have fallen and been lying there, two days at least.'

'I generally go over at weekends,' said Midgley.

'Pneumonia has set in. His heart is not strong. All things considered,' he looked at the clipboard again, 'we do not think he will last the night.'

As he went away he tucked the clipboard under his arm and Midgley saw there was nothing on it.

'ONLY THREE PHONES and two of them duff. You wouldn't credit it,' said a fat man. 'Say you were on standby for a transplant. It'd be just the same.' He jingled his coins and a young man in glasses on the working phone put his head outside the helmet.

'I've one or two calls to make,' he said cheerfully.

'Oh hell,' said the fat man.

'There's a phone outside Physio. Try there,' said a passing nurse.

'I'll try there,' said the fat man.

Midgley sat on.

'Hello,' said the young man brightly. 'Dorothy? You're a grandma.' He looked at Midgley while he was talking, but without seeing him.

'A grandma,' he shouted. 'Yes!' There was a pause. 'Guess,' said the young man and listened. 'No,' he said. 'Girl. Seven and a half pounds. 5.35. Both doing well. I'm ringing everybody. Bye, Grandma.'

Midgley half rose as the young man put the receiver back, but sat back as he consulted a bit of paper then picked it up again and dialled.

'Hello, Neil. Hi. You're an uncle ... You're an uncle. Today. Just now. 5.35. Well, guess.' He waited. 'No. Girl. No. I'm over the moon. So you can tell Christine she's an aunty. Yes, a little cousin for Josephine. How's it feel to be an uncle? ... Bye.'

Midgley got up and stood waiting. The young man took another coin and dialled again. It was a way of breaking news that could be adapted for exits as well as entrances, thought Midgley.

'Hello, Margaret. You're a widow. A widow ... This afternoon. Half-past two ... How's it feel to be bereaved?'

'Betty,' said the young man. 'Congratulations. You're an aunty. Aunty Betty. I won't ask you to guess,' he went on hurriedly. 'It's a girl. Susan's over the moon. And I am.'

With each call his enthusiasm had definitely decreased. Midgley reflected that this baby was well on the way to being a bore and it was only a couple of hours old.

'I'm just telephoning with the glad tidings. Bye, Aunty.'

The proud father put a new pile of coins on the box and Midgley was moved to intervene.

'Could I just make one call?'

'Won't it wait,' said the young man. 'I was here first. I'm a father.'

'I'm a son,' said Midgley. 'My father's dying.'

'There's no need to take that tone,' said the young man, stepping out of the helmet. 'You should have spoken up. There's a phone outside Physio.'

Midgley listened to the phone ringing along the passage at his father's brother's house.

'Uncle Ernest? It's Denis. Dad's been taken poorly.'

'You mean Frank?' said his uncle.

'Yes. Dad. He's had a stroke,' said Midgley. 'And a fall. And now he's got pneumonia.' Somehow he felt he ought to have selected two out of three, not laid everything on the line first go off.

'Oh dear, oh dear, oh dear,' said his uncle. 'Our Frank.'

'Can you ring round and tell anybody who might want to come. The doctor says he won't last the night.'

'From here? Me ring?'

It started pipping.

'Yes. I'm in a box. There are people waiting.'

'You never know,' said the young man. 'They can work miracles nowadays.'

'T HIS IS WHAT I'D CALL an industrial lift,' said Uncle Ernest, tapping the wall with his strong boot. 'It's not an ordinary passenger lift, this. It's as big as our sitting-room.'

It stopped and a porter slid a trolley in beside Midgley. A woman looked up at him and smiled faintly.

'Is it working?' said the porter. The little head closed its eyes.

'We've just had a nice jab and now we're going for a ta ta.'

Behind a glass panel Midgley watched the concrete floors pass.

'It's very solidly constructed,' said Uncle Ernest, looking at the floor. 'These are overlapping steel plates. We can still do it when we try.'

'Let the dog see the rabbit,' said the porter as the lift stopped.

'This is six,' said Midgley.

'Every floor looks the same to me,' said his uncle.

'Did you ring our Hartley?' Hartley was Uncle Ernest's son and a chartered accountant.

'He's coming as soon as he can get away.'

'Was he tied up?'

He had been.

'Secretary was it? Was he in a meeting? I'd like to know what they are, these meetings he's always in, that he can't speak to his father. "Excuse me, I have to speak to my father." That's no disgrace, is it? "I won't be a moment, my dad's on the line." Who's going to take offence at that? Who are they, in these meetings? Don't they have fathers? I thought fathers were universal. Instead of which I have to make an appointment to see my own son. Sons, fathers, you shouldn't need appointments. You should get straight through. You weren't like that with your dad. Frank thought the world of you.'

They were going down the long corridor again.

'I came on the diesel,' said Uncle Ernest. He was lame in one leg.

'I go all over. I went to York last week. Saw the railway museum. There's stock in there I drove. Museum in my own lifetime. I'll tell you one thing.'

They stopped.

'What,' said Midgley.

'I wouldn't like to have to polish this floor.'

They resumed.

'You still schoolteaching?'

Midgley nodded.

'Pleased your dad, did that. Though it won't be much of a salary. You'd have been better off doing something in our

Hartley's line. He's up there in the £30,000 bracket now. She was talking about a swimming pool.'

They stopped at the entrance to Intensive Care while his uncle stood, one arm stretched out to the wall, taking the weight off his leg.

'Is your Aunty Kitty here?'

'Yes.'

'I thought she would be. Where no vultures fly.'

A UNTY KITTY got up and did her 'I am too upset to speak' act. 'Hello, Kitty,' said Ernest.

'I always thought I should be the first, Ernest.'

'Well you still might be. He's not dead yet.'

'Go in, Ernest.' She dabbed her nose. 'Go in.'

Uncle Ernest stood by his brother's bed. Then he sat down.

'This is summat fresh for you, Frank,' he said. 'You were always such a bouncer.' He stood up and leaned over the bed to look closer at the bleeps on the scanner. They were bouncing merrily. A nurse looked in.

'You're not to touch that.'

'I was just interested.'

'He's very ill.'

She paused for a moment, came further into the room and looked at the scanner. She looked at Uncle Ernest (though not, he noticed, at Frank) and went out.

'It's all mechanised now,' he said.

There was no sound in the room. The brothers had never

had much to say to each other at the best of times. Without there being any animosity, they felt easier in the presence of a third party; alone they embarrassed each other. It was still the case, even though one of them was unconscious, and Uncle Ernest got up, thankful to be able to go.

'Ta-ra then, butt,' he said.

And waited.

He wanted to pat his brother's hand.

'I went to York last week,' he said. 'It hasn't changed much. They haven't spoiled it like they have Leeds. Though there's one of these precinct things. It's the first time I've been since we were lads. We went over on our bikes once.' Instead of touching his brother's hand he jogged his foot in farewell, just as the nurse was coming in.

'He's *very* ill,' she said, smoothing the coverlet over his brother's feet. 'And this is delicate equipment.'

'I went in,' she said in the canteen later, 'and there was one of them pulling a patient's leg about. He had hold of his foot. It's an uphill battle.'

UNCLE ERNEST'S SON Hartley came with his wife Jean and their children, Mark (14) and Elizabeth (10). Hartley hated hospitals, hence his demand for full family back-up. He was actually surprised that Mark had condescended to come: a big fourteen, Mark had long since passed beyond parental control and only appeared with the family on state occasions. The truth was that Miss Pollock, who took him for

Religious Knowledge and who was known to be fucking at least one of the sixth form, had pointed out only last week how rare were the opportunities these days of seeing a dead person, and thus of acquiring a real perspective on the human condition. Mark was hoping this visit might gain him some status in the eyes of Miss Pollock. Sensitive to the realities of birth and death, he hoped to be the next candidate for 'bringing out'.

They were all going up in the lift.

'Think on,' said Hartley. 'It's quite likely your grandad'll be here. I don't want you asking for all sorts in front of him.'

'No,' said his wife. 'We don't want him saying you're spoiled.'

'Though you are spoiled,' said Hartley.

'Whose fault is that?' said Jean.

The steel doors folded back to reveal Denis saying goodbye to Uncle Ernest.

'Now then, Dad,' said Hartley. 'Hello, Denis. This is a bad do.'

Jean kissed the old man.

'Give your grandad a kiss, Elizabeth.'

The child did so.

'Come on, Mark.'

'I don't kiss now,' said the boy.

'You kiss your grandad,' said Hartley and the boy did so and a nurse, passing, looked.

'How is he?' said Hartley.

'Dying,' said his father. 'Sinking fast.'

'Oh dear, oh dear, oh dear,' said Hartley, who had hoped it would be all over by now.

'And how've you been keeping?' said Jean, brightly.

'Champion,' said Uncle Ernest. 'Is that one of them new watches?' He took Mark's wrist.

'He had to save up for it,' said Jean. 'You had to save up for it, didn't you, Mark?'

Mark nodded.

'He didn't,' said the little girl.

'I never had a watch till I was twenty-one,' said the old man. 'Of course, they're twenty-one at eighteen now, aren't they?'

Denis pressed the button for the lift.

'We'd better get along to the ward if he's that critical,' said Jean.

'I've had the receiver in my hand to give you a ring once or twice,' said Hartley as they waited for the lift, 'then a client's come in.'

'I was thinking of going to Barnard Castle next week,' said Ernest.

'Whatever for?' said Jean, kissing him goodbye.

'I've never been.' He shook Denis's hand. The lift doors closed. Hartley and his family walked ahead of Midgley down the long corridor.

'I'll give you such a clatter when I get you home, young lady,' Jean was saying. 'He did save up.'

'Only a week,' said the child.

'When we get there,' said Hartley, 'we want to go in in twos. All together would be too much of a strain.'

'What's he doing going to Barnard Castle?' said Jean.

'He can't be short of money taking himself off to Barnard Castle.'

Midgley caught them up.

'You'd no need all to come,' he said. 'I wouldn't let Joyce bring ours.'

'They wanted to come,' said Jean. 'Our Mark did especially, didn't you Mark?'

'It's more handy for us, anyway,' said Hartley. 'What did we do before the M62?'

Mark was disappointed. The old man was quite plainly breathing. He could quite easily have been asleep. He wasn't even white.

'He's not my uncle, is he, Dad?'

'He's my uncle. He's your great-uncle.'

Hartley was looking at the screen.

'You see this screen, Mark? It's monitoring his heartbeats.'

Mark didn't look, but said wearily, 'I know, Dad.'

'I was only telling you.'

Hartley touched the screen where the beep was flickering.

'You want to learn, don't you?' his father said as they came out.

'Dad.' The boy stopped. 'We made one of those at school.'

Jean now led little Elizabeth in. ('Bless her,' said Aunty Kitty.)

They stood hand in hand by the bedside, and Jean bent down and kissed him.

'Do you want me to kiss him?' said the child.

'No. I don't think so, love,' and she rubbed her lips with her hanky where they had touched him.

'Are you crying, Mam?' said the child.

'Yes.'

The little girl looked up at her.

'There aren't any tears.'

'You can cry without tears,' said her mother, looking at the monitor. 'You can cry more without tears.'

'I can't,' said the child. 'How do you do it, Mam?'

'It comes when you're grown up.'

'I want to be able to do it now.'

'Listen, I'll give you such a smack in a minute,' said her mother. 'He's dying.'

Elizabeth began to cry.

'There, love.' Her mother hugged her. 'He doesn't feel it.'

'I'm not crying because of him,' said the child. 'I'm crying because of you.'

'I wouldn't have another Cortina,' said Hartley. 'I used to swear by Cortinas. No longer.'

Midgley was watching an Indian man and his son sat in the corner. The father's face ran with tears as he hugged the child to him so that he seemed in danger of smothering the boy.

'You still got the VW?'

Midgley nodded.

'I think I might go in for a Peugeot,' said Hartley. 'A 604. Buy British.' There was a pause, and he added: 'He was a nice old chap.'

Jean and Elizabeth returned and Mark, who had been in

the corridor, came in to ask how long they were stopping.

Hartley looked at Jean.

'I think we ought to wait just a bit, don't you, darling?'

'Oh yes,' said Jean. 'Just in case.'

Aunty Kitty came in. 'I've just had one coffee and a Wagon Wheel and it was 45p. And it's all supposed to be voluntary.'

'There isn't a disco, is there?' said Mark.

'Disco?' said Jean. 'Disco? This is a hospital.'

'Well. Leisure facilities. Facilities for visitors. Killing time.'

'Listen,' Jean hissed. 'Your Uncle Denis's father is dying and you talk about discos.'

'It's all right,' said Midgley.

'Here, go get yourself a coffee,' said Hartley, giving him a pound. Aunty Kitty looked away.

HARTLEY AND HIS FAMILY were going. They were congregated outside the lift.

'You'll wait, I expect,' said Hartley.

'Oh yes,' said Midgley, 'I want to be here.'

'You want to make it plain at this stage you don't want him resuscitating.'

'That's if he doesn't want him resuscitating,' said Jean. 'You don't know.'

'I wouldn't want my dad resuscitating,' said Hartley.

'Denis might, mightn't you Denis?'

'No,' said Midgley.

'You often don't get the choice,' said Hartley. 'They'll

resuscitate anybody given half a chance. Shove them on these life-support machines. It's all to do with cost-effectiveness. They invest in this expensive equipment then they feel they have to use it.' He pumped the lift button. 'My guess is that it'll be at four in the morning, the crucial time. That's when life's at its lowest ebb, the early hours.'

'Miracles do happen, of course,' said Jean. 'I was reading about these out-of-body experiences. Have you read about them, Denis? It's where very sick people float in the air above their own bodies. Personally,' Jean kissed Midgley, 'I think it won't be long before science will be coming round to an after-life. Bye bye. I wish it had been on a happier occasion.'

Midgley went down the long corridor.

'MONEY'S NO GOOD,' said Aunty Kitty. 'Look at President Kennedy. They've been a tragic family.'

The Indians slept, the little son laid with his head in the father's lap.

An orderly came in and tidied the magazines, emptied the waste-bin and took away a vase of flowers.

'Oxygen,' he said as he went out.

'The Collingwoods got back from Corfu,' said Aunty Kitty. 'They said they enjoyed it but they wouldn't go a second time.'

It was after ten and Midgley had assumed she was going to stay the night when she suddenly got up.

'If I go now I can get the twenty-to,' she said. 'I'll just get back before they're turning out. I never go upstairs. It's just asking for it.'

'I'll walk down with you,' said Midgley.

She tiptoed elaborately past the sleeping immigrants, favouring them with a benevolent smile.

'They've got feelings the same as us,' she whispered. 'They're fond of their families. More so, probably.' They came out into the corridor. 'But then they're less advanced than we are.'

He phoned Joyce.

She and Colin were watching a programme about dolphins that had been introduced by the Duke of Edinburgh. Her mother was asleep with her mouth open.

'What're you doing?' asked Midgley.

'Nothing. Colin's watching a programme about dolphins. How is he?'

Midgley told her.

'I've got to stay,' he finished.

'Why? You've done all that's necessary. Nobody's going to blame you.'

Midgley saw that somebody had written on the wall 'Pray for me'. A wag had added 'OK'.

'I must be here when he goes,' said Midgley. 'You can understand that.'

'I understand you,' she said. 'It's not love. It's not affection.' Colin looked up. 'It's yourself.'

She put the phone down.

'Dad?' said Colin.

She turned the television off. 'He's hanging on.'

'Who?'

'Your grandad.' She got up. 'Wake up, Mother. Time for bed.'

M IDGLEY WENT BACK and sat with his father. While he had been out the night nurse had come on. She was a plump girl, dark, less pert than the others, and, he thought, more human. Actually she was just dirty. The hair wasn't gathered properly under her cap and there was a ladder in her stocking. She straightened the bedclothes, bending over the inert form so that her behind was inches from Midgley's face. Midgley decided it wasn't deliberate.

'Am I in the way?' he asked.

'No,' she said. 'Why? Stop there.'

She looked at the television monitor for a minute or two, counting the jumps with her watch. Then she smiled and went out. Five minutes later she was back with a cup of tea.

'No sugar,' said Midgley.

'May I?' she said and put both lumps in her mouth.

'Slack tonight,' she said. 'Still it just needs one drunken driver.'

Midgley closed his eyes.

'I thought you were going to be a bit of company,' she said. 'You're tired out.' She fetched a pillow and they went out into the waiting room. The Indians had gone.

'Lie down,' she said. 'I'll wake you if anything happens.'

Around five an alarm went off, and there were two deaths

in quick succession. Midgley slept on. At eight he woke.

'You can't lie down,' said a voice. 'You're not supposed to lie down.' It was a clean, fresh nurse.

Two women he had not seen before sat watching him.

'The nurse said she'd wake me up.'

'What nurse?'

'If anything happened to my father.'

'Whose is that pillow?'

'Midgley. Mr Midgley.'

'It's a hospital pillow.' She took it, and went back inside to her desk.

'Midgley.' Her finger ran down the list. 'No change. But don't lie down. It's not fair on other people.'

Midgley went and looked at his father. No change was right. He felt old and dirty. He had not shaved and there was a cold sore starting on his lip. But with his father there was no change. Still clean. Still pink. Still breathing. The dot skipped on. He walked out to the car park where he had left his van and wondered if he dared risk going out to buy a razor.

He went back in search of the doctor.

He cut across the visitors' car park, empty now except for his van, and took a path round the outside of the hospital that he thought would take him round to the entrance. The buildings were long and low and set in the hillside. They were done in identical units, every ward the same. He was passing a ward that seemed just like his father's except where his father should have been a woman was just putting her breast to a baby's mouth. A nurse came to the window and stared at him.

He looked away hurriedly and walked on, but not so quickly as to leave her with the impression he had been watching. She was still staring at him as he turned the corner. He experienced a feeling of relief if not quite homecoming when he saw he was now outside Intensive Care. He picked out his father's room, saw the carnations on the window-sill and the head and shoulders of a nurse. She was obviously looking at the bed. She moved back towards the window to make room for someone else. Midgley stood on tiptoe to try and see what was happening. He thought there was someone else there in a white coat. The room was full of people.

Midgley ran round the unit trying to find a way in. There was a door at the end of the building with an empty corridor beyond. It was locked. He ran up to the path again, then cut down across the bank through some young trees to try another door. A man on the telephone watched him sliding down then put one phone down and picked up another. Midgley ran on and suddenly was in a muddy flower bed among bushes and evergreens. It was the garden around the entrance to the Reception Area. Upstairs he ran past the startled nurse at the desk and into his father's room. Nobody spoke. There was an atmosphere of reverence.

'Is he dead?' said Midgley. 'Has he gone?' He was panting. An older woman in blue turned round. 'Dead? Certainly not. I am the matron. And look at your shoes.'

Behind the matron Midgley caught a glimpse of his father. As a nurse bustled him out Midgley struggled to look back. He was sure his father was smiling.

'I've just been to spend a penny,' said Aunty Kitty. 'When you consider it's a hospital the toilets are nothing to write home about. Look at your shoes.'

She was beginning to settle in, had brought a flask, sandwiches, knitting.

'I know Frank,' she said, looking at Country Life. 'He'll make a fight of it. I wouldn't thank you for a place in Bermuda.'

Midgley went to the gents to have a wash. He got some toilet paper and stood by the basins wiping the mud off his boots. He was stood with the muddy paper in his hands when an orderly came in, looked at the paper then looked at him incredulously, shook his head and went into a cubicle saying: 'The fucking public. The fucking dirty bastard public.'

Midgley went down to ring his Uncle Ernest on the phone outside Physio. A youngish woman was just dialling.

'Cyril. It's ...' She held the mouthpiece away from her mouth and the earpiece from her ear. 'It's Vi. Vi. I am speaking into it. Mum's had her op. No. She's had it. Had it this morning first thing. She's not come round yet, but I spoke to the sister and apparently she's fine. FINE. And the sister says ...' She dropped her voice. 'It wasn't what we thought. It wasn't what we thought. No. So there's no need to worry.' She ran her finger over the acoustic headboard behind the phone, fingering the holes. 'No. Completely clear. Well I think it's good news, don't you? The sister said the surgeon is the best. Mr Caldecott. People pay thousands to have him. Anyway I'm so relieved. Aren't you? Yes. Bye.'

As Midgley took the phone she took out her handkerchief

and rubbed it over her lips, and safely outside the hospital, her ear.

UNCLE ERNEST had said on the phone that if this was going to go on he wasn't sure he could run to the fares, but he turned up in the late afternoon along with Hartley.

He went and sat with his brother for a bit, got down and looked under the bed and figured out how the mechanism worked that lifted and lowered it and finally stood up and said, 'Gillo, Frank,' which was what he used to say when they went out cycling between the wars. It meant 'hurry up'.

'It's Frank all over,' said Aunty Kitty, 'going down fighting. He loved life.'

There were a couple of newcomers in the waiting room, an oldish couple.

'It's their eldest daughter,' whispered Aunty Kitty. 'She was just choosing some new curtains in Schofields. Collapsed. Suspected brain haemorrhage. Their other son's a vet.'

They trailed down the long corridor to the lift.

'It's a wonder to me,' said Uncle Ernest, 'how your Aunty Kitty's managed to escape strangulation all these years. Was he coloured, this doctor?'

'Which?' said Midgley.

'That said he was on his last legs.'

Midgley reluctantly admitted he was.

'That explains it,' said the old railwayman.

'Dad,' said Hartley.

'What does that mean, "Dad"?' said his father.

'It means I'm vice-chairman of the community relations council. It means we've got one in the office and he's a tip-top accountant. It means we all have to live with one another in this world.' He pumped the button of the lift.

'I'll not come again,' said Uncle Ernest. 'It gets morbid.'

'We've just got to play it by ear,' said Hartley.

'You won't have this performance with me,' said the old man. 'Come once and have done.'

'Shall I drop you?' said Hartley as the doors opened.

'I don't want you to go out of your way.'

'No, but shall I drop you?'

'Press G,' said Uncle Ernest.

The lift doors closed.

MIDGLEY WAS SITTING with his father when the plump night nurse came on.

'I wondered if you'd be on tonight.' He read her tab. 'Nurse Lightfoot.'

'Waiting for me, were you? No change.' She took a tissue and wiped the old man's mouth. 'He doesn't want to leave us, does he?' She picked up the vase of carnations from the window-sill. 'Oxygen,' she said and took them outside.

Later, when she had made him a cup of tea and Aunty Kitty had gone home for the second night, he was sitting at the bed-side but got up when she started to give his father a bed bath.

'You're like one another.'

He stared out of the window, even moved to avoid seeing the reflection.

'No,' he said.

'You are. It's a compliment. He has a nice face.' She sponged under his arms.

'What are you?' she said.

'How do you mean?' He turned just as she had folded back the sheets and was sponging between his legs. Quickly he looked out of the window again.

'What do you do?'

'Teacher. I'm a teacher.' He wanted to go and sit in the waiting room.

'What was he?'

'Plumber.'

'He's got lovely hands. Real ladies' hands.'

And it was true. She had finished and the soft white hands of his father lay over the sheet.

'That happens in hospitals. People's hands change.' She held his father's hand. Midgley wondered if he could ask her to hold his. Probably. She looked even more of a mess than the night before.

'Is there anything you want to ask?'

'Yes,' said Midgley.

'If there is, doctor'll be round in a bit.'

It was a different doctor. Not Indian. Fair, curly-haired and aged not much more than fourteen.

'His condition certainly hasn't deteriorated,' the child said.

'On the other hand,' he glanced boyishly at the chart, 'it can't be said to have improved.'

Midgley wondered if he had ever had his ears pierced.

'I don't know that there's any special point in waiting. You've done your duty.' He gave him a winning smile and had Midgley been standing closer would probably have put his hand on his arm as he had been taught to do.

'After all,' he was almost conspiratorial, 'he doesn't know you're here.'

'I don't think he's dying,' said Midgley.

'Living, dying,' said the boy and shrugged. The words meant the same thing.

'You do want your father to live?' He turned towards the nurse and pulled a little face.

'I was told he wasn't going to last long. I live in Hull.'

'Our task is to make them last as long as possible.' The pretty boy looked at his watch. 'We've no obligation to get them off on time.'

'Some of them seem to think we're British Rail,' the doctor remarked to a nurse in the small hours when they were having a smoke after sexual intercourse.

'I don't like 15-year-old doctors, that's all,' said Midgley. 'I'm old enough to be his father. Does nobody else wait? Does nobody else feel they have to be here?'

'Why not go sleep in your van? I can give you a pillow and things.' She was eating a toffee. 'I'll send somebody down to the car park if anything happens.'

'What do you do all day?' asked Midgley.

'Sleep.' She was picking a bit of toffee from her tooth. 'I generally surface around three.'

'Maybe we could have a coffee. If he's unchanged.'

'OK.'

She smiled. He had forgotten how easy it was.

'I'll just have another squint at my dad.'

He came back. 'Come and look. I think he's moved.'

She ran ahead of him into the room. The old man lay back on the pillows, a shaded light by the bed.

'You had me worried for a moment,' she said. 'It's all right.'

'No. His face has changed.'

She switched on the lamp over the bed, the light so sudden and bright that that alone might have made the old man flinch. But nothing moved.

'It's just that he seemed to be smiling.'

'You're tired,' she said, put her hand against his face and switched out the light.

Midgley switched it on again.

'If you look long enough at him you'll see a smile.'

'If you look long enough,' she said, walking out of the room, 'you'll see anything you want.'

Midgley stood for a moment in the darkened room, wishing he had kissed her when he'd had the chance. He went out to look for her but there had been a pile-up on the M62 and all hell was about to break loose.

'WHAT DO YOU DO ALL DAY?' said his wife on the phone. 'Sit in the waiting room. Sit in his room. Walk round the hospital.'

'Don't they mind?'

'Not if they're going to die.'

'Is he, though?' said his wife, watching her mother who had taken up her station on the chair by the door, holding her bag on her knees, preparatory to going to bed. 'It seems a long time.' The old lady was falling asleep. Once she had slipped right off that chair and cracked her head on the sideboard. That had been a hospital do.

'I can't talk. Mum's waiting to go up. She's crying out for a bath. I'm just going to have to steel myself.' The handbag slipped to the floor.

'I need a bath,' said Midgley.

'Go over to your dad's,' said his wife. 'Mum's falling over. Bye.'

'What am I doing sat on this seat?' said her mother, as she got her up. 'I never sit on this seat. I don't think I've ever sat on this seat before.'

IN THE MORNING Midgley was woken by Nurse Lightfoot banging on the steamed-up window of the van. It was seven o'clock.

'I'm just going off,' she was mouthing through the glass.

He wound down the window.

'I'm just coming off. Isn't it a grand morning? I'm going to have a big fried breakfast then go to bed. I'll see you at teatime. You look terrible.'

Midgley looked at himself in the driving mirror, then started up the van and drove after her, hooting.

'You're not supposed to hoot,' she said. 'It's a hospital.'

'I forgot to ask you. How's my dad?'

'No change.' She waved and ran down a grass bank towards the nurses' flats. 'No change.'

His dad lived where he had lived once, at the end of a terrace of redbrick back-to-back houses. It was an end house, as his mother had always been careful to point out. It gave them one more window, which was nice, only kids used the end wall to play football against, which wasn't. His dad used to heave himself up from the fireside and go out to them, night after night. He let himself in with the key he had had since he was fourteen. 'You're twenty-one now,' his mother had said.

The house was neat and clean and cold. He looked for some sign of interrupted activity, even a chair out of place, some clue as to what his father had been doing when the blow fell. But there was nothing. He had a home help. She had probably tidied up. He put the kettle on, before having a shave. He knew where everything was. His dad's razor on the shelf above the sink, a shaving brush worn down to a stub and a half-used packet of Seven O'Clock blades. He scrubbed away the caked rust from the razor ('Your dad doesn't care,' said his mother) and put in a new blade. He had never gone in for shaving soap. Puritan soap they always bought, green Puritan soap. Then having shaved he took his shirt off to wash in the same sequence he had seen his father follow every night when he came in from work. Then, thinking of the coming afternoon, he did something he had never seen his father do, take off his trousers and his pants to wash his cock. He smelled his shirt. It stank. Naked, white and shivering he went through the neat sitting room and up the narrow stairs and stood on the cold lino of his parents' bedroom looking at himself in the dressing-table mirror. On top of the dressing-table, stood on little lace mats, was a toilet set. A round glass jar for a powder-puff, a pin tray, a cut-glass dish with a small pinnacle in the middle, for rings, and a celluloid-backed mirror and hair-brush. Items that had never had a practical use, but which had lain there in their appointed place for forty years.

He opened the dressing-table drawer, and found a new shirt still in its packet. They had given it to his father as a Christmas present two years before. He put it on, carefully extracting all the pins and putting them in the cut-glass dish. He looked for pants and found a pair that were old, baggy and gone a bit yellow. Some socks. Nothing quite fitted. He was smaller than his father. These days it was generally the other way round. He went downstairs, through into the scullery to polish his shoes. He remembered the brushes, the little brush to put the polish on which as a child he had always thought of as bad, the big noble brush that brought out the shine. He stood on the hearthrug and saw himself in the mirror, ready as if for a funeral, and sat down on the settee about to weep when he realised it was not his father's funeral he was imagining but his own. On the end of the tiled mantelpiece of which his mother had been so proud when they had had it put in in 1953 (a crime getting rid of that beautiful range, Joyce always said) was his dad's pipe. It was still half full of charred tobacco. He put it back but rolling over it fell on to the hearth. He stooped to pick it up and was his father suddenly, bending down, falling and lying there two days with the pipe under his hand. He dashed out of the house and drove wildly back to the hospital.

'No change,' said the nurse wearily (they were beginning to think he was mad). But if there was no change at least the old man didn't seem to be smiling.

'I'm wearing your shirt, Dad,' Midgley said. 'The one we gave you for Christmas. I hope that's all right. It doesn't really suit me, but I think that's why Joyce bought it. She said it didn't suit me but it would suit you.'

A nurse came in.

'They tell you to talk,' said Midgley. 'I read it in an article in the *Reader's Digest*,' (and as if this gave it added force), 'it was in the waiting room.'

The nurse sniffed. 'They say the same thing about plants,' she said, putting the carnations back on the window-sill. 'I think it's got past that stage.'

MIDGLEY WAS SITTING on the divan bed in Nurse Lightfoot's room in the nurses' quarters. The rooms were light and modern like the hospital. She was sitting by the electric fire with one bar on. There was a Snoopy poster on the wall.

'People are funny about nurses,' she said. 'Men.' She took a bite of her bun. They were muesli buns. 'You say you're a nurse and their whole attitude changes. Do you know what I mean?'

'No,' lied Midgley.

'I notice it at parties particularly. They ask you what you do, you say you're a nurse and next minute they've got you on the floor. Perfectly ordinary people turn into wild beasts.' She switched another bar on.

'I've given up saying I'm a nurse for that reason.'

'What do you say you are?' asked Midgley. He wondered whether he would be better placed if he went over to the fire or he got her to come over to the bed.

'I say I'm a sales representative. I don't mean you,' she said. 'You're obviously not like that. Course you've got other things on your mind at the moment.'

'Like what?'

'Your dad.'

'Oh yes.'

The duty nurse had been instructed to ring if there was any sign of a crisis.

'He is lovely,' she said, through mouthfuls of bun. 'I do understand the way you feel about him.'

'Do you?' said Midgley. 'That's nice.'

'Old people have their own particular attraction. He's almost sexy.'

Midgley stood up suddenly.

She picked something out of her mouth.

'Was your cake gritty?'

'No,' said Midgley, sitting down again.

'Mine was. Mine was a bit gritty.'

'It was probably meant to be gritty,' said Midgley, looking at his watch.

'No. It was more gritty than that.'

'What would you say,' asked Midgley, as he carefully examined a small stain on the bedcover, 'what would you say if I asked you to go to bed.'

'Now?' she asked, extracting another piece of grit or grain.

'If you like.' He made it sound as if she had made the suggestion.

'I can't now.' She gathered up the cups and plates.

'Why not? You're not on till seven.'

'It's Wednesday. I'm on early turn.' She wondered if he was going to turn into a wild beast.

'Tomorrow then?'

'Tomorrow would be better. Though of course it all depends.'

'What on?'

She was shocked.

'Your father. He may not be here tomorrow.'

'That's true,' said Midgley, getting up. He kissed her fairly formally.

'Anyway,' she smiled. 'Fingers crossed.'

M IDGLEY SAT BY HIS FATHER'S BED and watched the dot skipping on the screen.

'Hold on, Dad,' he muttered. 'Hold on.'

There was no change.

Before going down to sleep in the van he telephoned home. It was his son who answered. Joyce was upstairs with her mother.

'Could you ask her to come to the phone, please,' said Midgley. The 'please' was somehow insulting. He heard brief shouting.

'She can't,' said Colin. 'Gran's in the bath. Mum can't leave her. What do you want?'

'You go up and watch her while I speak to your mum.'

'Dad.' The boy's voice was slow with weary outrage. 'Dad. She's in the bath. She's no clothes on. I don't want to see her.'

He heard more distant shouting.

'Mum says if she can get a granny-sitter she may come over to see Grandad.'

'Colin.' Midgley was suddenly urgent. 'Colin. Are you still there?'

'Sure.' (Midgley hated that.)

'Tell her not to do that. Do you hear? Tell her there's no need to come over. Go on, tell her.'

'I'll tell her when she comes down.'

'No,' said Midgley. 'Now. I know you. Go up and tell her now.'

The phone was put down and he could hear Colin bellowing up the stairs. He came back.

'I told her. Is that all?'

'No,' said Midgley. 'Haven't you forgotten something? How's Grandad? Haven't you forgotten that? Well it's nice

of you to ask, Colin. He's about the same, Colin, thank
you.'

'How was your grandad?' said Joyce, coming downstairs
with a wet towel and a bundle of her mother's underclothes.

'About the same,' said Colin.

'And your dad?'

'No change.'

T HAT NIGHT MIDGLEY DREAMED it was morning when
the door opened and his father got into the van.

'I didn't know you drove, Dad,' he said as they were going
into town. 'When did you learn?'

'Just before I died.'

His mother, as a girl, met them outside the Town Hall.

'What a spanking van, Frank,' she said. 'Move up, Denis, let
me sit next to your dad.'

The three of them sat in a row until he saw her hand was on
his father's leg, when suddenly he was in a field alone with his
mother.

'What a grand field,' she said. 'It's spotless.'

He was a little boy and she was in a white frock, and some
terrible threat had just been lifted. Then he looked behind him
and saw something much worse. On the edge of the field,
ready to engulf them, was an enormous slag heap, glinting
black and shiny in the sun. His mother hadn't seen it and chat-
tered on how lovely this field was and slipping nearer came
this terrible hill. Someone ran down the slope, waving his

arms, a figure big and filthy, a miner, a coalman. He slid down beside them.

'Oh,' she said placidly, 'here's your father,' and he sat down beside her, coal and muck all over her white frock.

Then they were walking through Leeds Market. It was Sunday and the stalls were empty and shuttered. It was also a church and they walked up through the market to the choir screen. It was in the form of a board announcing Arrivals and Departures, slips of board clicking over with names on them, only instead of Arrivals and Departures it was headed Births and Deaths. Midgley wandered off while his parents sat looking at the board. Then his mam got up and kissed his dad, and went backwards through the screen just before the gates were drawn across. Midgley tried to run down the church and couldn't. He was shouting, 'Mam. Mam.' Eventually he got to the gates and started shaking them, but she had gone. He turned to look at his father who shook his head slowly and turned away. Midgley went on rattling the gates then someone was shaking the van. It was Nurse Lightfoot waking him up. 'You can call me Valery,' she chanted as she ran off to her big breakfast.

Later that morning Midgley went in to see his father to find a smartish middle-aged woman sat by the bed. She was holding his father's hand.

'Is it Denis?' she said without getting up.

'Yes.'

'I'm Alice Dugdale. Did he tell you about me?'

'No.'

'He wouldn't, being him. He's an old bugger. Aren't you?'

She shook the inert hand. She was in her fifties, Midgley decided, very confident and done up to the nines. His mother would have called her common. She looked like the wife of a prosperous licensee.

'He told me about you,' she said. 'He never stopped telling me about you. It's a sad sight.'

The nurse had said his father was a bit better this morning.

'His condition's stabilised,' said Midgley.

'Yes, she said that to me, the little slut. What does she know?' She looked at him. 'You're a bit scruffy.' She stood up and smoothed down her skirt. 'I've come from Southport.' She took the carnations from the vase and put them in the waste-bin. 'A depressing flower, carnations,' she said. 'I prefer freesias. I'm a widow,' she said. 'A rich widow. Shall we have a meander round? No sense in stopping here.' She kissed his father on the forehead. 'His lordship's not got much to contribute. Bye bye chick.'

She swept through the waiting room with Midgley in her wake. Aunty Kitty open-mouthed got up and went out to watch them going down the corridor.

'That'll be your Aunty Kitty, I take it.' She said it loudly enough for her to hear.

'It is, yes,' said Denis, glancing back and smiling weakly. 'Do you know her?'

'No, thank God. Though she probably knows me.'

They found a machine and had some coffee. She took a silver flask from her bag.

'Do you want some of this in it?'

'No thanks,' said Midgley.

'I'd better,' she said. 'I've driven from Southport. I wanted to marry your dad only he said no. I had too much money. My husband left me very nicely placed. He was a leading light in the soft furnishing trade. Frank would have felt beholden, you see. That was your dad all over. Still you know what he was like.'

Midgley was no longer sure he did.

'How do you mean?' he said.

'He always had to be the one, did Frank. The one who did the good turns, the one who paid out, the one who sacrificed. You couldn't do anything for him. I had all this money and he wouldn't even let me take him to Scarborough. We used to go sit in Roundhay Park. Roundhay Park!'

A woman went by, learning to use crutches.

'We could have been in Tenerife.'

Midgley was glad to have at least this aspect of his father's character confirmed.

'I didn't want to let him down,' said Midgley. 'That's why I've been waiting. He wants me to let him down, I know.'

'Poor soul,' she said, looking at the woman struggling down the corridor.

'What was your mam like?'

'She was lovely,' said Midgley.

'She must have had him taped. She looks a grand woman. He's showed me photographs.' She took out her compact and made up her face. 'I'll go back and have another look. Then

I've got to get over to a Round Table in Harrogate. Killed two birds with one stone for me, this trip.'

'YOUR MOTHER'D NOT BEEN DEAD A YEAR,' sniffed Aunty Kitty. 'I was shocked.'

'I'm not shocked.'

'You're a man.'

'It wasn't like your dad. She's a cheek showing her face.'

'I'm rather pleased,' said Midgley.

'That hair's dyed,' said Aunty Kitty, but it was a last despairing throw. 'They're sending him downstairs tomorrow. He must be on the mend.' The drama was about to go out of her life. 'I only hope when he does come round he's not a vegetable.'

'I'VE TOLD SHIRLEY to ring if anything happens,' Valery said. 'Not that it will. His chest is better. His heart is better. He's simply unconscious now.'

Midgley was brushing his teeth.

'I'm looking forward to him coming round.' She raised her voice above the running tap. 'I long to know what his voice is like.'

'What?' said Midgley turning off the tap.

'I long to know what his voice is like.'

'Oh,' said Midgley. 'Yes.' And turned the tap on again.

'I think I know what it's like,' she said. 'I'd just like to have it confirmed.'

'You don't seem to like talking about your father,' she said as she unzipped her skirt. 'Nice shirt.'

'Yes,' said Midgley. 'It's one of Dad's.'

'I like it.'

He went and had a pee and while he was out she took the receiver off the phone and put a cushion over it. When he came back she was already in bed.

'Hello,' he said, getting in and lying beside her. 'It's a bit daft is this.'

'Why?' she said. 'It happens all the time.'

'Yes,' said Midgley. 'So I'm told.'

They kissed.

'I ought to have done more of this.'

'What?'

'This,' said Midgley. 'This is going to be the rule from now on. I've got a lot of catching up to do.'

He ran his hand between her thighs.

'It's the nick of time.'

'First time I've heard it called that.'

'I hope this isn't one of those private beds,' said Midgley. 'I'm opposed to that on principle.'

'You've never asked me if I was married,' she said.

'You're a nurse. That puts you in a different category.' There was a pause. 'Are you married?'

'He's on an oil rig.'

'I hope so,' said Midgley.

Later on he had a cigarette and she had a cake.

'i was certain they were going to ring from the ward,' he said.

'No.' She lifted up the cushion and put the receiver back.

He frowned. Then grinned. 'No harm done,' he said.

They were just settling in again when the phone rang. She answered.

'Yes,' she said, looking at him. 'Yes.'

'What's the matter?' said Midgley.

She put the phone down and looked away.

He was already out of bed and pulling his trousers on.

'Had she rung before?'

She had turned to face the wall.

'Had she?' Midgley was shouting. 'Was she ringing?'

'Don't shout. There are night nurses asleep.'

A T THE END OF THE LONG CORRIDOR the doors burst open.

'It's the biggest wonder I'd not gone in to see Mrs Tunnicliffe,' said Aunty Kitty. 'She's in Ward 7 with her hip. She's been waiting two years. But I don't know what it was. Something made me come back upstairs. I was sat looking at a *Woman's Own* then in walks Joyce and next minute the nurse is calling us in and he has his eyes open! So we were both there, weren't we?'

Mrs Midgley nodded. They were all three stood by the bedside.

'He just said, "Is our Denis here? Is our Denis here?"' said Aunty Kitty, 'and I said: "He's just coming, Frank." And he smiled a little smile and it was all over. Bless him. I was his only sister.'

The body lay flat on the bed, the eyes closed, the sheet up to the neck.

'The dot does something different when you're dying,' said Aunty Kitty, looking at the screen which now showed a continuous line. 'I wasn't watching it, naturally, but I noticed out of the corner of my eye it was doing something different during the last moments.'

'I think he's smiling,' said Mrs Midgley.

'Of course he's smiling,' said Midgley. He went and looked out of the window. 'He's won. Scored. In the last minute of extra time.'

Mrs Midgley came over to the window and said in an undertone: 'You disgust me.'

A nurse came in and switched off the monitor.

They went out.

'It's a pity you weren't here, Denis,' said Aunty Kitty. 'I mean when it came to the crunch. You've been so good. You've been here all the time he was dying. What were you doing?'

'Living,' said Midgley.

'He's at peace anyway,' said Aunty Kitty.

They went out and got his clothes. As they were walking out a young man was on the phone. 'It's a boy!' he was saying. 'A boy! Yes. Just think. I'm a father.'

They stood in the car park.

'I suppose while we're here,' said Joyce, 'we could go up home and make a start on going through his things.'

THE LADY IN THE VAN

Good nature, or what is often considered as such, is the most selfish of all virtues: it is nine times out of ten mere indolence of disposition.

William Hazlitt, 'On the Knowledge of Character' (1822)

'I ran into a snake this afternoon,' Miss Shepherd said. 'It was coming up Parkway. It was a long, grey snake – a boa constrictor possibly. It looked poisonous. It was keeping close to the wall and seemed to know its way. I've a feeling it may have been heading for the van.' I was relieved that on this occasion she didn't demand that I ring the police, as she regularly did if anything out of the ordinary occurred. Perhaps this was too out of the ordinary (though it turned out the pet shop in

Parkway had been broken into the previous night, so she may have seen a snake). She brought her mug over and I made her a drink, which she took back to the van. 'I thought I'd better tell you,' she said, 'just to be on the safe side. I've had some close shaves with snakes.'

This encounter with the putative boa constrictor was in the summer of 1971, when Miss Shepherd and her van had for some months been at a permanent halt opposite my house in Camden Town. I had first come across her a few years previously, stood by her van, stalled as usual, near the convent at the top of the street. The convent (which was to have a subsequent career as the Japanese School) was a gaunt reformatory-like building that housed a dwindling garrison of aged nuns and was notable for a striking crucifix attached to the wall overlooking the traffic lights. There was something about the position of Christ, pressing himself against the grim pebbledash beneath the barred windows of the convent, that called up visions of the Stalag and the searchlight and which had caused us to dub him 'The Christ of Colditz'. Miss Shepherd, not looking un-crucified herself, was standing by her vehicle in an attitude with which I was to become very familiar, left arm extended with the palm flat against the side of the van indicating ownership, the right arm summoning anyone who was fool enough to take notice of her, on this occasion me. Nearly six foot, she was a commanding figure, and would have been more so had she not been kitted out in greasy raincoat, orange skirt, Ben Hogan golfing-cap and carpet slippers. She would be going on sixty at this time.

She must have prevailed on me to push the van as far as Albany Street, though I recall nothing of the exchange. What I do remember was being overtaken by two policemen in a panda car as I trundled the van across Gloucester Bridge; I thought that, as the van was certainly holding up the traffic, they might have lent a hand. They were wiser than I knew. The other feature of this first run-in with Miss Shepherd was her driving technique. Scarcely had I put my shoulder to the back of the van, an old Bedford, than a long arm was stretched elegantly out of the driver's window to indicate in textbook fashion that she (or rather I) was moving off. A few yards further on, as we were about to turn into Albany Street, the arm emerged again, twirling elaborately in the air to indicate that we were branching left, the movement done with such boneless grace that this section of the Highway Code might have been choreographed by Petipa with Ulanova at the wheel. Her 'I am coming to a halt' was less poised, as she had plainly not expected me to give up pushing and shouted angrily back that it was the other end of Albany Street she wanted, a mile further on. But I had had enough by this time and left her there, with no thanks for my trouble. Far from it. She even climbed out of the van and came running after me, shouting that I had no business abandoning her, so that passers-by looked at me as if I had done some injury to this pathetic scarecrow. 'Some people!' I suppose I thought, feeling foolish that I'd been taken for a ride (or taken her for one) and cross that I'd fared worse than if I'd never lifted a finger, these mixed feelings to be the invariable aftermath of any transaction involving Miss

Shepherd. One seldom was able to do her a good turn without some thoughts of strangulation.

It must have been a year or so after this, and so some time in the late sixties, that the van first appeared in Gloucester Crescent. In those days the street was still a bit of a mixture. Its large semi-detached villas had originally been built to house the Victorian middle class, then it had gone down in the world, and, though it had never entirely decayed, many of the villas degenerated into rooming-houses and so were among the earliest candidates for what is now called 'gentrification' but which was then called 'knocking through'. Young professional couples, many of them in journalism or television, bought up the houses, converted them and (an invariable feature of such conversions) knocked the basement rooms together to form a large kitchen/ dining- room. In the mid-sixties I wrote a BBC TV series, *Life in NW1*, based on one such family, the Stringalongs, whom Mark Boxer then took over to people a cartoon strip in the *Listener*, and who kept cropping up in his drawings for the rest of his life. What made the social set-up funny was the disparity between the style in which the new arrivals found themselves able to live and their progressive opinions: guilt, put simply, which today's gentrifiers are said famously not to feel (or 'not to have a problem about'). We did have a problem, though I'm not sure we were any better for it. There was a gap between our social position and our social obligations. It was in this gap that Miss Shepherd (in her van) was able to live.

October 1969. When she is not in the van Miss S. spends much of her day sitting on the pavement in Parkway, where she has a pitch outside Williams & Glyn's Bank. She sells tracts, entitled 'True View: Mattering Things', which she writes herself, though this isn't something she will admit. 'I sell them, but so far as the authorship is concerned I'll say they are anonymous and that's as far as I'm prepared to go.' She generally chalks the gist of the current pamphlet on the pavement, though with no attempt at artistry. 'St Francis FLUNG money from him' is today's message, and prospective customers have to step over it to get into the bank. She also makes a few coppers selling pencils. 'A gentleman came the other day and said that the pencil he had bought from me was the best pencil on the market at the present time. It lasted him three months. He'll be back for another one shortly.' D., one of the more conventional neighbours (and not a knocker-through), stops me and says, 'Tell me, is she a *genuine* eccentric?'

April 1970. Today we moved the old lady's van. An obstruction order has been put under the windscreen wiper, stating that it was stationed outside number 63 and is a danger to public health. This order, Miss S. insists, is a statutory order: 'And statutory means standing – in this case standing outside number 63 – so, if the van is moved on, the order will be invalid.' Nobody ventures to argue with this, but she can't decide whether her next pitch should be outside number 61 or further on. Eventually she decides there is 'a nice space' outside 62 and plumps for that. My neighbour Nick Tomalin and

I heave away at the back of the van, but while she is gracefully indicating that she is moving off (for all of the fifteen feet) the van doesn't budge. 'Have you let the handbrake off?' Nick Tomalin asks. There is a pause. 'I'm just in the process of taking it off.' As we are poised for the move, another Camden Town eccentric materialises, a tall, elderly figure in long overcoat and Homburg hat, with a distinguished grey moustache and in his buttonhole a flag for the Primrose League. He takes off a grubby canary glove and leans a shaking hand against the rear of the van (OLU 246), and when we have moved it forward the few statutory feet he puts on his glove again, saying, 'If you should need me I'm just round the corner' (i.e. in Arlington House, the working men's hostel).

I ask Miss S. how long she has had the van. 'Since 1965,' she says, 'though don't spread that around. I got it to put my things in. I came down from St Albans in it, and plan to go back there eventually. I'm just pedalling water at the moment. I've always been in the transport line. Chiefly delivery and chauffeuring. You know,' she says mysteriously – 'renovated army vehicles. And I've got good topography. I always have had. I knew Kensington in the blackout.'

This van (there were to be three others in the course of the next twenty years) was originally brown, but by the time it had reached the Crescent it had been given a coat of yellow. Miss S. was fond of yellow ('It's the papal colour') and was never content to leave her vehicles long in their original trim. Sooner or later she could be seen moving slowly round her immobile home, thoughtfully touching up the rust from a tiny tin of primrose paint, looking, in her long dress and sunhat, much as Vanessa Bell would have looked had she gone in for painting Bedford vans. Miss S. never appreciated the difference between car enamel and ordinary gloss paint, and even this she never bothered to mix. The result was that all her vehicles ended up looking as if they had been given a coat of badly made custard or plastered with scrambled egg. Still, there were few occasions on which one saw Miss Shepherd genuinely happy and one of them was when she was putting paint on. A few years before she died she went in for a Reliant Robin (to put more of her things in). It was actually yellow to start with, but that didn't save it from an additional coat, which she applied as Monet might have done, standing back to judge the effect of each brush-stroke. The Reliant stood outside my gate. It was towed away earlier this year, a scatter of yellow drops on the kerb all that remains to mark its final parking place.

January 1971. Charity in Gloucester Crescent takes refined forms. The publishers next door are bringing out some classical volume and to celebrate the event last night held a Roman dinner. This morning the au pair was to be seen knocking at the window of the van with a plate of Roman remains. But Miss S. is never easy to help. After twelve last night I saw her striding up the Crescent waving her stick and telling someone to be off. Then I heard a retreating middle-class voice say plaintively, 'But I only asked if you were all right.'

June 1971. Scarcely a day passes now without some sort of

incident involving the old lady. Yesterday evening around ten a sports car swerves over to her side of the road so that the driver, rich, smart and in his twenties, can lean over and bang on the side of the van, presumably to flush out for his grinning girlfriend the old witch who lives there. I shout at him and he sounds his horn and roars off. Miss S. of course wants the police called, but I can't see the point, and indeed around five this morning I wake to find two policemen at much the same game, idly shining their torches in the windows in the hope that she'll wake up and enliven a dull hour of their beat. Tonight a white car reverses dramatically up the street, screeches to a halt beside the van, and a burly young man jumps out and gives the van a terrific shaking. Assuming (hoping, probably) he would have driven off by the time I get outside, I find he's still there, and ask him what the fuck he thinks he's doing. His response is quite mild. 'What's up with you then?' he asks. 'You still on the telly? You nervous? You're trembling all over.' He then calls me a fucking cunt and drives off. After all that, of course, Miss S. isn't in the van at all, so I end up as usual more furious with her than I am with the lout.

These attacks, I'm sure, disturbed my peace of mind more than they did hers. Living in the way she did, every day must have brought such cruelties. Some of the stallholders in the Inverness Street market used to persecute her with medieval relish – and children too, who both inflict and suffer such casual cruelties themselves. One night two drunks systematically smashed all the windows of the van, the flying glass cutting her face. Furious over any small liberty, she was only mildly disturbed by this. 'They may have had too much to drink by mistake,' she said. 'That does occur through not having eaten, possibly. I don't want a case.' She was far more interested in 'a ginger feller I saw in Parkway in company with Mr Khruschev. Has he disappeared recently?'

But to find such sadism and intolerance so close at hand began actively to depress me, and having to be on the alert for every senseless attack made it impossible to work. There came a day when, after a long succession of such incidents, I suggested that she spend at least the nights in a lean-to at the side of my house. Initially reluctant, as with any change, over the next two years she gradually abandoned the van for the hut.

In giving her sanctuary in my garden and landing myself with a tenancy that went on eventually for fifteen years I was never under any illusion that the impulse was purely charitable. And of course it made me furious that I had been driven to such a pass. But I wanted a quiet life as much as, and possibly more than, she did. In the garden she was at least out of harm's way.

October 1973. I have run a lead out to the lean-to and now regularly have to mend Miss S.'s electric fire, which she keeps fusing by plugging too many appliances into the attachment. I sit on the steps fiddling with the fuse while she squats on her haunches in the hut. 'Aren't you cold? You could come in here. I could light a candle and then it would be a bit warmer. The toad's been in once or twice. He was in here with a slug. I think he may be in love with the slug. I tried to turn it out and it got very disturbed. I thought he was going to go for me.' She complains that there is not enough room in the shed and suggests I get her a tent, which she could then use to store some of her things. 'It would only be three feet high and by rights ought to be erected in a meadow. Then there are these shatterproof greenhouses. Or something could be done with old raincoats possibly.'

March 1974. The council are introducing parking restrictions in the Crescent. Residents' bays have been provided and yellow lines drawn up the rest of the street. To begin with, the workmen are very understanding, painting the yellow line as far as the van, then beginning again on the other side so that technically it is still legally parked. However, a higher official has now stepped in and served a removal order on it, so all this week there has been a great deal of activity as Miss S. transports cargoes of plastic bags across the road, through the garden and into the hut. While professing faith in divine protection for the van, she is prudently clearing out her belongings against its possible removal. A notice she has written declaring the council's action illegal twirls idly under the windscreen wiper.

'The notice was served on a Sunday. I believe you can serve search warrants on a Sunday but nothing else, possibly. I should have the Freedom of the Land for the good articles I've sold on the economy.' She is particularly concerned about the tyres of the van which 'may be miraculous. They've only been pumped up twice since 1964. If I get another vehicle'– and Lady W. is threatening to buy her one – 'I'd like them transferred.'

The old van was towed away in April 1974 and another one provided by Lady W. ('a titled Catholic lady', as Miss S. always referred to her). Happy to run to a new (albeit old) van, Lady W. was understandably not anxious to have it parked outside her front door and eventually, and perhaps by now inevitably, the van and Miss S. ended up in my garden. This van was roadworthy, and Miss S. insisted on being the one to drive it through the gate into the garden, a manoeuvre which once again enabled her to go through her full repertoire of hand signals. Once the van was on site Miss S. applied the handbrake with such determination that, like Excalibur, it could never thereafter be released, rusting so firmly into place that when the van came to be moved ten years later it had to be hoisted over the wall by the council crane.

This van (and its successor, bought in 1983) now occupied a paved area between my front door and the garden gate, the bonnet of the van hard by my front step, its rear door, which Miss S. always used to get in and out of, a few feet from the gate. Callers at the house had to squeeze past the back of the van and come down the side, and while they waited for my door to be opened they would be scrutinized from behind the murky windscreen by Miss Shepherd. If they were unlucky, they would find the rear door open with Miss S. dangling her large white legs over the back. The interior of the van, a midden of old clothes, plastic bags and half-eaten food, was not easy to ignore, but should anyone Miss S. did not know venture to speak to her she would promptly tuck her legs back and wordlessly shut the door. For the first few years of her sojourn in the garden I would try and explain to mystified callers how this situation had arisen, but after a while I ceased to care, and when I didn't mention it nor did anyone else.

At night the impression was haunting. I had run a cable out from the house to give her light and heating, and through the ragged draperies that hung over the windows of the van a visitor would glimpse Miss S.'s spectral figure, often bent over in prayer or lying on her side like an effigy on a tomb, her face resting on one hand, listening to Radio 4. Did she hear any movements she would straightaway switch off the light and wait, like an animal that has been disturbed, until she was sure the coast was clear and could put the light on again. She retired early and would complain if anyone called or left late at night. On one occasion Coral Browne was coming away from the house with her husband, Vincent Price, and they were talking quietly. 'Pipe down,' snapped the voice from the van, 'I'm trying to sleep.' For someone who had brought terror to millions it was an unexpected taste of his own medicine.

December 1974. Miss S. has been explaining to me why the old Bedford (the van not the music-hall) ceased to go, 'possibly'. She had put in some of her home-made petrol, based on a recipe for petrol substitute she read about several years ago in a newspaper. 'It was a spoonful of petrol, a gallon of water and a pinch of something you could get in every High Street. Well, I got it into my head, I don't know why, that it was bicarbonate of soda, only I think I was mistaken. It must be either sodium chloride or sodium nitrate, only I've since been told sodium chloride is salt and the man in Boots wouldn't sell me the other, saying it might cause explosions. Though I think me being an older person he knew I would be more responsible. Though not all old ladies perhaps.'

February 1975. Miss S. rings, and when I open the door she makes a bee-line for the kitchen stairs. 'I'd like to see you. I've called several times. I wonder whether I can use the toilet first.' I say I think this is pushing it a bit. 'I'm not pushing it at all. I just will do the interview better if I can use the toilet first.' Afterwards she sits down in her green mac and purple head-scarf, the knuckles of one large mottled hand resting on the clean, scrubbed table and explains how she has devised a method of 'getting on the wireless'. I was to ask the BBC to give me a phone-in programme ('something someone like you could get put on in a jiffy') and then she would ring me up from the house. 'Either that or I could get on *Petticoat Line.* I know a darn sight more on moral matters than most of them. I could sing my song over the telephone. It's a lovely song, called "The End of the World"' (which is pure *Beyond the Fringe*). 'I won't commit myself to singing it – not at this moment – but I probably would. Some sense should be said and knowledge known. It could all be anonymous. I could be called The Lady Behind the Curtain. Or A Woman of Britain.

You could take a *nom-de-plume* view of it.' This idea of The Woman Behind the Curtain has obviously taken her fancy and she begins to expand on it, demonstrating where the curtain could be, her side of it coincidentally taking in the television and the easy chair. She could be behind the curtain, she explains, do her periodic broadcasts, and the rest of the time 'be a guest at the television and take in some civilisation. Perhaps there would be gaps filled with nice classical music. I know one: "Prelude and Liebestraum" by Liszt. I believe he was a Catholic priest. It means "love's dream", only not the sexy stuff. It's the love of God and the sanctification of labour and so on, which would recommend it to celibates like you and me, possibly.' Shocked at this tentative bracketing of our conditions, I quickly get rid of her and, though it's a bitter cold night, open the windows wide to get rid of the smell.

The Woman Behind the Curtain remained a favourite project of hers, and in 1976 she wrote to Aiman (*sic*) Andrews: 'Now that *This is Your Life* is ended, having cost too much etc., I might be able to do a bit as The Lady Behind the Curtain. All you need do is put a curtain up to hide me but permit words of sense to come forth in answer to some questions. Sense is needed.' Hygiene was needed too, but possibly in an effort to persuade me about being behind the curtain she brought the subject up herself. 'I'm by nature a very clean person. I have a testimonial for a Clean Room, awarded me some years ago, and my aunt, herself spotless, said I was the cleanest of my mother's children, particularly in the unseen places.' I never fathomed her toilet arrangements. She only once asked me to buy her toilet rolls ('I use them to wipe my face'), but whatever happened in that department I took to be part of some complicated arrangement involving the plastic bags she used to hurl from the van every morning. When she could still manage stairs she did very occasionally use my loo, but I didn't encourage it; it was here, on the threshold of the toilet, that my charity stopped short. Once when I was having some building work done (and was, I suppose, conscious of what the workmen were thinking), I very boldly said there was a smell of urine. 'Well, what can you expect when they're raining bricks down on me all day? And then I think there's a mouse. So that would make a cheesy smell, possibly.'

Miss S.'s daily emergence from the van was highly dramatic. Suddenly and without warning the rear door would be flung open to reveal the tattered draperies that masked the terrible interior. There was a pause, then through the veils would be hurled several bulging plastic sacks. Another pause, before slowly and with great caution one sturdy slippered leg came feeling for the floor before the other followed and one had the first sight of the day's wardrobe. Hats were always a feature: a black railwayman's hat with a long neb worn slightly on the skew so that she looked like a drunken signalman or a French guardsman of the 1880s; there was her Charlie Brown pitcher's hat; and in June 1977 an octagonal straw table-mat, tied on with a chiffon scarf and a bit of cardboard for the peak. She also went in for green eyeshades. Her skirts had a telescopic appearance, as they had often been lengthened many times over by the simple expedient of sewing a strip of extra cloth around the hem, though with no attempt at matching. One skirt was made by sewing several orange dusters together. When she fell foul of authority she put it down to her clothes. Once, late at night, the police rang me from Tunbridge Wells. They had picked her up on the station, thinking her dress was a nightie. She was indignant. 'Does it look like a nightie? You see lots of people wearing dresses like this. I don't think this style can have got to Tunbridge Wells yet.'

Miss S. seldom wore stockings, and alternated between black pumps and brown carpet slippers. Her hands and feet were large, and she was what my grandmother would have called 'a big-boned woman'. She was middle class and spoke in a middle-class way, though her querulous and often resentful demeanour tended to obscure this; it wasn't a gentle or a genteel voice. Running through her vocabulary was a streak of schoolgirl slang. She wouldn't say she was tired, she was 'all done up'; petrol was 'juice'; and if she wasn't keen on doing something she'd say 'I'm darned if I will'. All her conversation was impregnated with the vocabulary of her peculiar brand of Catholic fanaticism ('the dire importance of justice deeds'). It was the language of the leaflets she wrote, the 'possibly' with which she ended so many of her sentences an echo of the 'Subject to the Roman Catholic Church in her rights etc.' with which she headed every leaflet.

May 1976. I have had some manure delivered for the garden

and, since the manure heap is not far from the van, Miss S. is concerned that people passing might think the smell is coming from there. She wants me to put a notice on the gate to the effect that the smell is the manure, not her. I say no, without adding, as I could, that the manure actually smells much nicer.

I am working in the garden when Miss B., the social worker, comes with a boxful of clothes. Miss S. is reluctant to open the van door, as she is listening to *Any Answers*, but eventually she slides on her bottom to the door of the van and examines the clothes. She is unimpressed.

MISS S.: I only asked for one coat.

MISS B.: Well, I brought three just in case you wanted a change.

MISS S.: I haven't got room for three. Besides, I was planning to wash this coat in the near future. That makes four.

MISS B.: This is my old nursing mac.

MISS S.: I have a mac. Besides, green doesn't suit me. Have you got the stick?

MISS B.: No. That's being sent down. It had to be made specially.

MISS S.: Will it be long enough?

MISS B.: Yes. It's a special stick.

MISS S.: I don't want a special stick. I want an ordinary stick. Only longer. Does it have a rubber thing on it?

When Miss B. has gone, Miss S. sits at the door of the van slowly turning over the contents of the box like a chimpanzee, sniffing them and holding them up and muttering to herself.

June 1976. I am sitting on the steps mending my bike when Miss S. emerges for her evening stroll. 'I went to Devon on Saturday,' she said. 'On this frisbee.' I suppose she means freebie, a countrywide concession to pensioners that BR ran last weekend. 'Dawlish I went to. People very nice. The man over the loudspeaker called us Ladies and Gentlemen, and so he should. There was one person shouted, only he wasn't one of us – the son of somebody, I think.' And almost for the first time ever she smiled, and said how they had all been bunched up trying to get into this one carriage, a great crowd, and how she had been hoisted up. 'It would have made a film,' she said. 'I thought of you.' And she stands there in her grimy raincoat, strands of lank grey hair escaping from under her headscarf. I am thankful people had been nice to her, and wonder what the carriage must have been like all that hot afternoon. She then tells me about a programme on Francis Thompson she'd heard on the wireless, how he had tried to become a priest but had felt he had failed in his vocation, and had become a tramp. Then, unusually, she told me a little of her own life, and how she tried to become a nun on two occasions, had undergone instruction as a novice, but was forced to give it up on account of ill-health, and that she had felt for many years that she had failed. But that this was wrong, and it was not a failure. 'If I could have had more modern clothes, longer sleep and better air, possibly, I would have made it.'

'A bit of a spree,' she called her trip to Dawlish. 'My spree.'

June 1977. On this the day of the Jubilee, Miss S. has stuck a paper Union Jack in the cracked back window of the van. It is the only one in the Crescent. Yesterday she was wearing a headscarf and pinned across the front of it a blue Spontex sponge fastened at each side with a large safety pin, the sponge meant to form some kind of peak against the (very watery) sun. It looked like a favour worn by a medieval knight, or a fillet to ward off evil spirits. Still, it was better than last week's effort, an Afrika Korps cap from Lawrence Corner: Miss Shepherd – Desert Fox.

September 1979. Miss S. shows me a photograph she has taken of herself in a cubicle at Waterloo. She is very low in the frame, her mouth pulled down, the photo looking as if it has been taken after death. She is very pleased with it. 'I don't take a good photograph usually. That's the only photograph I've seen looks anything like me.' She wants two copies making of it. I say that it would be easier for her to go back to Waterloo and do two more. No – that would 'take it out of her'. 'I had one taken in France once when I was twenty-one or twenty-two. Had to go into the next village for it. I came out cross-eyed. I saw someone else's photo on their bus-pass and she'd come out looking like a nigger. You don't want to come out like a nigger if you can help it, do you?'

June 1980. Miss S. has gone into her summer rig: a raincoat turned inside out, with brown canvas panels and a large label declaring it the Emerald Weatherproof. This is topped off with a lavender chiffon scarf tied round a sun visor made from an old cornflakes packet. She asks me to do her some shopping. 'I want a small packet of Eno's, some milk and some jelly babies. The jelly babies aren't urgent. Oh and, Mr Bennett, could you get me one of those little bottles of whisky? I believe Bell's is very good. I don't drink it – I just use it to rub on.'

August 1980. I am filming, and Miss S. sees me leaving early each morning and returning late. Tonight her scrawny hand comes out with a letter marked 'Please consider carefully':

An easier way for Mr Bennett to earn could be possibly with my cooperative part. Two young men could follow me in a car, one with a camera to get a funny film like 'Old Mother Riley Joins Up' possibly. If the car stalls they could then push it. Or they could go on the buses with her at a distance. Comedy happens without trying sometimes, or at least an interesting film covering a Senior Citizen's use of the buses can occur. One day to Hounslow, another to Reading or Heathrow. The bus people ought to be pleased, but it might need their permission. Then Mr Bennett could put his feet up more and rake it in, possibly.

October 1980. Miss S. has started hankering after a caravan trailer and has just missed one she saw in Exchange and Mart: 'little net curtains all round, three bunks'. 'I wouldn't use them all, except,' she says ominously, 'to put things on. Nice little windows – £275. They said it was sold, only they may have thought I was just an old tramp . . . I was thinking of offering to help Mrs Thatcher with the economy. I wouldn't ask any money, as I'm on social security, so it would come cheap for her. I might ask her for some perks, though. Like a caravan. I would write to her but she's away. I know what's required. It's perfectly simple: Justice.'

No political party quite catered to Miss S.'s views, though the National Front came close. She was passionately anti-Communist, and as long ago as 1945 had written a letter to Jesus 'concerning the dreadful situation feared from the Yalta agreement'. The trouble was that her political opinions, while never moderate, were always tempered by her idiosyncratic view of the human physiognomy. Older was invariably wiser, which is fair if debatable, except that with Miss S. taller was wiser too. But height had its drawbacks, and it was perhaps because she was tall herself that she believed a person's height added to their burdens, put them under some strain. Hence, though she was in sympathy with Mr Heath on everything except the Common Market, 'I do think that Mr Wilson, personally, may have seen better in regard to Europe, being on the Opposition bench with less salary and being older, smaller and under less strain.' She was vehemently opposed to the Common Market – the 'common' always underlined when she wrote about it on the pavement, as if it were the sheer vulgarity of the economic union she particularly objected to. Never very lucid in her leaflets, she got especially confused over the EEC. 'Not long ago a soul wrote, or else was considering writing [she cannot recall as to which and it may have been something of either] that she disassociated from the Common Market entry and the injustices feared concerning it, or something like that.' 'Enoch', as she invariably called Mr Powell, had got it right, and she wrote him several letters telling him so, but in the absence of a wholly congenial party she founded her own, the Fidelis Party. 'It will be a party caring for Justice (and as such not needing opposition). Justice in the world today with its gigantic ignorant conduct requires the rule of a Good Dictator, possibly.'

Miss S. never regarded herself as being at the bottom of the social heap. That place was occupied by 'the desperate poor' – i.e. those with no roof over their heads. She herself was 'a cut above those in dire need', and one of her responsibilities in society she saw as interceding for them and for those whose plight she thought Mrs Thatcher had overlooked. Could it be brought to her attention (and she wrote Mrs T. several letters on the subject), alleviation would surely follow.

Occasionally she would write letters to other public figures. In August 1978 it was to the College of Cardinals, then busy electing a Pope. 'Your Eminences. I would like to suggest humbly that an older Pope might be admirable. Height can count towards knowledge too probably.' However this older (and hopefully taller) Pope she was recommending might find the ceremony a bit of a trial, so, ever the expert on headgear, she suggests that 'at the Coronation there could be a not so heavy crown, of light plastic possibly or cardboard for instance.'

February 1981. Miss S. has flu, so I am doing her shopping. I wait every morning by the side window of the van and, with the dark interior and her grimy hand holding back the tattered purple curtain, it is as if I am at the confessional. The chief items this morning are ginger nuts ('very warming') and grape juice. 'I think this is what they must have been drinking at Cana,' she says as I hand her the bottle. 'Jesus wouldn't have wanted them rolling about drunk, and this is non-alcoholic. It wouldn't do for everyone, but in my opinion it's better than champagne.'

October 1981. The curtain is drawn aside this morning and Miss S., still in what I take to be her nightclothes, talks of 'the discernment of spirits' that enabled her to sense an angelic presence near her when she was ill. At an earlier period, when she had her pitch outside the bank, she had sensed a similar angelic presence, and now, having seen his campaign leaflet, who should this turn out to be, 'possibly', but Our Conservative Candidate Mr Pasley-Tyler. She embarks on a long disquisition on her well-worn theme of age in politics. Mrs Thatcher is too young and travels too much. Not like President Reagan. 'You wouldn't catch him making all those U-turns round Australia.'

January 1982. 'Do you see he's been found, that American soldier?' This is Colonel Dozo, kidnapped by the Red Brigade and found after a shoot-out in a flat in Padua. 'Yes, he's been found,' she says triumphantly, 'and I know who found him.' Thinking it unlikely she has an acquaintance in the Italian version of the SAS, I ask whom she means. 'St Anthony of course. The patron saint of lost things. St Anthony of Padua.' 'Well,' I want to say, 'he didn't have far to look.'

May 1982. As I am leaving for Yorkshire, Miss S.'s hand comes out like the Ancient Mariner's: do I know if there are any steps at Leeds station? 'Why?' I ask warily, thinking she may be having thoughts of camping on my other doorstep. It turns out she just wants somewhere to go for a ride, so I suggest Bristol. 'Yes, I've been to Bristol. On the way back I came through Bath. That looked nice. Some beautifully parked cars.' She then recalls driving her reconditioned army vehicles and taking them up to Derbyshire. 'I did it in the war,' she says. 'Actually I overdid it in the war,' and somehow that is the thin end of the wedge that has landed her up here, yearning for travel on this May morning forty years later.

'Land' is a word Miss S. prefers to 'country'. 'This land . . .' Used in this sense, it's part of the rhetoric if not of madness at any rate of obsession. Jehovah's Witnesses talk of 'this land', and the National Front. Land is country plus destiny – country in the sight of God. Mrs Thatcher talks of 'this land'.

February 1983. A. telephones me in Yorkshire to say that the basement is under three inches of water, the boiler having burst. When told that the basement has been flooded, Miss S.'s only comment is 'What a waste of water'.

April 1983. 'I've been having bad nights,' says Miss S., 'but if I were elected I might have better nights.' She wants me to get her nomination papers so that she can stand for Parliament in the coming election. She would be the Fidelis Party candidate. The party, never very numerous, is now considerably reduced.

Once she could count on five votes but now there are only two, one of whom is me, and I don't like to tell her I'm in the SDP. Still, I promise to write to the town hall for nomination papers. 'There's no kitty as yet,' she says, 'and I wouldn't want to do any of the meeting people. I'd be no good at that. The secretaries can do that (you get expenses). But I'd be very good at voting – better than they are, probably.'

May 1983. Miss S. asks me to witness her signature on the nomination form. 'I'm signing,' she says: 'are you witnessing?' She has approached various nuns to be her nominees. 'One sister I know would have signed but I haven't seen her for some years and she's got rather confused in the interim. I don't know what I'll do about leaflets. It would have to be an economy job – I couldn't run to the expense. Maybe I'll just write my manifesto on the pavement; that goes round like wildfire.'

May 1983. Miss S. has received her nomination papers. 'What should I describe myself as?' she asks through the window slit. 'I thought Elderly Spinster, possibly. It also says Title. Well my title is' – and she laughs one of her rare laughs – 'Mrs Shepherd. That's what some people call me out of politeness. And I don't deny it. Mother Teresa always says she's married to God. I could say I was married to the Good Shepherd, and that's what it's to do with, Parliament, looking after the flock. When I'm elected, do you think I shall have to live in Downing Street or could I run things from the van?'

I speak to her later in the day and the nomination business is beginning to get her down. 'Do you know anything about the Act of 1974? It refers to disqualifications under it. Anyway, it's all giving me a headache. I think there may be another election soon after this one, so it'll have been good preparation anyway.'

June 1984. Miss S. has been looking in *Exchange and Mart* again and has answered an advert for a white Morris Minor. 'It's the kind of car I'm used to – or I used to be used to. I feel the need to be mobile.' I raise the matter of a licence and insurance, which she always treats as tiresome formalities. 'What you don't understand is that I am insured. I am insured in heaven.' She claims that since she had been insured in heaven there has not been a scratch on the van. I point out that this is less to do with the celestial insurance than with the fact that the van is parked the whole time in my garden. She concedes that when she was on the road the van did used to get the occasional knock. 'Somebody came up behind me once and scratched the van. I wanted him to pay something – half-a-crown I think it was. He wouldn't.'

October 1984. Some new staircarpet fitted today. Spotting the old carpet being thrown out, Miss S. says it would be just the thing to put on the roof of the van to deaden the sound of rain. This exchange comes just as I am leaving for work, but I say that I do not want the van festooned with bits of old carpet – it looks bad enough as it is. When I come back in the evening I find half the carpet remnants slung over the roof. I ask Miss S. who has put them there, as she can't have done it herself. 'A friend,' she says mysteriously. 'A well-wisher.' Enraged, I pull down a token piece but the majority of it stays put.

April 1985. Miss S. has written to Mrs Thatcher applying for a post in 'the Ministry of Transport advisory, to do with drink and driving and that'. She also shows me the text of a letter she is proposing to send to the Argentinian Embassy on behalf of General Galtieri. 'What he doesn't understand is that Mrs Thatcher isn't the Iron Lady. It's me.'

To Someone in Charge of Argentina. 19 April 1985

Dear Sir,

I am writing to help mercy towards the poor general who led your forces in the war actually as a person of true knowledge more than might be. I was concerned with Justice, Love and, in a manner of speaking, I was in the war, as it were, shaking hands with your then leader, welcoming him in spirit (it may have been to do with love of Catholic education for Malvinas for instance) greatly meaning kindly negotiators etc. ... but I fear that he may have thought it was Mrs Thatcher welcoming him in that way and it may hence have unduly influenced him.

Therefore I beg you to have mercy on him indeed. Let him go, reinstate him, if feasible. You may read publicly this letter if you wish to explain mercy etc.

I remain.

Yours truly

    A Member of the Fidelis Party

      (Servants of Justice)

P.S. Others may have contributed to undue influence also.

P.P.S. Possibly without realizing it.

Translate into Argentinian if you shd wish.

Sometime in 1980 Miss S. acquired a car, but before she'd managed to have more than a jaunt or two in it ('It's a real goer!') it
was stolen and later found stripped and abandoned in the basement of the council flats in Maiden Lane. I went to collect what
was left ('though the police may require it for evidence, possibly') and found that even in the short time she'd had the Mini
she'd managed to stuff it with the usual quota of plastic bags,
kitchen rolls and old blankets, all plentifully doused in talcum
powder. When she got a Reliant Robin in 1984 it was much the
same, a second wardrobe as much as a second car. Miss
Shepherd could afford to splash out on these vehicles because
being parked in the garden meant that she had a permanent
address, and so qualified for full social security and its various
allowances. Since her only outgoings were on food, she was
able to put by something and had an account in the Halifax and
quite a few savings certificates. Indeed I heard people passing
say, 'You know she's a millionaire,' the inference being no one
in their right mind would let her live there if she weren't.

    Her Reliant saw more action than the Mini, and she would
tootle off in it on a Sunday morning, park on Primrose Hill

('The air is better'), and even got as far as Hounslow. More often than not, though, she was happy (and I think she was happy then) just to sit in the Reliant and rev the engine. However, since she generally chose to do this first thing on Sunday morning, it didn't endear her to the neighbours. Besides, what she described as 'a lifetime with motors' had failed to teach her was that revving a car does not charge the battery, so that when it regularly ran down I had to take it out and recharge it, knowing full well this would just mean more revving. ('No,' she insisted, 'I may be going to Cornwall next week, possibly.') This recharging of the battery wasn't really the issue: I was just ashamed to be seen delving under the bonnet of such a joke car.

March 1987. The nuns up the road – or, as Miss S. always refers to them, 'the sisters' – have taken to doing some of her shopping. One of them leaves a bag on the back step of the van this morning. There are the inevitable ginger nuts, and several packets of sanitary towels. I can see these would be difficult articles for her to ask me to get, though to ask a nun to get them would seem quite hard for her too. They form some part of her elaborate toilet arrangements, and are occasionally to be seen laid drying across the soup-encrusted electric ring. As the postman says this morning, 'The smell sometimes knocks you back a bit.'

May 1987. Miss S. wants to spread a blanket over the roof (in addition to the bit of carpet) in order to deaden the sound of the rain. I point out that within a few weeks it will be dank and disgusting. 'No,' she says, '– weather-beaten.'

She has put a Conservative poster in the side window of the van. The only person who can see it is me.

This morning she was sitting at the open door of the van and as I edge by she chucks out an empty packet of Ariel. The blanket hanging over the pushchair is covered in washing powder. 'Have you spilt it?' I inquire. 'No,' she says crossly, irritated at having to explain the obvious. 'That's washing powder. When it rains, the blanket will get washed.' As I work at my table now I can see her bending over the pushchair, picking at bits of soap flakes and redistributing them over the blanket. No rain is at the moment forecast.

June 1987. Miss S. has persuaded the social services to allocate her a wheelchair, though what she's really set her heart on is the electric version.

MISS S.: That boy over the road has one. Why not me?

ME: He can't walk.

MISS S: How does he know? He hasn't tried.

ME: Miss Shepherd, he has spina bifida.

MISS S: Well, I was round-shouldered as a child. That may not be serious now, but it was quite serious then. I've gone through two wars, an infant in the first and not on full rations, in the ambulances in the second, besides being failed by the ATS. Why should old people be disregarded?

Thwarted in her ambition for a powered chair, Miss S. compensated by acquiring (I never found out where from) a second wheelchair ('in case the other conks out, possibly'). The full inventory of her wheeled vehicles now read: one van; one Reliant Robin; two wheelchairs; one folding pushchair; one folding (two-seater) pushchair. Now and again I would thin out the pushchairs by smuggling one on to a skip. She would put down this disappearance to children (never a favourite), and the number would shortly be made up by yet another wheelie from Reg's junk stall. Miss S. never mastered the technique of self-propulsion in the wheelchair because she refused to use the inner handwheel ('I can't be doing with all that silliness'). Instead, she preferred to punt herself along with two walking sticks, looking in the process rather like a skier on the flat. Eventually I had to remove the handwheel ('The extra weight affects my health').

July 1987. Miss S. (bright green visor, purple skirt, brown cardigan, turquoise fluorescent ankle socks) punts her way out through the gate in the wheelchair in a complicated manoeuvre which would be much simplified did she just push the chair out, as well she can. A passer-by takes pity on her, and she is whisked down to the market. Except not quite whisked, because the journey is made more difficult than need be by Miss S.'s refusal to take her feet off the ground, so the Good Samaritan finds himself pushing a wheelchair continually slurred and braked by these large, trailing, carpet-slippered feet. Her legs are so thin now the feet are as slack and flat as those of a camel.

Still, there will be one moment to relish on this, as on all these journeys. When she had been pushed back from the market, she will tell (and it is tell: there is never any thanks) whoever is pushing the chair to leave her opposite the gate but on the crown of the road. Then, when she thinks no one is looking, she lifts her feet, pushes herself off, and freewheels the few yards down to the gate. The look on her face is one of pure pleasure.

October 1987. I have been filming abroad. 'When you were in Yugoslavia,' asks Miss S., 'did you come across the Virgin Mary?' 'No,' I say, 'I don't think so.' 'Oh, well, she's appearing there. She's been appearing there every day for several years.' It's as if I've missed the major tourist attraction.

January 1988. I ask Miss S. if it was her birthday yesterday. She agrees guardedly. 'So you're seventy-seven.' 'Yes. How did you know?' 'I saw it once when you filled out the census form.' I give her a bottle of whisky, explaining that it's just to rub on. 'Oh. Thank you.' Pause. 'Mr Bennett. Don't tell anybody.' 'About the whisky?' 'No. About my birthday.' Pause. 'Mr Bennett.' 'Yes?' 'About the whisky either.'

March 1988. 'I've been doing a bit of spring cleaning,' says Miss S., kneeling in front of a Kienholz-like tableau of filth and decay. She says she has been discussing the possibility of a bungalow with the social worker, to which she would be prepared to contribute 'a few hundred or so'. It's possible that the bungalow might be made of asbestos, 'but I could wear a mask. I wouldn't mind that, and of course it would be much better from the fire point of view.' Hands in mittens made from old socks, a sanitary towel drying over the ring, and a glossy leaflet from the Halifax offering 'fabulous investment opportunities'.

April 1988. Miss S. asks me to get Tom M. to take a photograph of her for her new bus-pass. 'That would make a comedy, you know – sitting on a bus and your bus-pass out of date. You could make a fortune out of that with very little work involved, possibly. I was a born tragedian,' she says, 'or a comedian possibly. One or the other anyway. But I didn't realise it at the time. Big feet.' She pushes out her red, unstockinged ankles. 'Big hands.' The fingers stained brown. 'Tall. People trip over me. That's comedy. I wish they didn't, of course. I'd like it easier, but there it is. I'm not suggesting you do it,' she says hastily, feeling perhaps she's come too near self-revelation, 'only it might make people laugh.' All of this is said with a straight face and no hint of a smile, sitting in the wheelchair with her hands pressed between her knees and her baseball cap on.

May 1988. Miss S. sits in her wheelchair in the road, paintpot in hand, dabbing at the bodywork of the Reliant, which she will shortly enter, start, and rev for a contented half-hour before switching off and paddling down the road in her wheelchair. She has been nattering at Tom M. to mend the clutch, but there are conditions. It mustn't be on Sunday, which is the feast of St Peter and St Paul and a day of obligation. Nor can it be the following Sunday apparently, through the Feast of the Assumption falling on the Monday and being transferred back to the previous day. Amid all the chaos of her life and now, I think, more or less incontinent, she trips with fanatical precision through this liturgical minefield.

September 1988. Miss S. has started thinking about a flat again, though not the one the council offered her a few years ago. This time she has her eye on something much closer to home. My home. We had been talking outside, and I left her sitting on the step in the hall while I came back to work. This is often what happens: me sitting at my table, wanting to get on, Miss S. sitting outside rambling. This time she goes on talking about the flat, soliloquising almost, but knowing that I can hear. 'It need only be a little flat, even a room possibly. Of course, I can't manage stairs, so it would have to be on the ground floor. Though I'd pay to have a lift put in.' (Louder.) 'And the lift wouldn't be wasted. They'd have it for their old age. And they'll have to be thinking about their old age quite soon.' The tone of it is somehow familiar from years ago. Then I realise it's like one of the meant-to-be-overheard soliloquies of Richmal Crompton's William.

Her outfit this morning: orange skirt, made out of three or four large dusters; a striped blue satin jacket; a green headscarf – blue eyeshield topped off by a khaki peaked cap with a skull-and-crossbones badge and Rambo across the peak.

February 1989. Miss S.'s religion is an odd mixture of traditional faith and a belief in the power of positive thinking. This morning, as ever, the Reliant battery is running low and she asks me to fix it. The usual argument takes place:

ME: Well, of course it's run down. It will run down unless you run the car. Revving up doesn't charge it. The wheels have to go round.

MISS S.: Stop talking like that. This car is not the same. There are miracles. There is faith. Negative thoughts don't help. (*She presses the starter again and it coughs weakly.*) There, you see. The devil's heard you. You shouldn't say negative things.

The interior of the van now indescribable.

March 1989. Miss S. sits in the wheelchair trying to open the sneck of the gate with her walking-stick. She tries it with one end, then reverses the stick and tries with the other. Sitting at my table, trying to work, I watch her idly, much as one would watch an ant trying to get round some obstacle. Now she bangs on the gate to attract the attention of a passer-by. Now she is wailing. Banging and wailing. I go out. She stops wailing, and explains she has her washing to do. As I manoeuvre her through the gate, I ask her if she's fit to go. Yes, only she will need help. I explain that I can't push her there. (Why can't I?) No, she doesn't want that. Would I just push her as far as the corner? I do so. Would I just push her a bit further? I explain that I can't take her to the launderette. (And anyway there is no launderette any more, so which launderette is she going to?) Eventually, feeling like Fletcher Christian (only not

Christian) abandoning Captain Bligh, I leave her in the wheel-chair outside Mary H.'s. Someone will come along. I would be more ashamed if I did not feel, even when she is poorly, that she knows exactly what she's about.

March 1989. There is a thin layer of talcum powder around the back door of the van and odd bits of screwed-up tissues smeared with what may or may not be shit, though there is no doubt about the main item of litter, which is a stained inconti-nence pad. My method of retrieving these items would not be unfamiliar at Sellafield. I don rubber gloves, put each hand inside a plastic bag as an additional protection, then, having swept the faecal artefacts together, gingerly pick them up and put them in the bin. 'Those aren't all my rubbish,' comes a voice from the van. 'Some of them blow in under the gate.'

April 1989. Miss S. has asked me to telephone the social ser-vices, and I tell her that a social worker will be calling. 'What time?' 'I don't know. But you're not going to be out. You haven't been out for a week.' 'I might be. Miracles do happen. Besides, she may not be able to talk to me. I may not be at the door end of the van. I might be at the other end.' 'So she can talk to you there.' 'And what if I'm in the middle?'

Miss C. thinks her heart is failing. She calls her Mary. I find this strange, though it is of course her name.

April 1989. A staple of Miss S.'s shopping-list these days is sherbet lemons. I have a stock of them in the house, but she insists I invest in yet more so that a perpetual supply of sherbet lemons may never be in doubt. 'I'm on them now. I don't want to have to go off them.'

I ask her if she would like a cup of coffee. 'Well, I wouldn't want you to go to all that trouble. I'll just have half a cup.'

Towards the end of her life Miss S. was befriended by an ex-nurse who lived locally. She put me in touch with a day centre who agreed to take Miss Shepherd in, give her a bath and a medical examination and even a bed in a single room where she could stay if she wanted. In retrospect I see I should have done something on the same lines years before, except that it was only when age and illness had weakened Miss Shepherd that she would accept such help. Even then it was not easy.

27 April 1989. A red ambulance calls to take Miss S. to the day centre. Miss B. talks to her for a while in the van, gradually coaxing her out and into the wheelchair, shit streaks over her swollen feet, a piece of toilet roll clinging to one scaly ankle. 'And if I don't like it,' she keeps asking, 'can I come back?' I reassure her, but, looking at the inside of the van and trying to cope with the stench, I find it hard to see how she can go on living here much longer. Once she sees the room they are offering her, the bath, the clean sheets, I can't imagine her wanting to come back. And indeed she makes more fuss than usual about locking the van door, which suggests she accepts that she may not be returning. I note how, with none of my distaste, the ambulance driver bends over her as he puts her on

the hoist, his careful rearrangement of her greasy clothing, pulling her skirt down over her knees in the interests of modesty. The chair goes on the hoist, and slowly she rises and comes into view above the level of the garden wall and is wheeled into the ambulance. There is a certain distinction about her as she leaves, a Dorothy Hodgkin of vagabonds, a derelict Nobel Prize-winner, the heavy folds of her grimy face set in a kind of resigned satisfaction. She may even be enjoying herself.

When she has gone I walk round the van noting the occasions of our battle: the carpet tiles she managed to smuggle on to the roof, the blanket strapped on to muffle the sound of the rain, the black bags under the van stuffed with her old clothes – sites of skirmishes all of which I'd lost. Now I imagine her bathed and bandaged and cleanly clothed and starting a new life. I even see myself visiting and taking flowers.

This fantasy rapidly fades when around 2.30 Miss S. reappears, washed and in clean clothes, it's true, and with a long pair of white hospital socks over her shrunken legs, but obviously very pleased to be back. She has a telephone number where her new friends can be contacted, and she gives it to me. 'They can be reached,' she says, 'any time – even over the holiday. They're on a long-distance bleep.'

As I am leaving for the theatre, she bangs on the door of the van with her stick. I open the door. She is lying wrapped in clean white sheets on a quilt laid over all the accumulated filth and rubbish of the van. She is still worrying that I will have her taken to hospital. I tell her there's no question of it and that she can stay as long as she wants. I close the door, but there is another bang and I reassure her again. Once more I close the door, but she bangs again. 'Mr Bennett.' I have to strain to hear. 'I'm sorry the van's in such a state. I haven't been able to do any spring cleaning.'

28 April. I am working at my table when I see Miss B. arrive with a pile of clean clothes for Miss Shepherd, which must have been washed for her at the day centre yesterday. Miss B. knocks at the door of the van, then opens it, looks inside and – something nobody has ever done before – gets in. It's only a moment before she comes out, and I know what has happened before she rings the bell. We go back to the van where Miss Shepherd is dead, lying on her left side, flesh cold, face gaunt, the neck stretched out as if for the block, and a bee buzzing round her body.

It is a beautiful day, with the garden glittering in the sunshine, strong shadows by the nettles, and bluebells out under the wall, and I remember how in her occasional moments of contemplation she would sit in the wheelchair and gaze at the garden. I am filled with remorse for my harsh conduct towards her, though I know at the same time that it was not harsh. But still I never quite believed or chose to believe she was as ill as she was, and I regret too all the questions I never asked her. Not that she would have answered them. I have a strong impulse to stand at the gate and tell anyone who passes.

Miss B. meanwhile goes off and returns with a nice doctor from St Pancras who seems scarcely out of her teens. She gets into the van, takes the pulse in Miss S.'s outstretched neck, checks her with a stethoscope and, to save an autopsy, certifies death as from heart failure. Then comes the priest to bless her before she is taken to the funeral parlour, and he, too, gets into the van – the third person to do so this morning, and all of them without distaste or ado in what to me seem three small acts of heroism. Stooping over the body, his bright white hair brushing the top of the van, the priest murmurs an inaudible prayer and makes a cross on Miss S.'s hands and head. Then they all go off and I come inside to wait for the undertakers.

I have been sitting at my table for ten minutes before I realise that the undertakers have been here all the time, and that death nowadays comes (or goes) in a grey Ford transit van that is standing outside the gate. There are three undertakers, two young and burly, the third older and more experienced – a sergeant, as it were, and two corporals. They bring out a rough grey-painted coffin, like a prop a conjuror might use, and, making no comment on the surely extraordinary circumstances in which they find it, put a sheet of white plastic bin-liner over the body and manhandle it into their magic box, where it falls with a bit of a thud. Across the road, office workers stroll down from the Piano Factory for their lunch, but nobody stops or even looks much, and the Asian woman who has to wait while the box is carried over the pavement and put in the (other) van doesn't give it a backward glance.

Later I go round to the undertakers to arrange the funeral, and the manager apologises for their response when I had originally phoned. A woman had answered, saying, 'What exactly is it you want?' Not thinking callers rang undertakers with a great variety of requests, I was nonplussed. Then she said briskly, 'Do you want someone taking away?' The undertaker explains that her seemingly unhelpful manner was because she thought my call wasn't genuine. 'We get so many hoaxes these days. I've often gone round to collect a corpse only to have it open the door.'

9 May. Miss Shepherd's funeral is at Our Lady of Hal, the Catholic church round the corner. The service has been slotted into the ten o'clock mass, so that, in addition to a contingent of neighbours, the congregation includes what I take to be regulars: the fat little man in thick glasses and trainers who hobbles along to the church every day from Arlington House; several nuns, among them the ninety-nine-year-old sister who was in charge when Miss S. was briefly a novice; a woman in a green straw hat like an upturned plant pot who eats toffees throughout; and another lady who plays the harmonium in tan slacks and a tea-cosy wig. The server, a middle-aged man with white hair, doesn't wear a surplice, just ordinary clothes with an open-necked shirt, and, but for knowing all the sacred drill, might have been roped in from the group on the corner outside The Good Mixer. The priest is a young Irish boy with a big, red peasant face and sandy hair, and he, too, stripped of his cream-coloured cassock, could be wielding a pneumatic drill in the roadworks outside. I keep thinking about these characters during the terrible service, and it reinforces what I

have always known: that I could never be a Catholic because I'm such a snob, and that the biggest sacrifice Newman made when he turned his back on the C of E was the social one.

Yet kindness abounds. In front of us is a thin old man who knows the service backwards, and seeing we have no prayer books he lays down his own on top of his copy of the *Sun*, goes back up the aisle to fetch us some, and hands them round, all the time saying the responses without faltering. The first hymn is Newman's 'Lead Kindly Light', which I try and sing, while making no attempt at the second hymn, which is 'Kum Ba Ya'. The priest turns out to have a good strong voice, though its tone is more suited to 'Kum Ba Ya' than to Newman and J. B. Dykes. The service itself is wet and wandering, even more so than the current Anglican equivalent, though occasionally one catches in the watered-down language a distant echo of 1662. Now, though, arrives the bit I dread, the celebration of fellowship, which always reminds me of the warm-up Ned Sherrin insisted on inflicting on the studio audience before *Not So Much a Programme*, when everyone had to shake hands with their neighbour. But again the nice man who fetched us the prayer books shames me when he turns round without any fuss or embarrassment and smilingly shakes my hand. Then it is the mass proper, the priest distributing the wafers to the ninety-nine-year-old nun and the lady with the plant pot on her head, as Miss S. lies in her coffin at his elbow. Finally there is another hymn, this one by the (to me) unknown hymnodist Kevin Norton, who's obviously reworked it from his unsuccessful entry for the Eurovision

Song Contest; and with the young priest acting as lead singer, and the congregation a rather subdued backing group, Miss Shepherd is carried out.

The neighbours, who are not quite mourners, wait on the pavement outside as the coffin is hoisted on to the hearse. 'A cut above her previous vehicle,' remarks Colin H.; and comedy persists when the car accompanying the hearse to the cemetery refuses to start. It's a familiar scene, and one which I've played many times, with Miss S. waiting inside her vehicle as wellwishers lift the bonnet, fetch leads and give it a jump start. Except this time she's dead.

Only A. and I and Clare, the ex-nurse who lately befriended Miss S., accompany the body, swept around Hampstead Heath at a less than funereal pace, down Bishop's Avenue and up to the St Pancras Cemetery, green and lush this warm, sunny day. We drive beyond the scattered woods to the furthest edge where stand long lines of new gravestones, mostly in black polished granite. Appropriately, in view of her lifelong love of the car, Miss S. is being buried within sight and sound of the North Circular Road, one carriageway the other side of the hedge, with juggernauts drowning the words of the priest as he commits the body to the earth. He gives us each a go with his little plastic bottle of holy water, we throw some soil into the grave, and then everybody leaves me to whatever solitary thoughts I might have, which are not many, before we are driven back to Camden Town – life reasserted when the undertaker drops us handily outside Sainsbury's.

In the interval between Miss Shepherd's death and her funeral ten days later I found out more about her life than I had in twenty years. She had indeed driven ambulances during the war, and was either blown up or narrowly escaped death when a bomb exploded nearby. I'm not sure that her eccentricity can be put down to this any more than to the legend, mentioned by one of the nuns, that it was the death of her fiancé in this incident that 'tipped her over'. It would be comforting to think that it is love, or the death of it, that imbalances the mind, but I think her early attempts to become a nun and her repeated failures ('too argumentative', one of the sisters said) point to a personality that must already have been quite awkward when she was a girl. After the war she spent some time in mental hospitals, but regularly absconded, finally remaining at large long enough to establish her competence to live unsupervised.

The turning-point in her life came when, through no fault of hers, a motorcyclist crashed into the side of her van. If her other vans were any guide, this one too would only have been insured in heaven, so it's not surprising she left the scene of the accident ('skedaddled', she would have said) without giving her name or address. The motorcyclist subsequently died, so that, while blameless in the accident, by leaving the scene of it she had committed a criminal offence. The police mounted a search for her. Having already changed her first name when she became a novice, now under very different circumstances she changed her second and, calling herself Shepherd, made her way back to Camden Town and the vicinity of the convent where she had taken her vows. And though in the years to come she had little to do with the nuns, or they with her, she was never to stray far from the convent for the rest of her life.

All this I learned in those last few days. It was as if she had been a character in Dickens whose history has to be revealed and her secrets told in the general setting-to-rights before the happy-ever-after, though all that this amounted to was that at long last I could bring my car into the garden to stand now where the van stood all those years.

POSTSCRIPT (1994)

This account of Miss Shepherd condenses some of the many entries to do with her that are scattered through my diaries. Unemphasised in the text (though deducible from the dates of the entries) is the formality of her last days. The Sunday before she died she attended mass, which she had not done for many months; on the Wednesday morning she allowed herself to be taken to be bathed and given clean clothes and then put to bed in the van on clean sheets; and that same night she died. The progression seemed so neat that I felt, when I first wrote it up, that to emphasise it would cast doubt on the truth of my account, or at least make it seem sentimental or melodramatic. However, the doctor who pronounced Miss Shepherd dead said that she had known other deaths in similar circumstances; that it was not (as I had facetiously wondered) the bath that had killed her but that to allow herself to be washed and put into clean clothes was both a preparation and an acknowledgement that death was in the offing.

Nor is it plain from the original account how in the period after her death I got to know the facts of her life that she had so long concealed. A few months before, a bout of flu must have made her think about putting her affairs in order and she had shown me an envelope that I might need 'in case anything happens to me, possibly'. I would find the envelope in the place under the banquette where she kept her savings books and other papers. What the envelope contained she did not say, and, when in due course she got over the flu and struggled on, nothing more was said about it.

It was about this time, though, that I had the first and only hint that her name might not be her own. She had, I knew, some money in the Abbey National, and periodically their bright brochures would come through my door – young and happy home-owners pictured gaily striding across their first threshold and entering upon a life of mortgaged bliss.

'Some post, Miss Shepherd.' I would knock on the window and wait for the scrawny hand to come out (nails long and grey; fingers ochre-stained as if she had been handling clay). The brochure would be drawn back into the dim and fetid interior, where it would be a while before it was opened, the packet turned over and over in her dubious hands, the Society's latest exciting offer waiting until she was sure it was not from the IRA. 'Another bomb, possibly. They've heard my views.'

In 1988 the Abbey National were preparing to turn themselves from a building society into a bank, a proposal to which Miss Shepherd for some reason (novelty, possibly) was very much opposed. Before filling in her ballot form, she asked me (and she was careful to couch the question impersonally) if a vote would be valid had the purchaser of the shares changed their name. I said, fairly obviously, that if the shares had been bought in one name then it would be in order to vote in that name. 'Why?' I asked. But I should have known better, and, as so often, having given a teasing hint of some revelation, she refused to follow it up, just shook her head mutely, and

snapped shut the window. Except (and this was standard pro-
cedure too) as I was passing the van next day her hand came
out.

'Mr Bennett. What I said about change of name, don't mention it to anybody. It was just in theory, possibly.'

For some days after Miss Shepherd's death I left the van as
it was, not from piety or anything to do with decorum but
because I couldn't face getting into it, and though I put on a
new padlock I made no attempt to extract her bank books or
locate the necessary envelope. But the news had got round,
and when one afternoon I came home to find a scrap dealer
nosing about I realised I had to grit my teeth (or hold my nose)
and go through Miss Shepherd's possessions.

To do the job properly would have required a team of
archaeologists. Every surface was covered in layers of old
clothes, frocks, blankets and accumulated papers, some of
them undisturbed for years and all lying under a crust of
ancient talcum powder. Sprinkled impartially over wet slippers, used incontinence pads and half-eaten tins of baked
beans, it was of a virulence that supplemented rather than
obliterated the distinctive odour of the van. The narrow aisle
between the two banks of seats where Miss Shepherd had
knelt, prayed and slept was trodden six inches deep in sodden
debris, on which lay a top dressing of old food, Mr Kipling
cakes, wrinkled apples, rotten oranges and everywhere batteries – batteries loose, batteries in packets, batteries that had
split and oozed black gum on to the prehistoric sponge cakes
and ubiquitous sherbet lemons that they lay among. A hand-

kerchief round my face, I lifted one of the banquettes where in the hollow beneath she had told me her bank books were hidden. The underside of the seat was alive with moths and maggots, but the books were there, together with other documents she considered valuable: an MOT certificate for her Reliant, long expired; a receipt for some repairs to it done three years before; an offer of a fortnight of sun and sea in the Seychelles that came with some car wax. What there was not was the envelope. So there was nothing for it but to excavate the van, to go through the festering debris in the hope of finding the note she had promised to leave, and with it perhaps her history.

Searching the van, I was not just looking for the envelope; sifting the accumulated refuse of fifteen years, I was hoping for some clue as to what it was that had happened to make Miss Shepherd want to live like this. Except that I kept coming across items that suggested that living 'like this' wasn't all that different from the way people ordinarily lived. There was a set of matching kitchen utensils, for instance – a ladle, a spatula, a masher for potatoes – all of them unused. They were the kind of thing my mother bought and hung up in the kitchen, just for show, while she went on using the battered old-faithfuls kept in the knife drawer. There were boxes of cheap soap and, of course, talcum powder, the cellophane wrapping unbreached; they too had counterparts in the dressing-table drawer at home. Another item my mother hoarded was toilet rolls, and here were a dozen. There was a condiment set, still in its box. When, amid such chaos, can she have hoped to use that particular appurtenance of gentility? But when did we ever use ours, stuck permanently in the sideboard cupboard in readiness for the social life my parents never had or ever really wanted? The more I laboured, the less peculiar the van seemed – its proprieties and aspirations no different from those with which I had been brought up.

There was cash here too. In a bag Miss Shepherd carried round her neck there had been nearly £500, and peeling off the soggy layers from the van floor I collected about £100 more. Taking into account the money in various building societies and her National Savings certificates, Miss Shepherd had managed to save some £6,000. Since she was not entitled to a pension, most of this must have been gleaned from the meagre allowance she got from the DHSS. I am not sure whether under the present regime she would have been praised for her thrift or singled out as a sponger. Arch-Tory though she was, she seems a prime candidate for Mr Lilley's little list, a paid-up member of the Something for Nothing society. I would just like to have seen him tell her so.

Modest though Miss Shepherd's estate was, it was more than I'd been expecting and made the finding of the envelope more urgent. So I went through the old clothes again, this time feeling gingerly in the pockets and shaking out the greasy blankets in a blizzard of moth and 'French Fern'. But there was nothing, only her bus-pass, the grim photograph looking as if it were taken during the siege of Stalingrad and hardly auguring well for the comedy series she had once suggested I write on the subject. I was about to give up, having decided that she must have kept the envelope on her and that it had been taken away with the body, when I came upon it, stiff with old soup and tucked into the glove compartment along with another cache of batteries and sherbet lemons, and marked 'Mr Bennett, if necessary'.

Still looking for some explanation ('I am like this, possibly, because ...'), I opened the envelope. True to form, even in this her final communication Miss Shepherd wasn't prepared to give away any more than she had to. There was just a man's name, which was not her own, and a phone number in Sussex.

I finished cleaning out the van, scraped down the aisle, and opened all the windows and doors so that for the first time since she had moved in it was almost sweet-smelling – only not, because sweet in an awful way was how she had made it smell. My neighbour, the artist David Gentleman, who ten years before had done a lightning sketch of Miss Shepherd watching the removal of an earlier van, now came and did a romantic drawing of this her last vehicle, the grass growing high around it and the tattered curtains blowing in the spring breeze.

2 May 1989. This afternoon comes a rather dapper salvage man who, fifteen years ago, refused to execute a council order for the removal of one of Miss Shepherd's earlier vans on the grounds that someone was living in it. So he says anyway, though it's perhaps just to establish his claim. He stands there on the doorstep, maybe waiting to see if I am going to mention a price; I wait too, wondering if he is going to mention a charge. Silence on both sides seems to indicate that the

transaction is over with no payment on either side, and within the hour he is back with his lifting-gear. Tom M. takes photographs as the van is hauled like an elephant's carcass through the gate and up the ramp, the miraculous tyres still happily inflated; the salvage man scrawls 'On Tow' in the thick dirt on the windscreen; stood by the bonnet I pose for a final photograph (which doesn't come out); and the van goes off for the last time up the Crescent, leaving the drive feeling as wide and empty as the Piazza San Marco.

5 May 1989. 'Mr Bennett?' The voice is a touch military and quite sharp, though with no accent to speak of and nothing to indicate this a man who must be over eighty. 'You've sent me a letter about a Miss Shepherd, who seems to have died in your drive. I have to tell you I have no knowledge of such a person.' A bit nonplussed, I describe Miss Shepherd and her circumstances and give her date of birth. There is a slight pause.

'Yes. Well it's obviously my sister.'

He tells me her history and how, returning from Africa just after the war, he found her persecuting their mother, telling her how wicked she was and what she should and shouldn't eat, the upshot being that he finally had his sister committed to a mental hospital in Hayward's Heath. He gives her subsequent history, or as much of it as he knows, saying that the last time he had seen her was three years ago. He's direct and straightforward and doesn't disguise the fact that he feels guilty – about having her committed yet cannot see how he could have done otherwise, how they never got on, and how he cannot see how I have managed to put up with her all these years. I tell him about the money, slightly expecting him to change his tune and stress how close they had really been. But not a bit of it. Since they hadn't got on he wants none of it, saying I should have it. When I disclaim it too, he tells me to give it to charity.

Anna Haycraft (Alice Thomas Ellis) had mentioned Miss S.'s death in her *Spectator* column, and I tell him about this, really to show that his sister did have a place in people's affections and wasn't simply a cantankerous old woman. 'Cantankerous is not the word,' he says, and laughs. I sense a wife there, and after I put the phone down I imagine them mulling over the call.

I mull it over too, wondering at the bold life she has had and how it contrasts with my own timid way of going on – living, as Camus said, slightly the opposite of expressing. And I see how the location of Miss Shepherd and the van in front but to the side of where I write is the location of most of the stuff I write about; that too is to the side and never what faces me.

Over a year later, finding myself near the village in Sussex where Mr F. lived, I telephoned and asked if I could call. In the meantime I'd written about Miss Shepherd in the *London Review of Books* and broadcast a series of talks about her on Radio 4.

17 June 1990. Mr and Mrs F. live in a little bungalow in a modern estate just off the main road. I suppose it was because of

the unhesitating fashion in which he'd turned down her legacy that I was expecting something grander; in fact Mrs F. is disabled and their circumstances are obviously quite modest, which makes his refusal more creditable than I'd thought. From his phone manner I'd been expecting someone brisk and businesslike, but he's a plumpish, jolly man, and both he and his wife are full of laughs. They give me some lovely cake, which he's baked (Mrs F. being crippled with arthritis) and then patiently answer my questions.

The most interesting revelation is that as a girl Miss S. was a talented pianist and had studied in Paris under Cortot, who had told her she should have a concert career. Her decision to become a nun put an end to the piano, 'and that can't have helped her state of mind,' says Mr F.

He recalls her occasional visits, when she would never come in by the front door but lope across the field at the back of the house and climb over the fence. She never took any notice of Mrs F., suspecting, rightly, that women were likely to be less tolerant of her than men.

He says all the fiancé stuff, which came via the nuns, is nonsense; she had no interest in men, and never had. When she was in the ambulance service she used to be ribbed by the other drivers, who asked her once why she had never married. She drew herself up and said, 'Because I've never found the man who could satisfy me.' Mystified by their laughter she went home and told her mother, who laughed too.

Mr F. has made no secret of the situation to his friends, particularly since the broadcasts, and keeps telling people he's spent his life trying to make his mark and here she is, having lived like a tramp, more famous than he'll ever be. But he talks about his career in Africa, how he still works as a part-time vet, and I come away thinking what an admirable pair he and his wife are, funny and kind and as good in practice as she was in theory – the brother Martha to his sister's Mary.

Sometimes now hearing a van door I think, 'There's Miss Shepherd', instinctively looking up to see what outfit she's wearing this morning. But the oil patch that marked the site of the van has long since gone, and the flecks of yellow paint on the pavement have all but faded. She has left a more permanent legacy, though, and not only to me. Like diphtheria and Brylcreem, I associate moths with the forties, and until Miss Shepherd took up residence in the drive I thought them firmly confined to the past. But just as it was clothes in which the plague was reputedly spread to the Derbyshire village of Eyam so it was a bundle of Miss Shepherd's clothes, for all they were firmly done up in a black plastic bag, that brought the plague to my house, spreading from the bag to the wardrobe and from the wardrobe to the carpets, the appearance of a moth the signal for frantic clapping and savage stamping. On her death my vigorous cleaning of the van broadcast the plague more widely, so that now many of my neighbours have come to share in this unwanted legacy.

Her grave in the Islington St Pancras Cemetery is scarcely less commodious than the narrow space she slept in the previous twenty years. It is unmarked, but I think as someone so reluctant to admit her name or divulge any information about herself, she would not have been displeased by that.